Apocalypse Yesterday

Also available by Brock Adams

Ember

Apocalypse Yesterday

A Novel

BROCK ADAMS

CROOKED LANE

NEW YORK

Copyright © 2020 by Brock Adams

All rights reserved.

Published in the United States by Crooked Lane Books, an imprint of The Quick Brown Fox & Company LLC.

Crooked Lane Books and its logo are trademarks of The Quick Brown Fox & Company LLC.

Library of Congress Catalog-in-Publication data available upon request.

ISBN (hardcover): 978-1-64385-553-0
ISBN (ebook): 978-1-64385-554-7

Cover illustration: Adams Carvalho

Printed in the United States.

www.crookedlanebooks.com

Crooked Lane Books
34 West 27th St., 10th Floor
New York, NY 10001

First Edition: September 2020

10 9 8 7 6 5 4 3 2 1

For Katla

SATURDAY, OCTOBER 26

Imagine the machete in your hand and the sky on fire. The blade feels like an extension of your arm, a bone grown long and honed to the finest edge—a part of you as much as your teeth, your boots, your scars. Now imagine the feeling when that blade hits home, when you catch a zombie right in the middle of its skull and open it up like a watermelon on the Fourth of July. Can you feel it?

But it isn't just the killing; it's the little things. The stars spread like shattered glass blinking through rents in the smoke-screened sky. A bonfire of busted-up beach chairs burning on the concrete while you drink warm beer with your friends. No—your family. And the woman you love, the fiercest fieriest woman alive, asleep beside you, the two of you in your pirate-ship palace in the water park, your kingdom, the zombies held at bay on the other side of the lazy-river moat. Your subjects asleep around you, each in their own special place—under the big fiberglass mushrooms, tucked into the bottom of the spiral tube slide, cozy on a bed of inflatable rafts spread out in the abandoned margarita hut. All of them safe because of you. Looking up to you. Depending on you. Their king.

You see it now, don't you? You see it.

Imagine they took it all away from you.

It's the kind of thing that makes you want to die, but you can't die now, not after everything you've survived. So instead you just want to scream at the sky and tear the rebuilt world down around you. You'd do anything to have it back. Anything.

I would, anyway. I did. That's what got me here. Middle of the night at an Air Force base with two zombies banging around in the back of a landscaping trailer and a twentysomething security guard pointing an M16 at my head.

"Get on the ground!" he says.

I hold my hands out in front of me, take a step back. "Hang on," I say.

"On the fucking ground!"

"We gonna die, Rip," Rodney says. He's already facedown on the asphalt, hands laced around the back of his head. "This was so stupid. The stupidest goddamn thing."

"We're not going to die," I say to him. Then, to the guard, "Look, just let us go. We're almost out. Let us go, and you'll never see us again."

The gun is shaking in his hands. His upper lip twitches like a rabbit's. One of the zombies roars inside the trailer, and it echoes and vibrates against the metal and the guard says, "Down! Now!"

So I get on my knees and put my hands behind my head and the guard takes a step forward, and then I see Mo. He comes around the other side of the trailer and he's got his decap-itator in his hands, the moonlight glinting on the blade, that monster blade nearly as tall as the guard, and Mo raises it like he did before cleaving so many zombies in two, and the guard turns but too late and I know now that we are well and truly fucked.

TUESDAY, OCTOBER 22

"She's a part of me, man," I say. "You can't take her away."

"Her?" says the cop. He's standing over my booth at McDonald's, looking down at me, at the machete resting on the table next to my burger.

Everyone else in McDonald's is looking at me too. The kids over in the play area, their faces all lit up as they press against the window and point at me. Some mom grabs one by the wrist and drags him away. Behind the counter, the cashier is laughing. She snaps a picture with her phone. And this old woman two tables over, face like a crumpled paper bag. I watch her out the corner of my eye as she eats her fries like a turtle, three, four bites per fry. Staring. Judging. She's the one that called the cop. I know it.

"Santana," I say.

"What?" says the cop.

"Machete's named Santana, if you want to know." I touch her black blade with my finger and the cop shifts, rests a hand on his gun. I put my hands in my lap. "I know you carried. Everyone did. That gun, I bet. It was a part of you, wasn't it?"

The cop sighs. "What's your name?" he says.

"Rip."

He sits down across from me in the booth. He's a few years younger than me—thirty, maybe—but it's hard to tell; everyone aged weird during the outbreak. Four months with the grid shut down and zombies trying to eat you. Some people grew old. Their hair shot white and the struggle etched heavy lines in their faces. Others came out younger. Tan and lean and brimming with verve. I'm one of those. This cop is one of them too. Scar running down the left side of his face, worn skin on his knuckles, but supernovas swimming in his eyes.

We know each other. We know.

"Listen, Rip," he says. "You gotta put the knife away."

"Santana."

"It doesn't matter. I don't need to know her name. I don't need to know your story. I just need to do my job." He looks over at the old woman, who pretends to be real interested in her fries. Then he rests his elbows on the table, puts two fingers on Santana's hilt. He speaks low. "It's not fair, I know. I get to carry. I've got the gun, the baton. I can't imagine what it'd be like if they took them away. So I feel you, man. I feel you. But I got to do my job, and you're freaking people out."

"They carried too," I say. We all did. Everyone and their weapons in some symbiotic relationship, each making the other stronger. Like Rodney and his knuckles, his actual knuckles that he'd used for fighting his whole life and the spiky brass things he wore later, the logical evolution of a brawler's fists. Or Bob's shotgun, the big-ass boomstick as loud and bombastic as he is. Mo's decapitator, a hunk of steel torn from its machine and reforged into something far deadlier, just like its owner. "They had their weapons. Wouldn't be alive if they didn't."

"And they've put them away. They're following the law." He lingers on the hilt a moment and I feel this tightness inside of me like he's got his hands on my woman, and I guess he kind of does. Then he pushes her across the table to me. "You got to follow the law too. It's been two months since the U.S. all-clear. Three weeks since the new weapons ordinances. We can't let you skate by any longer."

"It's that old woman called you, isn't it?"

"I can't say." He rolls his eyes, smiles. "Time to hang her up, Rip," he says, and he gets up and leaves.

I put Santana in my bag next to my work stuff and my go-bag stuff, the canteen and the easy-pack food and the cash. Feel that old woman's smirk from across the room.

I want to leave then, but I finish the burger because I paid for it, goddamn it, paid twice what I should have because who knows what they're going through to get that meat to my plate. Most of the cows are dead. Zombies tore them up, easy food when they'd eaten all the low-hanging fruit people-wise. Plus some of the roads are still busted up from strafing runs from the A-10s and the Apaches, so the trucks have to drive all over hell and back to get here. And there's the lack of manpower: a bunch of people doing jobs all up and down the chain—sunburned migrants pulling tomatoes from the vine, aging white women standing on assembly lines at a bun bakery in California, CEOs and marketing execs arguing in half-empty boardrooms—are dead, their brains gobbled up. So much ruin, but already we've got burgers again, except now they cost six bucks. 'Course I'm going to finish the son of a bitch.

Might not be cow meat in the burger, come to think of it, unless they're shipping it in from the NewSSR. Tastes like it, though, so good enough, because god you miss burgers when you're eating whatever canned stuff you can scrounge for four months in a row.

I shove the last bite in my mouth and go to the door and feel the heads swivel to follow me. I'm naked without her. Santana. Her weight tugging on my belt, the *tunk tunk* as she bounces off my leg when I walk. *I'm sorry, girl.*

Outside the sun is bright white in the sky and the blue stretches around it forever. The smoke and haze that smothered everything all summer has blown away. Can't look at the sun without it burning your eyes. Used to be it was orange up there behind the veil; you could watch it track its way through the half-light, like some old man carrying a lantern through a swamp. Could smell it, the light working on the smoke, acrid particles of ash flaming up in miniature under the spindly sun-beams. Lit your nose like smelling salts, like cocaine. Made all the cylinders in your brain fire at once.

Now it's October and the only smell in the air is the late-blooming honeysuckle. Maybe some salt and seaweed from the bay just down the road. But the smoke is gone. Never knew I'd miss it so much.

I wait at the light to cross the street. A school bus goes by, kids laughing playing in the back on their way to a midday field trip. The light turns and I walk and the traffic doesn't move. Horns honk and I see that the woman in front of the line of traffic is texting, and there's more honking and she leans out the window and says, "Just hold on a fucking second!" and then people are tearing around her, laying on the horn, cussing back at her. Like this is the worst thing that's ever happened.

Two months. Two months since the all-clear.

Back in front of the call center, this low, squat building with no windows. Down near the corner it's still charred up where a car crashed into it in the first week of the outbreak. Black flames creeping up the stucco. I rub my hand on the soot shadow and my fingers come away black. I hold them to my face and sniff and it's rapturous; all the memories at once flood through me, synapses like lightning screaming *fire* and *war* and *victory* and *Davia*, so I press my face right up against the wall and inhale like I'm drowning, about to go under.

It smells like destruction, like death. It smells like heaven.

"The fuck you doing?"

It's Rodney. He's standing at the door to the office, paper cup of coffee in his hand. Behind him my other coworkers are coming back from lunch, talking among themselves, laughing. The cars buzz by and the streets are full of the noise of the day.

"You coming, Rip?" Rodney says.

"Yeah," I say. I put my hand on the stucco. It's warm, rough. The soot pungent, the inside of a spent shotgun shell. "Yeah, I'm coming."

We are civilized and innocent again and I wonder what the world is coming to.

BACK THEN

Killed my first one in a grocery store. First one I saw, matter of fact. It was late and the store was empty except for me and the kid at the checkout counter. He was all tired and didn't look at me and dragged my stuff across the electric eye *beep beep* so slow like no one had anywhere else to be.

It was after midnight and the fluorescents were burning white like midday desert sun.

She came in through the automatic doors. Girl, nineteen maybe. A blonde, thin, hair in sort of a pixie cut. She stops a few feet inside and the doors start to close, but the sensor picks her up again and they jerk back open. Close and open like that a few times while she sways in the doorway and the checkout kid keeps scanning my stuff. Soup, most of it. Pop-Tarts. Shit like that. *Beep.*

Girl is looking at the mat beneath her feet where it says *Welcome to Arnie's!*

Door does the open-close thing again and checkout kid turns around. "In or out," he says.

She looks up now. Something with her eyes—out of whack, like she's looking at some invisible thing hanging in the air way past me and the kid. A little reddish. Brown stuff smeared on her cheek.

"Come on," kid says, "you're letting the AC out."

Then the girl goes *urrrrrrrgggh* and lurches our way and the kid turns to push her away but she's on him, and she's smaller than this kid but she's wrapped around his chest, her arms her fingers digging into him and she's climbing him like she's a spider monkey and he's a tree in a cloud forest in Costa Rica. She bites him on top of the head. Bites hard, and the kid is screaming and beating at her and there's blood running down the side of his face and she's tearing into him, rips an ear off and chews. He throws her off and tries to run but slips on his own blood, and then she's on him again, and goddamn, the way he's screaming.

I'm not sure what I'm supposed to do, if I still have to pay if she eats him or if I can just go. Got to bag my own stuff now, I guess. Start putting the soup in the bag.

Kid's on the ground, blood coming out of his head, his neck, and he's still trying to push her away but not very hard.

Girl looks up at me. Eyes like they're cut loose from whatever hangs them in her skull.

"I'm gonna go," I say.

She jumps up on the checkout counter. Her foot hits the switch that controls the conveyor belt, and the belt starts moving and it pulls her off her feet and she falls on her side and goes *raaaarrrrgh!* I try to step back, but she's got me by the shirt collar and she's clawing like a feral cat gone crazy, rabid, yowling and staring at me with those weird eyes, and the kid's blood is all over her teeth and her lips. Belt keeps moving, and every time she wants to get up it sweeps her back down, but she's still chomping at me with those red teeth.

"Let go!" I yell at her. "Fucking let go!"

Rooooaaarrraaahh!

I've got this can of soup in my hand. Campbell's, so familiar, red on white like a baseball. Heavy, the edges fierce. I grip it in my fist and swing it at her. I'm the caveman from that movie with the spaceships and I just discovered tools; I'm the one, the first to make the leap from beast to man with this tool, the first tool a weapon, of course, because isn't every tool a weapon—a weapon against another man or against hunger or nature or whatever?

I clock her in the head with it, leave a bean-with-bacon-shaped hole in her skull. She goes *grrrooooaag?* and I hit her again, again, until she's still. The belt keeps whirring by and she bleeds onto it. Blood streaks the belt, goes under the counter, comes back up the other end.

The electric eye is painting a red X on her chest and I put the can in front of it. *Beep.*

Kid's still gurgling on the floor, but there's a lot of blood. Don't know what I'm supposed to do about that, so I bag up my stuff and get.

TUESDAY, OCTOBER 22

So this email says:

> *I wasn't halfway through my can of Pringles when I came across one broken in half. By the time I reached the bottom of the package, the chips were nothing more than crumbs. If the can is designed to keep the chips whole, I ought to receive a full can of whole chips. I didn't pay for crumbs. Please reimburse my $1.49 immediately.*

This is what I look at all day long. Our company makes just about everything, it seems, and people buy their shit from us and then they complain. You know those numbers on the side of the box where you call for questions and comments? Used to be the number went to a call center in India, but people kept calling the call center to complain about the accents of the people at the call center, so now the complaints come to me. The emails, anyway. Boss put me on emails because she says my writing skills are better than my oral ones. Don't know if that's a compliment or not.

The job made some sort of sense before everything, I guess. Now every email pisses me off. This guy's emailing from Pennsylvania. Half his state got overrun in the first month and they evacuated and firebombed Pittsburg, and now the world's barely back to normal and he's complaining about his broken chips.

I look up and Rodney's beside my desk. He's flipping the pages on my calendar.

"Leave it," I say.

"You're like six months behind."

"I like the picture." Tell the truth, I'm not crazy about the picture. Some cliffs in Ireland or somewhere, all tall and black beside the ocean. But it's the March picture, and March is when it all started, and I like to look at it and think maybe it's all going to start again.

"Bungalow?" Rodney says.

Bungalow's our bar.

Rodney's drumming his fingers on top of my cubicle wall. He looks like LeBron James's little brother, tall but not that tall, fit but not that fit. Looking at him now makes me think of the real LeBron and how it took half of LA to bring him down. That was one of the last things the media covered before the power went out: Zombie LeBron stalking around outside the arena, still in his Lakers jersey, and man, it was something to see. People coming at him and him swiping them away like gnats. News played it over and over, and I'd be lying if I said I wasn't impressed. He was like the LeBron James of zombies.

"Yeah," I say. "One second." It's 4:49, so too close to closing to do any real work. I look at that email again and I type:

Fuck your chips.

And then Rodney and I head outside. We blink in the afternoon light, feel the sun on our shoulders. Summer goes long in Spanish Shanty, in all of Florida, really, so even though it's October it's hot out, but the sun's going down and the breeze is coming in over the bay. We walk. Our building sits at the east end of the main road, out where things start getting ugly and industrial. Head west toward the water and it's cutesy red-brick streets with lots of cafés and antique shops and a cupcake place. Woman reopened her cupcake place before the Army had even lifted the curfew.

Bungalow is down on the bayou where the beach curls around and folds in on itself and the water is black and still and the trees aren't palms like out near the Gulf but old oaks and maybe a weeping willow. The bar looks like you think it does. Sits over the bayou on barnacle-covered pilings, docks leading from shore to the bar and out to the porch. Wood paneling and a cheap neon sign and rusted beer cans sunk a foot below the murky water.

We go in and Bob's behind the bar. He looks up and says, "Rip! How you been?" Bob's got the Jamaican flag hanging behind the bar. He was born there but he moved to Topeka when he was like three. He's got the dreads and all, though, and he even looks a little like Marley, so you know he's milked that for everything it's worth.

"Hey Bob," I say. Inside, the place is dark, the light coming in from the plastic skylight and the door that leads out over the water. We can go out there, yeah, but for right now I feel like sitting inside. We'll go out later, later when the sun is hitting the water and bleeding orange into the black. In here it's warm and quiet and smells like beer, and Bob gets us a couple of beers and we sit at the bar, just me and Rodney and down at the end Guillermo. Mo, we call him. Drunk already, probably gained thirty pounds since the all-clear. Got his forehead on the bar, half a glass of whiskey in front of him.

"Mo," Rodney says. "Hey, Mo!"

Mo looks up and mutters something in Spanish and puts his head back down. Makes me sad to see him like this now. He owned a landscaping company before—Guillermo's Gardens— and now there's nothing for him to do since all the lawns dried up when the water shut off and no one's that concerned with regrowing them yet with winter coming anyway. Maybe next spring, but now there's just a stretch of short days and long nights and dead grass between him and work. He survived the zombies to have them ruin him after the fact. No one could touch him back then. He was hard and wiry, and he patrolled the streets while the sun turned him a deeper brown than he'd been even after all those days in the yards. Mo pulled the blade off the big thirty-six-inch mower and filed one end down to a handle, honed the other till it flamed white in sunlight. Called it el decapitador. Wore it on his back like a greatsword. Man, he was a beast.

"He's not much use after five," Bob says. "He starts in right after I open and he's passing out before dark. It's hard to watch."

We drink the beers and listen to the water moving against the pilings beneath us. I take Santana out of my bag and set her on the bar in front of me. Run my fingers along the sheath.

"Still got your girl," Bob says.

I nod. "She goes where I go. Where's yours?"

"Under the bar, where she belongs." Bob has a double-barreled ten-gauge, huge fucker like it was made to hunt pterodactyls. He holed himself up in the bar during the outbreak. Pushed the refrigerators and the kegs up against the door and poked his head through the skylight to shoot any zombies that wandered too close. Lived off beer and peanuts and pretzels.

He was still wearing the shotgun on a sling last time I saw him. Now it's gone. I'm the only one who's still carrying.

Bob's got the TV on in the corner. They cut into the show with this big banner for a special news bulletin. The anchor comes on, smiling at the camera. Picture of a soldier in the corner, boot on the skull of a dead zombie. The anchor says they've killed the last one, a straggler wandering the banks of the Yangtze in central China. North America's been clear for six weeks, Europe for a month. They took down the last ones in Africa and South America over the last couple of weeks—big announcement on TV every time a country was clear, bigger announcement every time it was a continent. Australia was all up its own ass as the first continent clear. Like it's so hard to keep zombies away from a big-ass desert in the middle of the ocean.

And now Asia. The last continent. "So that's it, I say."

"So they say," Bob says.

"Now we're really fucked," Rodney says. He looks at his beer. It's a Three Bears Light, cheap import from the NewSSR.

Brown bottle the size of your head with a pissed-off Russian soccer player on the label, scowling at these bears standing in the goal. "We hit four twenty-five today. Saw it online."

He means parts per million. Carbon in the atmosphere. Some professor showed him *An Inconvenient Truth* in college and he's been obsessed with carbon ever since, rants about it every time a milestone ticks by. Feels like 420 wasn't very long ago.

"It went down during the outbreak, you know that?" Rodney says. "Even with the forests burning and all that exhaust from the jets and the tanks, it still went down. And now we're right back to where we were." He sets the empty bottle on the bar and spins it, and it wobbles and falls over. "This shit right here. Think about it. They're growing hops and barley and whatever else over there in the NewSSR, driving tractors to harvest it, running big factories to brew the beer and bottle it. Putting it on trucks, hauling it to harbors, sailing it across the fucking ocean. Burning, burning, burning fuel all day, every day. Unsustainable."

"People got to have their beer," Bob says.

"But is it worth destroying the world for beer?"

"Depends on the beer," I say.

He glares at me but he smiles a little. "Not beer, then. All the other bullshit that we don't really need. Fast food every day and a car for every single person and a new smartphone every year. We don't need it. The outbreak showed us that. We didn't have any of that stuff, and we got along just fine. But now the zombies are gone, and we're right back where we were." He shakes his head. "I thought the zombies were a correction. The earth telling us to slow down. I figured we'd come back afterwards and we'd live differently. Or if not that, then at least there'd be fewer of us around. Fewer people, less waste, lower emissions—all that. There might have been time."

"The zombies were the good guys, then?" I say.

He's quiet for a minute. There's a NASCAR race on TV now. The cars fly around the track, gas flaming through those engines, exhaust clouding the air. Round and round.

"They weren't the good guys," Rodney says. "But they were the only ones who could save us."

We finish the beers and Bob gets us a couple more and Rodney and I take them outside and sit at one of the white plastic tables. Cheap patio furniture, the wood of the dock rough beneath us. The sun's going down, turning all red like it does, and I love this time of evening, when the breeze is switching from the sea breeze to land and the seagulls and the pelicans are coming by in their echelons heading to wherever it is they go at night. I would watch this even during the outbreak. The world was falling apart but the birds kept flying through the smoke, nature doing what it does. The beer's cold in my hand and tastes of salt water and I think, *Yeah, this isn't the worst thing in the world,* but I look at Santana sitting useless on the table and think of her going back to cutting weeds and picture all those days sitting in the office answering emails just so I can come to this dock and look at the water and the sun, and man, I don't know.

"You're going to have to leave her at home at some point," Rodney says.

I take Santana out of the sheath. She's still so sharp I could cut this table in half without even swinging that hard. Oiled just right, and she seems to vibrate while the sun streaks over her like napalm.

"Cops are going to take her away," Rodney says. "Only a matter of time."

"Don't feel right without her." I wet my finger on the bottle of beer and run it down Santana's keen edge. It hums a clean low tone, like a fingertip circling the rim of a wineglass.

Santana wasn't always a *she*. Once she was an *it*: the thing that I used to clear away the kudzu when it climbed too high up the trees or to cut down the rotten elephant-ear stalks if we got a freeze in the winter. It was a blade for gardening.

Santana was born before the sirens started, before the fires lit the night. After the girl at the grocery store, I came home and turned on the TV, and it was on the news just like I'd thought it would be. Reporter was at the hospital talking about an unknown virus and strange symptoms and all that: all over the place in Finland and the Scandinavian Peninsula; some cases popping up in China, in the UK, here in the States. Just like a movie. In the movies everyone sits around and wonders what's going on until it's too late and the zombies are everywhere. No one knows what to do, doesn't even know what the things are. No one in the movies ever calls a zombie a zombie—always *the dead* or *walkers* or something stupid like that, and I wonder, don't they watch zombie movies in the zombie movies?

So they were unprepared, but not me. I'd seen *Dawn of the Dead*. I knew how shit was going to go down.

I brought the machete inside from the carport and stood in the kitchen and swung it a few times. It whispered *whurmp*

whurmp as it sliced the air. I got the electric knife sharpener out of the cabinet and turned it on and ran the machete through it for half an hour until the blade glistened and sang like I could hear oxygen molecules splitting in half when they drifted into the edge.

Before everything it was just a tool: a twenty-two-inch blade, wider and curved at the end, black but shiny gray along its edge with a black rubber handle that fit my palm like it was crafted just for me, its balance its weight perfect like a swordsmith had made it for a knight, a king—but still just a tool. It hung on the rack at Home Depot. Ordinary. Utilitarian.

In my hand, though, with the world on fire, she was something different and I was something different. Like magic flowed from her into me and back. Black magic. She was my black magic woman.

Hence the name.

"Gotta give her up sometime," Rodney says. "Got to give it all up. Back to normal. We're just going to ride the *Titanic* all the way down to the bottom." He's looking at his beer bottle and shaking his head. "I guess it's the way it ought to be."

"Maybe so," I say. "But shit, man, we had some fun, didn't we?"

Rodney laughs. "Yeah, we did. Watching Mo in there do his thing. Or watching you. You were hell on wheels, Rip. You were the fucking king."

"The king."

"The fucking king." He finishes his beer and leans back so the chair's on two legs that bend under his weight and look like they're going to snap. Crosses his arms, scowls at me. "So what we going to do?"

"What do you mean?"

"I mean what we going to do now?"

And I don't know what to tell him, because what he's asking has no answer. What do we do now? We won and the world is back and we push forward, but what are we pushing toward? I can hear Santana weeping in her sheath and it forces the tears out of my own eyes, and I let them sit on my face while the sun goes lower out there beyond the bayou and the bay until the Gulf swallows it up.

BACK THEN

I thought the day I killed zombie girl was going to be Day 1, so I came home and sharpened the machete and sat on the couch and watched the news, waiting for it all to start. Listening for screams, for growls and groans, sirens.

None of that. Birds start singing around five like they always do.

Not Day 1 yet. Day 0, maybe. The day before The Day.

It's on the news, but still no word of zombies. Just unexplained sickness in Norway. Rioting in Finland. CNN says Anderson Cooper's on the way to Oulu. Then they start talking about whatever Trump tweeted this morning.

They all act like they don't know. But they know. Wouldn't send AC to Finland for your standard riot.

Sun's coming up, the sky getting dusty blue outside. I sigh and put the machete on a shelf and get dressed for work. Step into the front yard where the squirrels are skittering around the tree trunks. The wind's picking up, blowing in from across the bay.

Spanish Shanty isn't big. We've got downtown and the industrial crap to the east of it, and we've got the aging neighborhoods that follow the bay as it dips and curves in bay-ous and inlets. Big oaks with Spanish moss hanging from them, the water blue out there and wind-whipped on the stormy days. Dirty seafoam and driftwood on the beaches. Used to be the bay was full of oysters and scallops and fish, and people spent a few generations pulling them out and replacing them with garbage and oil. They turned the sea life into money and turned the money into beautiful houses all along the bay, prime real estate when they were built seventy-five, a hundred years ago. Now the bay is mostly dead and the houses are wilting, the salt air working on the delicately-carved columns and crown molding, the foundations sinking a millimeter at a time into the sandy dirt. The bay reclaiming it all. We live in these houses, these and the trailer parks and the projects and the wasting waterfront condos. We, the people of Spanish Shanty, five thousand of us or so, and none of us cares that the city is crumbling. It's like your body as you get older: all right, my gut's a little bigger, but I'm forty now; can't expect to be all washboard abs my entire life. Hair's gray, but that's okay. You deal, you accept.

That's me. I've accepted. Yes, I have a gut, and my hair is gray, and I can't run a mile without getting so tired I can't get out of bed the next day. But I'm forty. Show me the forty-year-old who can.

Yes, I know that plenty of forty-year-olds can.

And that's what my house is too. It's a two-bedroom set back among a bunch of elephant ears that start growing in spring and end up these monsters that shoot up taller than the roof, make it like I'm living in the jungles of Vietnam. Driveway is cracked and the weeds and grass are always creeping onto it, and I fight them back with the machete when I can.

There are a couple of houses across the street, but between them is a straight shot from my house to the water, so I keep a folding lawn chair at the end of my driveway where I watch the sun go down while the fighter jets from the Air Force base do maneuvers out over the Gulf. F-15s, F-22s, some F-16s. Can hear the distant groan of their engines, see their metal bodies radiant high up in the blue.

It's a ten-minute walk along the bay to work. Things are normal at the call center, the low hum of work getting done. I sit down and look at the first email. Some guy bitching about detergent turning his pants the wrong color. Nope. Can't do this yet.

Cubicle next to me is empty. Normally it's Marie sitting there, answering calls live. Fifty-something, Paula Deen fat, speaks with a southern accent heavy even for the Panhandle. Pictures of horses on her cubicle walls, pictures of ugly grandchildren. It's quiet with her gone.

I go over to Rodney's cube. "Where's Marie?"

He has a spreadsheet up on his screen. Rodney's the only one here—other than the boss—who actually finished college, so he gets to be floor manager. Sometimes it makes me think I ought to go back to school. I was fifteen credits short of an English degree from FSU twenty years ago, but they told me I had to take Chaucer if I wanted to graduate. Nah. Anyway, Rodney's really more of a glorified record keeper, so that shows what a degree gets you. All my emails get copied to him, and all the live-call people send reports to him after they hang up.

Rodney shrinks the spreadsheet and leans back in his chair. "Marie's sick," he says.

"With what?"

"Didn't say." He folds his hands behind his head, puts his feet up on the desk. "Why you look so excited about it?"

I'm trying not to look excited, but I can feel it bubbling around inside me. I'm thinking, *This is it*, this is Oulu, this is the girl at the grocery store. I don't know why it feels that way. Excitement over something different, I guess, something new that's going to happen. "You seen the news?" I say.

"You mean the Finland shit?"

"Yeah. Finland and Norway."

"Uh-huh." Rodney looks bored. He rolls his eyes and says, "The real deal, then. End of the world."

I look around the office. Everyone's on the phone or quiet at their computers. I kneel beside him. "I think it's zombies."

"For real?" He sits up.

I study him a moment, trying to see if he's fucking with me, stringing me along. He looks serious. I've known Rodney a few years now, and he's never fucked with me before. We're straight with one another. He knows I'm being straight with him now. 'Course he'll believe it. If I say zombies, he'll say how many.

"Yeah," I say. And I tell him about the girl at the grocery store.

"So you a murderer," he says.

"No, because she was already dead."

"You had her checked out? Like, you got your zombie detector out?"

"I told you. She ate the checkout guy." I lean out of the cubicle and look up and down the aisle. No one else around. Turn back to Rodney. "Why else would she eat the checkout guy? She's a zombie. Zombies all over Europe. Coming here too."

Rodney looks nervous now. "Like *Dawn of the Dead*," he says. "Shit, man, black guy always dies first. Always the black guy."

"Not *Dawn of the Dead*. Ving Rhames makes it to the end."

"So I'm Ving Rhames?"

"You're Ving Rhames."

Rodney's nodding now. "Bad motherfucker, Ving Rhames."

"That's right."

"So what we do?"

"I guess we play this shit by ear." I go back to my desk and there's a new email. I open it up:

My son was bitten by another toddler at preschool today. I sprayed Antibax on the bite, and he vomited blood all over the sofa. I'm writing you from the hospital. My son went into convulsions. He is with the doctors now. This will not stand. You will be hearing from my lawyers.

Sometimes people get rashes from Antibax, but no one vomits blood. Maybe the kid just had an allergic reaction. Maybe it's something he ate.

Or maybe shit's going down.

I ignore the Antibax stuff when I write back. Send her an e-coupon for Easyout! upholstery cleaner instead.

* * *

Rodney comes over that night. It's Friday, and we sit in front of the TV and eat nachos and drink beer. Feels like we're watching football. Fun.

First thing is Anderson Cooper in Oulu. It's the middle of the night over there and he's standing in some sort of square, a cathedral behind him. People run by in the background. One's in the foreground, cutting between Anderson and the camera, bumping the cameraman, shaking the view. There's a building on fire off to the side of the screen, every window lit orange with tentacles of smoke cascading out, like there's a black monster inside reaching for the sky. Can hear sirens but can't see any fire trucks.

Anderson himself looks bad. He's coughing in the smoke, his eyes red and watery. His hair is sloppy and sticking up in the back when it's usually so neat, smooth gray over his coyote face. He's practically yelling to be heard over the din around him. "Authorities have declared a state of emergency," he says. "The outbreak has been upgraded to Level 1. The military has been mobilized to aid in peacekeeping. Shit!" He runs toward the camera. The view is half of Anderson's shoulder as a screaming woman sprints by, her sleeve on fire. Behind her are more screams, but not screams of terror like hers; these are animal war cries coming from three more women who chase her. They enter the frame, lunging, stumbling, fast but uncoordinated. "What the fuck?" Anderson says.

"That's them," I say.

"The zombies?" Rodney leans closer to the screen. "Rewind it."

I rewind the DVR, wait for the women. The screamer comes by again, her arm aflame. Then the zombies. I pause it. Two of them are turned wrong, can't see them, but one of them is front and center. Rodney and I kneel in front of the TV.

She's young, dressed for the club. Probably a college kid. Slinky black dress and one black high heel, but she doesn't seem slowed by her missing shoe. Her hair is long and colored like an oil spill.

"Goddamn," Rodney says. He points at her arm. There's a chunk missing from her triceps, a big, bite-shaped chunk.

Her face is twisted into a snarl like nothing a human's supposed to make. Lips so wide, teeth practically jutting out. And her eyes. They're small on the TV but I can still see what's going on in them. It's emptiness and it's rage. The mindless fury of the reptile brain. Black holes dispassionately annihilating the universe as they careen through space. No wonder the woman they're chasing screams. The zombie is an unpiloted machine of terror.

"Goddamn is right," I say.

I unpause the TV and Anderson says, "What the fuck?" again and the women are gone, and he steps back in front of the camera. He looks off in the direction they ran. "Military is mobilized." There's a voice from offscreen—the cameraman— and Anderson shakes his head. "No, Matt," he says. "We're staying. We're getting the story." And then the camera jerks, points skyward, crashes to the pavement.

"Oh, shit!" Rodney says. He jumps to his feet in front of the TV. "You see that shit? They got him. They got the cameraman."

On-screen are Anderson's feet, and he's backing away, and then he's knocked out of frame and his microphone rolls across the asphalt. There's yelling for a moment; then his face slams to the ground just in front of the camera's lens.

"Ooooohhhh!" Rodney's yelling and bouncing around the room like his team just pulled off a Hail Mary on the final play. "Look. At. That. Shit," he says.

Anderson's face is bloody. He drags himself forward, grabs the mic. "I've been tackled by a woman," he says. He rolls onto his back. "I believe"—he kicks a couple of times at something off-camera—"I believe she may be infected. She's trying to bite me." And then he's dragged away.

The camera stays on, pointed sideways at the burning building. Black blood on the asphalt reflects the flames as Anderson continues to narrate. "Yes. Yes, she has bitten me on the arm. And now, ah, ahhhh, she's—" And then he's screaming.

Got to give it to him. A pro right up to the end.

The feed cuts back to Atlanta, and the anchor is sitting with her mouth open, her eyebrows up, her face so clean and makeup polished. She looks at the teleprompter, then at someone else in the room. "Really?" She waits. "Okay, then." Back to the camera. "We go live to Christina, who reports that Kim Kardashian and Kanye West are separating."

WEDNESDAY, OCTOBER 23

It's a little after lunch the next day when the boss calls me into her office. She's this tiny woman, five foot if she's on her tiptoes. She was pregnant a few years ago—twins—and I swear they took up half the space inside her. No idea how she survived it all; looks like the wind would knock her over. Who knows what a zombie'd do to her. Probably she latched on to someone and made that pour sap drag her through everything and out the other side.

Boss gives me her big sweetsie smile, the one she uses when she's leading workshops that are supposed to Promote Synergy or when she's slicing up someone's grocery-store birthday cake. "Well, Rip," she says, "I suppose you know why you're here."

I shrug. "No?"

She smiles even bigger, cocks her head. "Really? Think hard." Voice practically dripping with high-fructose corn syrup. "You can't think of any little bitty reason you might be here?" She turns the monitor of her computer so that I can see it and she's got her email open, so yeah, that's where this is going. She reads from the screen: "'Fuck your chips.'"

However this ends, it's worth it just to hear her read it out loud. "Yeah?"

"Why would you write something like that to a customer?"

"Because fuck his chips."

She sighs. She's been with the company who knows how long, probably her whole adult life, followed it around to half a dozen towns by now. That's what they do: they show up in some small town because the town gives them all these sweet tax incentives to open a new business, but the incentives run out in three years or so and they close up shop and go somewhere new with new incentives. You can follow them to Buttfuck, North Dakota, or you can find a new job. It's a predatory cycle that leaves in its wake a bunch of unemployed schmucks and ruined local economies. They came to Spanish Shanty two years before the outbreak, so I guess we're already in the final days. The boss shakes her head and says, "You're not yourself."

"So who am I?"

"I don't know. You didn't do this kind of thing before."

"Yeah, but I wanted to."

"But you didn't. Why now?"

"Because I could fake it before. Now it's just ridiculous. Like, who gives a shit about your Pringles? They put them in a can and ship them across the country and put them on the shelf, and you get to eat them for a dollar fifty? How amazing is that? A few months ago it was land of the living dead and today you can have Pringles again? And you want to bitch that the ones at the bottom are broken?"

"But Rip." Still the smile, but tension written across the lines on her forehead, in the set of her jaw. "It's their right to bitch. And it's our job to make them happy."

"The crumbs are the best part anyway. Just upend the can, drink them, like. You know?"

She reads the screen. "A customer complained about Starburst. The customer got a tube that was all oranges. He doesn't like the oranges. Your reply: 'Bullshit.'" She looks at me and shakes her head again. "'Bullshit'? That's all you can muster?"

"It is bullshit. How can you get nothing but oranges? Doesn't work that way. He's playing us for the free candy."

"So give him the candy. It costs nothing. Look. Look at this one. The customer's baby was getting diaper rash from our diapers. And you write: 'Yo baby's ass nasty.'"

I'm grinning at her now, but she's stopped smiling.

"That's not even correct grammar, Rip."

"Yeah, but it's funnier if you write it like that."

"You're fired."

"What?"

"You're fired. Go."

Guess that's what I figured would happen, so I don't say anything to her and I go back out to the cubicle. Rodney's there waiting for me.

"It was only a matter of time," I say.

"Sorry, man."

"Couldn't do it anymore anyway. Not another day. Not another fucking day."

"Bungalow later?"

"Yeah. See you." He goes back to his cubicle and I get my stuff and put it in a box and then I say fuck that. Don't need it. What, my plant? My calendar stuck on March? I leave it all and get Santana out of my bag and put her on my hip where everyone can see her. That's right, she's right there, I dare you to say something. Then I stand up on my desk and everyone's looking at me and I feel like I ought to say something meaningful, but all I can come up with is "I have no fucks left to give. Good-bye."

And then I'm gone, down the stairs and out to the street, and it's weird to be there in the middle of the afternoon. Sun's high overhead but not so hot, just a kind of nice and milky light spilling all over everything. The sky blue like a bucket of paint. People everywhere moving about in the stores, the restaurants. I walk past them, the McDonald's, the Long John Silver's. The hippie coffee shop they just reopened last week, now booming business again. Where they're getting the beans for their pumpkin lattes and mochaccinos, I don't know, since half of South America is a wasteland, but they're getting them somewhere. Maybe not. Maybe it's all just chemicals, but no one cares because goddamn did people miss coffee. So they're all crammed in there as I walk by, and I almost walk straight into her as she's coming out the door. Takes my breath away because it's *her*.

"Davia," I say.

She blinks, and then her eyes, those eyes like points of charcoal, light up, and her skin goes from its normal ashy amber to this glow like sun on the Sahara the way it always used to. Her lips pull back and she smiles those small teeth like a shark's, fierce, with probably other rows hidden underneath, and yes it is her, it's her. I wouldn't recognize her if not for her face, because so much of her is different. She's in a business suit, smart and gray but dull, and I never saw her before in anything but her hunting clothes, these short jean shorts and a black wifebeater.

So she stayed cool, she used to say. So she could move fast. I thought it was so she looked sexy as hell. Those hunting clothes are gone and now her hair is longer, almost hanging to her ears, no trace of the Mohawk she had before. She's a different woman outside, but her eyes—in her eyes she's the same woman my woman my Davia.

"Rip," she says. She's frozen, and people are bumping into her trying to leave the store, and she turns and curses at them in Russian.

I touch her elbow. "D," I say. "Where have you been?"

And now she looks back and she's changed. The shadow comes over her face and she looks at the paper coffee cup in her hands and she seems smaller than before. "I can't," she says, and then she's walking.

She's heading up the street, almost at a run, so I chase after her. "Davia, wait. Wait!"

She turns and holds out her hand, and I'm held like she's put up a force field. "Rip," she says. "No, Rip."

"Why?" But she's gone, and I'm glued to the spot and I watch her disappear up the street.

My starshina. Soviet warrior woman. Haven't seen her since we left the water park.

She said she'd worked in a hotel before the outbreak. Hotels, amusement parks, restaurants—they all fly in teenagers, twentysomethings from Russia, from Estonia, Ukraine, the long cold wall of Eastern Europe. Pay them garbage, work them all day, store them in packed dorms while they're sleeping. Ship them home at the end of the season and close the place down for the winter. Cheap, efficient. As cheap and efficient as indentured servitude.

Davia said she'd killed her boss when he turned zombie, tore his head in half with her poleaxe—broomstick with the sweeper part removed and a circular saw blade screwed on in its place. She called the poleaxe Putin. It was not a term of endearment, not like Santana. She called it Putin because it was steely, emotionless. And it fucking killed people.

Best kill she ever had, her boss. Sent shivers all through her like an orgasm.

She was pretty sure he'd turned, anyway.

I looked for her after the all-clear. Stood in hotel lobbies, stuck my head back through the kitchen doors of the restaurants. Rode every ride at the amusement park. Got to the point I was wondering if she'd gone back to Russia somehow, caught one of the first few flights when the jets finally took to the skies again.

And here she is, all my wildfire memories made real, and she's receding from me. I think to run after her again, but she turns the corner and is gone and I'm there in the sun blinking after her, fake coffee smell wafting onto the street.

What I want is a beer, cold beer on the porch at Bungalow, but Bob doesn't open the place until three and I'm not going to sit in the parking lot waiting on him like Mo, so I go into the coffee shop. They've redecorated. The walls are covered with pictures from the outbreak. Some of them selfies with zombie hordes in the background. One of the owner's wife standing on a big stack of boxes of coffee beans, a baseball bat raised above her head while dead hands reach up for her. Others of squadrons of jets flying far overhead, streaming condensation, or close to the ground with their machine guns rattling. Soldiers with their M16s and their Humvees rolling into town like they think they're saviors, like they think we need them.

Biggest picture is on the wall behind the counter. The owner shaking hands with the mayor. The last zombie is chained behind them, and the mayor has the golden gun on his hip.

I go to the counter. "Coffee," I say.

"What flavor?"

"Coffee flavored."

The kid behind the counter looks like he's just out of high school. His hair is long and slicked over to one side, like he's trying to cover his ear. Doesn't matter because the other one's sticking out and everyone can see what he's hiding. Earlobe's torn in two, two spongy bits of flesh dangling and scabbed. He tried to keep his earrings in. Zombies loved to grab people by the earrings. Like they were corncob holders. This kid probably had some big-ass silver hoops. Just give them handles, why don't you? But he's still alive. Standing behind the counter with a bored look on his face. Douchebag owner's alive, and his wife. All these people in the shop in their fedoras and their skinny jeans: alive. Alive like me.

I was the king. I kept my people alive. They must have found their own king. Takes a man like me to drag people like this through the fire.

Kid's still looking at me. "Like, mocha, or caramel?" he says. "Pumpkin spice, since it's fall?"

"Just pour coffee into a cup and give it to me."

I take my coffee and head all the way west through downtown to the marina. A quiet concrete road leads down one side and back up the other, with piers jutting off the sides. Covered boat slips, motorboats in a few of them, a sailboat here and there in the uncovered slips at the end. Marina was mostly empty before the outbreak anyway, leftovers from when the town was full of the kind of people who own boats. Then the outbreak came and a lot of people just went to sea, stayed on their boats bobbing on the swells while the land roiled and seethed. Sailed back in afterward and acted like survivors. Ha. Could they smell the smoke, the decay? Did they ever hold a machete, feel the rotting hands on their skin?

The marina ends and the road goes in a circle around the statue. Some benches nearby so people can sit and admire it. I take one of the benches and sip the coffee and yeah, it tastes like slow-roasted free-trade chemicals, but it's good enough. I look past the statue. Don't want to look at it. Look instead out into the bay where a couple of sailboats tool along. A heron strides in the shallows.

Beyond the bay the barrier island sprawls low and sandy, the buffer between the bay and the Gulf of Mexico. The island ends, and there's the pass, a channel of black water where the Gulf surges in with the tide and slurps out again, and on the other side of the pass is The Beach. The first condo so close to the pass it seems to lean over it. Twenty stories high. Then it's just condos all the way down, monsters, a thousand units strong some of them. They are a wall between land and water. You can drive down Beach Boulevard and you'd never know you were at the beach. They've colonized the shore and pushed nature back and back until it's just something you see from your window while you eat room-service shrimp cocktail. The whole city's a glossy tourist trap with its restaurants and mini-golf courses, its bars and clubs, its water park—Lazy River. Spring break and the place is swarming with college kids flashing their tits and fucking in the sand. Summer it's families eating snow cones and taking bay tours in a big yellow speedboat. Winter the Canadians come down and walk around in tank tops and flip-flops like fifty degrees is warm for them.

You have to cross the Halfway Bridge to get to The Beach, and that's what everyone did. A couple generations of movement and now The Beach is where everyone lives, where all the jobs are. Spanish Shanty is forgotten over here on the far side of the bridge.

I watch the heron for a while as it tiptoes among the breaking wavelets. After a while, it stops, dips its long beak into the water, and comes up with a fish. The heron tosses its head back and works the thing down his throat. Then it takes flight and sails off across the rippling waters toward The Beach. The condos are lit bright by the midday sun, the windows glinting, concrete glowing white, peach, teal.

The whistling sound of engines and two A-10s from the Air Force base fly by a half a mile out in the bay. Don't know where the F-15s and the other agile fighter jets went. Now it's all low-flying beasts, the slow-moving armored birds that cleared the roads with Avenger machine guns and Maverick missiles. I watch them bank and head toward The Beach.

Statue's looking down at me, so I think, *Fine, fine, I'll admire you, your eminence.* It's the mayor on the day of the all-clear. Twice life-size, so he's standing twelve feet tall, and the sculptor has given him muscles he never had, shoulders like

Arnold and arms like The Rock. He's got the golden gun in his hand, and he's pointing it down on the last zombie in Spanish Shanty. The zombie is carved to be ferocious—a monster, a huge, raving beast—but I was there, I remember. That's not how he was.

We all came to watch the Final Bullet. They'd turned it into a big deal. By then the military was running things and we were out of the refugee camp. I was sleeping in my house, in my bed, alone. Davia'd gone to wherever she went. The Final Bullet was on a Friday, and everyone was supposed to be back at work on Monday.

The high school band played. Half a band, I guess. The ones who were left. No percussion, somehow, though I'd thought they'd be the ones to survive, big guys carrying big drums. Lot more piccolos than you'd think.

A few hundred people gathered at the end of the marina in a circle, the wind coming light from the north with storm clouds rumbling way up there in the top of the state, up near Alabama. The wind still carried the smell of civilization burning, not as strong now but there, smoke wraithing up from the torched paper mill, the flaming cotton fields near the state line.

The zombie sat in the middle of the circle. Chained up, but he hardly needed the chains. They hung slack around him. He was a kid, used to be a kid, maybe even part of the high school band. Skinny like a zombie is skinny but more so, like he was already thin before anything started. White kid, short blond hair and his right arm half gone, raw and black and rotting at the elbow. He looked at the ground, turned his eyes up now and then and stared at the crowd, his eyes the eyes of a deer that's been shot. A deer on the ground, pink blood coming up from its punctured lung and onto its tawny fur, rasping its last few breaths. Those black and glassy eyes looking up at the sky for the last time. The rage gone.

That happened to them at the end. They slowed down, the fire drained out of them. Only so much energy in a body, I guess, if it's not actually metabolizing all the shit it eats. Geriatric zombies—easy kills for all the grunts who marched in with their M16s, their tanks, their jets. Wasted monsters with eyes like TV screens scrambled with static. Try taking on the newborn army with nothing but a machete.

And this chained-up zombie kid looked at us all with those empty eyes and judged us.

Around the circle were the survivors. Men and women I'd seen before the outbreak but leaner now, their faces brown with sun, stony and calm. Children played around the edges of the crowd. They played zombie versus survivor. *Raaaawwr! Bang, bang!* A few zombie-rights activists leaned on their protest signs. They'd been all over the place when the outbreak started; hardly any left now. Zombies ate most of them.

I looked for Davia. She wasn't there.

The band finished the song and the mayor stepped forward and smiled at us. He waited for applause and none came, so he looked over at the band and they started clapping and then the rest of the crowd joined in with this weak smattering of claps like rain dripping from the roof after the storm has moved on. Mayor nodded anyway. "Thank you, thank you," he said. "We're gathered here today to celebrate a return to normalcy. A return to the wonderful life we live in our beautiful town of Spanish

Shanty." He paused again—crickets—and then he sighed and went on. He said he wanted us to remember those we'd lost. He wanted us to be grateful to the soldiers who'd saved us.

I could see Rodney on the other side of the circle. He had his spiked knuckles on, and he flexed his fingers. I touched Santana. The soldiers who'd saved us. Like we'd needed saving.

The mayor finished his speech and brought out some dignitaries. A new chief of police, since the other had died. Local business owners, part of the rebuilding; people like coffee-shop guy shook the mayor's hand and grinned for the camera.

And then it was the big finish. The mayor took the golden gun from the holster and held it above his head. "This gun was made right here in town," he said. "It's the product of a symbolic partnership between Pemberton's Jewelry and Roger's Guns and Ammo. You'd never think a jewelry store would be working with an armory, but that's exactly the kind of partnership that kept us all alive. Teachers working with fishermen. Bakers working with doctors. Students and maids and soldiers, all of us together, working to keep Spanish Shanty safe. Together, we survived. So it's in the spirit of togetherness that I kill the last zombie."

Across the circle a woman sobbed, and she put her hands in her hair and buried her face in the chest of the man beside her. A thin man with short blond hair, an older version of the zombie.

The kid's parents.

The mayor pointed the gun at the zombie's head and grinned for another round of pictures. The zombie looked up at the barrel, cocked his head. "Let this be the last bullet fired in our fair town," the mayor said. "Sic semper zombius." He pulled the trigger. There were all these sounds at once: a crack from the gun and a grunt from the zombie and a clink on the concrete and then screaming. The zombie collapsed forward and the chains caught him, so his knees were on the ground but his chest hovered an inch or so off of it, and he swayed with pieces of his brain seeping out of the bullet holes while his mother cried. The screaming came from a man in the crowd downrange of the gun. Asian man, middle-aged. He sat on the ground, gripping his bleeding shin, while the people around him looked down and took a step back, two steps, cleared another small circle.

Gold's denser than lead. Fucking golden gun with a gold bullet. It went right through the soft zombie skull with no mushrooming, no slowing. Came out the back of the zombie's head and smacked against the concrete road and shattered that poor guy's leg. Thought he'd made it out unscathed, and here he was, last casualty of the war.

A couple of cops came and dragged him away. One of them was scrambling to put on a face mask.

So the sculptor is lying, I guess. Mayor The Rock is the action hero and the zombie is the beast to be slain. And already I'm wondering if that's how it really was. I was there, I saw it, but what is that memory but some flashes inside my head? This is stone. This is a statue chiseled from a boulder to show us the past. Does anyone else remember it the way I do? That the mayor didn't save us, that no one saved us. That we saved ourselves. That death came to Spanish Shanty and we the normals were the ones who looked in its rotting face and said *No*, that we were the ones with the machetes, the knuckles, the poleaxes who drove them back. It was our kingdom. There was no mayor. Only a king.

Coffee's gone. Clouds are building up north of town today too. I take the cup and impale it on the barrel of the golden gun. Then I look around and I'm alone here with the boats knocking against the pilings and the water sloshing through the breakwater, so I unzip my pants and piss all over the mayor's bodybuilder legs, all over his stone shoes, all over the gun.

And by now it's almost three. Bungalow.

BACK THEN

We watch the news coverage until late.

CNN has a split screen with the anchor on the left and Times Square on the right. The big building in the middle, the one where they do the New Year's thing, is on fire. Like a Roman candle shooting sparks in the night, flames up up higher than the buildings that surround it. The square itself is deserted.

The anchor keeps repeating the same thing. "Please keep in mind the World Health Organization's recommendations," she says. "Stay in your home if possible. Do not come into contact with anyone you believe to be suffering from the infection." She goes down the usual list of zombie-prevention protocol presented as if it's just regular disease-prevention protocol.

"Just like a movie," Rodney says.

"Never works in a movie," I say. "Everything she's saying. We know it and they know it. Not going to work."

"We're seeing symptoms in major cities across the country, across the world," the anchor says. She's reading quickly, like she's trying to get the shit done and get out of there. "Some cases have been reported in smaller towns—" and she looks off-screen and her eyes are wide and the feed cuts. Blue screen.

"Like a fucking movie," Rodney says again.

We watch the blue screen for a while. Then we sleep, Rodney crashing on the couch, until the signal comes back around midday.

Camera's pointed at a podium with the White House emblem on it. It's set up in a makeshift press room down at Mar-a-Lago in Florida. Before the anchors can say anything, Trump stalks to the podium and starts talking. "This is not a crisis," he says. "Everyone needs to stop worrying, because we've got this all under control. We've got a plan for dealing with this, a tremendous plan. I've got people on this right now. The people working on this, you wouldn't believe. Just the best people. And the fake news media wants you to believe that we don't know what we're doing, but trust me, we do. Everyone just calm down, and you'll all be fine." And then he's walking away and reporters are shouting questions—What's the plan? Is the military involved? Is there a cure? What should the American people do?—but Trump ignores them and then he's gone.

They cut back to a split screen, this time split into four: Times Square. Brooklyn Bridge. The Champs-Élysées in Paris and the Houses of Parliament in London. It's dark over in Europe, but you can see smoke in the air near the Arc de Triomphe, flames at the base of Big Ben.

We take Rodney's car and go get burgers. Spanish Shanty looks normal. Quiet, maybe, but normal. Kid at McDonald's doesn't say a word to us. We go back to my place and watch until dark.

There's been a crowd on the Brooklyn Bridge for a few hours, a steady stream of people fleeing Manhattan on foot. Now something else is happening in its corner of the split screen. There is no sound, no anchor, but the camera zooms in, pivots. People are pushing, scattering. A spot of pavement opens up, a circle of people forming around someone as the crowd shoves to get away. The other three images disappear and the bridge takes up the whole screen. It's a woman, on her back on the pavement, shaking like she's going to break her own bones, crack her skull. And then she's still. The crowd calms, begins to edge closer to her.

Then she's on her feet, and she leaps and pulls down the man nearest to her. He flails, tries to push her away. The camera zooms closer. She's at his throat. Blood sprays like waves breaking on rocks.

Panic. There are fifty thousand people on the bridge and they all want to be anywhere else. They shove and trample. People are going over the sides—some jump, some are forced over when the wall of bodies surges and there's no room left to surge. They fall into the East River. It's March, thirty degrees in New York. They splash into the frigid water and it closes black and cold over the top of them. Except for the people closest to Brooklyn, where the bridge continues past the river. There, they splash onto the cement.

The camera catches it all. It doesn't cut away. One unblinking, unwavering eye in the sky, witness to the madness.

And I wish I'd been there. I could have done something. The moment that zombie woman stood up, I could have brought her right back down. Calmed the crowd. Saved the trampled from the crushing feet of the horde, saved the fallen from the frozen grip of the water, the hard truth of the cement. I could have saved them.

"Shit, man," Rodney says, a whisper, a breath. "Shit."

I grab the machete from the shelf. Take it from the sheath and run my finger along its glinting edge. I grab an orange from the fridge and put it on the cutting board and give it an experimental chop. I barely put any force into it; gravity alone pulls the blade straight through the skin, the fleshy insides of the fruit. One smooth silent slice and the two clean halves wobble on the board. I toss one to Rodney and start to eat the other. Wipe the juice off the blade with a dish towel and put the machete back in its sheath.

"You going to get a zombie with that thing?" Rodney says.

"You bet."

"What am I supposed to use?"

"You got a gun?"

"You just figure all black guys got guns?"

I shrug. "I thought you might have a gun."

"No gun."

I start digging through the drawers. I find a chef's knife, a hammer, a crowbar. A three-foot chunk of rebar in the carport, left over from when I was going to build a wall at the end of the driveway so people'd quit driving through my goddamn lawn. "Want one of these things?"

Rodney looks them over. He hefts the rebar. Takes it out into the front yard and swings it. "This'll work for now. Got to get something better, though." He drums the rebar against the side of his foot. It's quiet out. Getting close to nine, so it's dark, and the wind is shifting from the bay so that now it's coming in warm over the land. We walk together to the end of the driveway and look past the neighbor's house and over the water. Black and glassy. A three-quarter moon hangs above the island. It looks warped, too fat to be a crescent or a half, too small to be full. A bulbous thing looking down at its own reflection shimmering in the calm.

And then a roar and the jets come right overhead. Normally they stay high, far out over the Gulf. These are low, racing north. Three F-16s tearing across the darkened land.

"Where they going?" Rodney says.

"Don't know," I say. "Hey, you want something better? We can go to the pawnshop. We go now we can get there before they close."

We get in Rodney's car and drive. We head into town and east through the closed-up shops into the industrial district. Paper mill is looming on the horizon, its lights casting white above it and blocking out the stars, smoke and steam curling up in billowing artificial clouds. The smell hangs over everything out here, a sulfurous fart smell.

There are a dozen cars outside the pawnshop, and a line of a few people trails out the door.

Rodney parks and we walk up to the end of the line. There's an old man in front of us. Shotgun in his hands. He turns, looks Rodney up and down, shifts the gun from one shoulder to the other. Rodney narrows his eyes. The man is silent. A woman comes out, cradling a pistol in her palms like it's an injured bird, and the line moves and the old man goes inside.

We wait.

Rodney's looking at his phone.

"What about your mom?" I say. My mom's been dead for years—my dad too, both of lung cancer, since they'd smoked since they were fifteen. Rodney's got family, though. Doesn't talk about them much.

"She's with my brother," Rodney says. "I haven't seen them in a month. And they're up in Briggsport. It's forty-five minutes."

"We could go up there after. Check on them."

"Getting late, though." He looks younger now. I'm not sure how old he actually is. I always figured like thirty, but you know what, he could be twenty-five, twenty-two. Right now, thinking about his mom, his brother, he looks like a kid. His clothes seem too big for him, his body thinner than before. He checks his phone again, looks north. "Man, I don't know."

More cars are pulling up. The line grows behind us. "We go if you want," I say.

The old man comes out of the store with a new gun, a revolver, sitting in a new holster around his waist. He's also got three bags full of boxes of ammo. "No more shells," he says to us. He stares at Rodney.

"Do I look like I got a shotgun?" Rodney says.

"Somewheres you do."

"Worry about the zombies, motherfucker," Rodney says, and he pushes past the old man and goes inside.

I follow him. Inside everything is lit yellow with old incandescent bulbs. Smells like gun oil and leather. A skinny woman stands behind the counter. She wears a flower-printed dress that hangs from her shoulders like a blanket over a birdcage. "What you need?" she says. "Make it quick. Got customers."

One wall of the shop is dominated by a row of shotguns and rifles. I pick up a double-barrel twelve-gauge, break it, look down the barrels.

"Ain't got no more shells," the shopkeeper says.

Rodney picks up an assault rifle. Bushmaster. He looks like Rambo holding it. "How much for this one?" he says.

She squints at it. "I give you that for three hundred. Five hundred if you want to skip the waiting period."

"You can't waive that? Considering the circumstances?"

"Rules is rules. It's not the goddamn end of the world. You got to wait three days. Unless you got that extra two hundred."

"Fine." Rodney takes the gun to the counter and slaps down his credit card.

"No credit," the woman says.

"I got good credit."

"Not taking credit from anyone."

She reaches across the counter and pulls the rifle from Rodney's hands. He has a look on his face like a kid who dropped his ice cream on the sidewalk. "Why not?" Rodney says.

"Cash only. Who knows if the credit companies'll ever pay me again."

"You said it's not the end of the world," I say.

She grins, and her teeth are yellow with tobacco. "Maybe not the end," she says. "But we're in the home stretch."

Rodney takes out his wallet. "I got twenty bucks."

The shopkeeper looks through the glass at the pistols and the knives, and then she perks up and says, "I know!" and shuffles over to a cabinet in the corner of the store. She digs through one of the drawers and comes out with a pair of brass knuckles and hands them to Rodney.

He slips them over his fingers. The subtle curve of the metal fits smoothly against Rodney's skin. The four spikes jut up in short, fierce points an inch long. Rodney clenches his fists, turns them in the light, the brass glowing dull and milky in the incandescent yellow. He waggles his fingers, then clenches them again and takes a couple of experimental punches.

"They's from World War Two," the shopkeeper says. "Guy who pawned them said they come from a dead Nazi. Don't know if I believe him, but they sweet little things, right?"

Rodney nods as he throws an uppercut.

"I give you those for twenty," the shopkeeper says.

Rodney slips her the bill.

"What you want for that machete?" she says. She's looking at the blade on my hip.

"Not for sale," I say.

She nods. "Smart man. That girl's going to treat you right."

We leave. The parking lot's full now. Line of people stretches to the end of the store. "Can you drive?" Rodney says. "I'm gonna text my mom."

We drive back toward town. Near McDonald's, a kid is running. Teenager, sprinting full out, looking over his shoulder. Big bloody hole torn in his shirt. Rodney rolls the window down beside him. "Hey!" he says, and the kid glances at Rodney and back over his shoulder and then turns down an alley. "You think it's here already?" Rodney says.

"I told you about the girl in the store."

"Thought you might be making it up." He looks at his phone. "She's not answering."

We head along the bay back toward my house. The moon has set now, and the night is thick around us. It's nearly ten, and the lights in the houses are out. Quiet all over except for the leaves shuffling against each other in the wind.

I pull into my driveway, and there's a kid standing in it.

"Zombie!" Rodney says.

It's my neighbor's kid. I can recognize him from behind because he has this long stupid curly hair, like he hasn't had a haircut in the eight years he's been alive. The headlights are on him and he's still staring at my house. I honk the horn. Nothing. I lay on the horn and the kid is motionless.

"Fucking zombie, man," Rodney says. "I'm telling you."

I pull up farther and nudge the kid with the bumper, and now he wheels around, puts his hands on the hood. He looks at the metal like it's some alien material. Bangs his palms against it, scrapes it with his fingernails. I honk again and the kid looks up and yeah, Rodney's right. Zombie. His eyes are wide open and his pupils seem to stretch black across the whole surface of the eyeball. Bloody tears trickle down past his nose. His mouth hangs open like someone's sliced the jaw muscles that hold it shut. He says *uuurrrrrrr*.

"All right," Rodney says. He slips his knuckles over his fingers. "I'm going to get him. Watch this." He starts to open the door and the kid says *ahhrrarrraaaaarrrrrr* and in an instant he's on Rodney's side, smacking bloody handprints on the window, reaching through the cracked door, pawing at Rodney's arm. "Shit!" Rodney says, and he slams the door on the kid's arm a few times until he lets go.

The kid jumps onto the hood and claws at the windshield. I turn on the wipers and they streak blood in long arcs, and then the kid grabs the wipers and tears them off. He throws one aside and tries to eat the other, and then he starts banging with his fist.

"He can't get in, can he?" Rodney says.

"He's small. I don't know."

We watch him. He's punching methodically, weak eight-year-old punches, but they're hitting the same spot again and again. Pressure. *Bang.* Repetition. *Bang.* Time. *Bang, bang, bang,* and then a splinter in the glass.

"Yep," I say. "Done with this."

I throw the car into reverse and hit the gas, and the kid rolls backward off the hood and crashes into the driveway. We wait in the road and watch him. He's still for a minute or so, and then he gets up, turns to us. *Riiiiiguhguhguh,* he says, and he runs toward us, but I put the car in drive and fly forward and hit him, and he sails back a few feet, thuds on the concrete. He jumps up, his face a snarl of confusion and rage. I hit him again, and this time he's stuck on the hood, so I keep going and push him all the way up the driveway and slam him against the back of the carport.

I turn the car off and Rodney and I get out. The kid is still moving. The middle of his body is crushed between the car and the wall, and some of his insides—brown and yellow slippery bits—have spilled onto the floor. The rest of his body is tangled up in the stuff I've got stored in the carport. An arm is caught in the bent handle of a weed trimmer. Another piece of rebar is sticking through his thigh. One arm is still free, though, and he's reaching for me with it. The thin arm of a child, clawing and grasping with bloody fingers. Bite marks on the wrist. Thumb missing.

"He's not dead yet," Rodney says. "What we got to do to kill him?"

"You know what we got to do."

Rodney nods. "Yeah, man. I know. I just didn't want it to be like that." He looks at the spikes on his knuckles. They glint in the headlights. "You going to do it?"

He's got this pleading look in his eyes. "I thought you wanted to get him," I say.

"Yeah, but that was when he was up and about. It's different now, him all pinned up. Don't feel the same."

The kid is wrenching his head from side to side, biting at the air. Growling, something quiet and guttural. His eyes don't focus on anything. I pull the machete from its sheath and turn it in the light. A white glow on its blade like a miniature sun. I hold it out and touch the blade to the kid's skull. Take a couple of practice swings, bringing the machete way over my head and stopping an inch away. One hand? Two hands? It's a weird angle with the car in the way, but I don't want to back out and risk the kid crawling around, leaking guts all over the carport. Hard enough to clean up already. So one hand, then. "Okay," I say. "All right. I'm going to do this."

"Hang on," Rodney says. He finds a paint-stained drop cloth and holds it in front of him so that just his eyes are sticking out over the top. "What? These are nice pants."

"All right. Going to count. One." I hold the blade an inch from the kid's head. "Two." Bring it high over my own. "Three."

Down, down, rushing slicing the blade cutting through the night the dark the head lamps the cool salt air; down through the kid's curly hair that has grown since he was a toddler wobbling along on shaky knees and falling on his ass in the grass of their front yard, the hair that his mother brushed and teased before the first day of kindergarten, that she smoothed and fluffed for Christmas-card pictures; down, down, down through his skin white and soft, protected from the sun by all that hair, cleaned by no-more-tears shampoos, softened by conditioner that comes in a bottle shaped like a dolphin; down through his skull, the skull that came out of his mother warped from the pressure of the birth canal and landed in his father's waiting hands, that rested against his mother's breast his father's shoulder on late nights and sleepy mornings as the bones inside it came together, piece by piece, fusing into one solid whole that protects its cargo, the precious, precious cargo; and down into the brain, repository of everything, everything this kid ever was—his memories his emotions his make-believe games, his multiplication tables his states and capitals, the rules of baseball and Monopoly and hide-and-seek, the girls he liked and pretended to hate—and everything he'd never be.

There's a *thwack* sound, and the blade sinks three inches into the kid's head before it runs out of momentum. His body goes limp. His head rests on the hood, the machete sticking out of it.

Rodney and I look at him for a while. Then I reach over and yank the machete out. "Give me that," I say to Rodney, and he hands me the drop cloth. It's spattered in blood, and I look down and see that my shirt is too, my pants, the tops of my shoes. I wipe the blade with the cloth and set the machete on the hood, and then I try to clean myself off. The blood stays where it is. Permanent stains.

"Well," Rodney says. "I guess you got him."

"I guess so."

Rodney tries to laugh, but it comes out forced. "You're a badass with that machete, Rip. Maybe *you're* Ving Rhames." He laughs again, but it's hollow in the quiet night.

"It didn't feel badass," I say. "Why am I always stuck killing kids? This kid"—I point at him with the machete—"and the girl at the grocery store. Goddammit, they're never killing kids in the movies. Kids all over the place; there's going to be kid zombies, right? But they're never killing kid zombies. Because it fucking sucks." I look over at the kid again and he doesn't look like a zombie anymore, just some dead kid in my carport, and this is not fun the way I wanted it to be. I wanted to be Ving Rhames. I didn't want to cut the neighbor kid's head in half.

"But you did what you had to do. Look, man," Rodney says, and he walks around the back of the car to come to my side, and there's a shrieking and this whir of white and blonde and Rodney's on the ground. I run to him, and he's there on the concrete with the kid's mom on top of him. She's in a nightgown and her teeth are red with blood and her hair is matted with black stuff, and she's clawing for Rodney's face but he's holding her off. I reach for the machete in its sheath but it's not there, it's still on the hood. I run back and grab it and when I turn around, Rodney has spun her over. She's a powerful woman, tall and covered with lean muscle from years of yoga and Pilates and whatever else I see her coming home from with her mat rolled under her arm and her ass so round in those tight black pants. Now those muscles are fighting for Rodney, but he's got her on her back and he puts one knee on her chest and one foot on the ground, and she's reaching for him but he rears back and puts his fist into her face. The knuckles go in deep and she says *urk*. She's still moving, so Rodney gives her another right to the face and then a left hook to the side of the head, and she goes limp.

Rodney's out of breath. He looks behind me. "Rip."

I spin with the blade ready because I know he's there. I could see it in Rodney's face. I could feel him there. Didn't hear him, didn't smell him, just felt him—the electricity in the air or the movement of atoms against my skin, I don't know. I know just where he'll be, and I spin and the blade cuts a clean path through the dad's neck, flesh muscle bone muscle flesh, right through and out the other side. Zombie dad's head rolls off and lands under the elephant ears, a confused look on his face, face all bloody with bite marks on his cheeks. One ear missing. His body stumbles around for a second and falls over.

"Ving Fucking Rhames," Rodney says.

And yeah, I'll admit it. That part was pretty cool.

WEDNESDAY, OCTOBER 23

There's no one in Bungalow except Bob and Mo. Clouds have come in and covered up the sun, so there's not much light coming through the skylight. The neon Coors sign glows pink in the dimness and reflects on the bar top. Bob hands me a Three Bears Light and goes in the back to do whatever he does back there, and I sit down beside Mo.

He smiles at me. Not that drunk yet. "Hey Rip," he says. "Long time."

It hasn't been a long time, but I guess he's been wasted the last few times I talked to him, so this is the first time that really counts. "Hey, Mo."

"King Rip," he says. "Rip, el rey del Río Perezoso."

"I don't speak Spanish, Mo."

"You should learn. Don't be ignorant." He swirls his whiskey and takes a sip. "You live in Florida, man. It's almost the native language."

"In Miami, maybe. Not up here."

"Still. You've got neighbors that speak it. Your coworkers. Your friends, huh?" He puts his palm on his chest. "A little respect. We all learned your language."

"Yeah, well, it's my country."

"I'm an American too, Rip." He grins at me.

I raise my beer. "You know I'm fucking with you, right?" I tink the bottle against his glass. I don't care what language he speaks. He can kill zombies like no one I've seen, except me, maybe. He can play the guitar and sing on a long night with no electric power. He can repair an old generator with nothing but a busted-up tire and some crazy glue.

"I know," Mo says. "You're one of the good ones."

"I'm still not learning Mexican," I say.

"Spanish."

"What's the difference?"

"Fuck you."

I smile at him and sip my beer.

Mo finishes his whiskey and reaches across the bar and pours himself another. The liquor fills the glass, two fingers, three, four. He takes a swig straight from the bottle before putting it back.

"I'm charging you for that," Bob yells from the back.

"Fine, fine." He's already slurring a little more than he was five minutes ago. Makes me wonder if he could still wield el decapitador, if he even knows where it is. If he's pawned it.

"Any business?" I say.

Mo shrugs. "I talked to a guy this morning. I drove out to that neighborhood near the bridge, Queen's Point, you know. The big houses. I saw one of Freddy's trucks out there, his guys working in a yard, putting down new sod."

"I thought Freddy got ate."

"He did. Someone else taken over his stuff." Mo shakes his head. "I don't even know where they got the sod. I talked to my distributors and none of them have any. Didn't grow right this summer since there wasn't enough light. The grass was in shadow all summer because of the smoke. It grew yellow. Weak. You can't transplant that stuff." He points at my beer. "It's probably commie grass. Ship it in like they ship in the beers."

Seems like half our stuff comes from the NewSSR now. Russia was the only country to come through the outbreak unscathed. They reforged the union, wrapped that Iron Curtain right back around Eastern Europe and most of the 'stans and even Mongolia. All those people perfectly happy to go back to the eighties in exchange for an army that would clean up the zombie mess. Now their economy's in overdrive, flush with resources and infrastructure and people while the rest of the world's lurching back to its feet.

People act mystified as to how Russia made it through so easily. I know how. Davia told me.

She used to stand at the edge of the lazy river and watch them at night. Ten yards of slow-flowing chlorinated blue between her and the dead. She leaned on her poleaxe, her eyes lost in the calculus of their movements.

I asked her why she watched them like that.

"So that I know them," she said.

They moved slow in the darkness, groaning, bumping into one another. Toeing the edge of the moat but never stepping in.

She shook her head and swirled the water with the saw blade. "Your country is pathetic. To let this happen."

"What were we supposed to do?" I said. "They were nowhere, and then they were everywhere. You can't practice for something like this."

"We did," she said. And she told me about the Upyr, the zombies of Russian lore. Thousands of years ago, an outbreak had plagued her continent, and Davia's ancestors had banded together to fight them. Killed most of them, drove the rest north, up to the farthest reaches of Siberia where the glaciers had scraped the land clean with the receding ice age. They wandered until they fell. They lay frozen for generations while the world warmed and the people turned the story into legend. Then they started thawing out. One or two a year clawed their way from the soggy permafrost and slouched southward to the barren villages at the cold edge of the world. The villagers knew an Upyr when they saw one. With the hatchet, the sledgehammer, the pipe wrench, they struck the monsters down and went about their lives.

One came to Davia's village when she was five. She killed it with a tire iron.

When the mass thaw came this spring and hundreds of zombies advanced, the Russians had been ready. They knew the legend of the Upyr, and the random encounters of the Industrial Age had spread by word of mouth. They were armed. They were practiced. The zombies didn't stand a chance.

"No one takes Russia from the Russians," Davia said. "Not Napoleon. Not Hitler. And not the Upyr."

The zombies spread out, wandering among the bougainvillea. Only a couple were across from us. Davia slipped into the water as quiet as a crocodile, came out the other side slick and dripping. She took down the zombies with two swings of her poleaxe, and then she knelt beside the lazy river and washed the saw blade clean. She looked at me across the water, her eyes filled with the terrible knowledge of the Siberian winter, of the snow red with blood, of the world that had turned her to steel.

So of course Russia made it through just fine. A whole country of Davias.

I drink my Three Bears Light. "I got fired today," I say.

"For what?" Mo says.

"I don't know. For being me, I guess."

"That makes sense."

"Does it?"

Mo nods. "How are you going to be you now? Not the same you, anyway. Not the you that you were. That you doesn't work at a call center. That you kills zombies."

Bob comes out and gives me another beer. "Sorry to hear it, Rip."

It's a Coors Light. They've changed the bottle since the outbreak: the Rockies are still there, but there's jets flying across them, trailing red-white-and-blue smoke. "I can't afford this, Bob." Even cheap American beer costs a fortune now with all the factories looted and the crops burned up.

"This one's on me." Bob looks at me a moment. "You told someone off, didn't you?"

I drink the beer. It tastes just like it used to—like corn and metal and sweat. Like America. "Yeah," I say.

"Who?"

"Everyone."

Bob laughs. "'Course they fired you."

"How am I supposed to do that job, though? How am I supposed to care about people's bullshit complaints? Did you ever think we'd have this again?" I gesture at the beer, the liquor, the bar in general, everything dark and musty but still so much more than what anyone had in the summer. "You know it," I say. "You thought the world was over. I did."

Bob nods. "I thought I'd be stuck in this bar until I died. And I figured I'd have died by now."

"I know. Everyone should be dead. But we're not. We're alive, somehow, and no one cares. It's all the same as it was. Same bullshit. I'm sick of it."

"This bullshit's better than the zombie bullshit."

"Is it, though?" I say, and I wonder what I'm saying.

"You got your beer. No one trying to eat you."

"Are you happy, though?" I say to Bob. He shrugs. "Mo? How about you, Mo? You happy?"

Mo looks into his whiskey. "Gabriela left me last week."

Bob sighs, fills Mo's glass again. "You didn't tell me that, man. Why didn't you tell me?"

"Thought she might come back. Not this time. It's for good this time."

Mo fought through it all for Gabriela and his daughter, Lupita. Kept digging through the ruins long after we'd left them for dead. And then he found them, *he found them*, pulled them from the rubble and brought them home and nursed them back to health. And then the way he lost Lupita. Gabriela was all he had left. And now she's gone. "I'm sorry, Mo," I say.

He nods.

Bob takes out a rag and wipes the bar while we drink. "What about Davia, Rip? You ever see her?"

I want to tell them about today, but already it feels like maybe I imagined it. She was a different woman there on the street, except for that flash of recognition, that instant when she saw me and lit up, but then it was gone. Maybe she was never there to begin with. "No," I say. "I don't know where she is."

Mo raises his glass. "To the women we've loved, the women who've left," he says. And Bob opens a beer too and we touch the glass bottle to bottle to rim, and we drink. The clouds are dark overhead and the rain starts to *dibble dop* on the roof and in the bayou around us, the sound cleansing rushing like water through pipes.

* * *

I'm four beers in and Mo's nearly unconscious when the Air Force guys show up. Base is ten miles out of town, down where the bay curves around toward the Gulf, nearly meeting up with the barrier island, and it's practically a city in itself, so they don't come to Spanish Shanty that often. It's obvious when they do, though. Usually they come in their flight jackets, sometimes even in those green flight suits. Even when they don't, though, you can tell because they look like their jets. The F-15 guys are long and lean. Angled faces, high cheekbones, narrow noses. They drink expensive beer and look down on the bar since they're so used to being high above everything. And the ones who fly the F-22s, the other air-to-air fighters, are even worse because they know they're in the hot-shit jet, the $150 million war machine. I've seen them drinking wine. F-16 pilots are different—smaller, scrappy-looking guys who come in loud, have one drink or maybe two, and take off for the next bar.

These two fly the A-10s. I know it immediately. They're short, stocky guys. Muscular chests and shoulders, their arms hanging a few inches from their sides like they're flexing in front of the mirror. Their jets are heavy and slow, but armored. They'll take a hundred bullets and cruise home. I even heard someone landed one after a missile blew a hole in his wing. The A-10 Warthog. Ugly beast that gets the job done.

The pilots sit down at one of the few tables in the bar, and Bob talks to them and brings them their drinks. Cheap commie beers—Three Bears and Baltika 3. One nods at me. He's still got his aviator shades on. I raise my hand and turn back to Mo.

"Up their own asses, huh?" I say.

Mo lifts his head off his forearms and gives them a glance and shrugs. Puts his head back down.

I look at my reflection in the mirror and try to figure out what jet I'd fly. I'm too tall for the Warthog. Not tall enough to be an Eagle, a Raptor—the F-15s, the 22s. Not an F-16 Falcon either; I'm too fat. Mostly, though, I'm too old. Dark under my eyes like I've been wearing swim goggles all day. Hair mostly gray by now. Used to be solid black, combed over nice and slick, but now it's gray and brittle and it doesn't stay where I put it. Don't care enough to make it stay. Just a sloppy gray mess on top of my head that needs cutting.

I sit up straighter so that it doesn't look like I have tits. I'm not *fat* fat, but I lost a lot of weight during the summer, got all light and solid from the running and from swinging Santana, and now that it's coming back I'm embarrassed of it. Never gave a shit before, but now it's like I know what I could be. What I ought to be. But the fat that comes with this soft world is growing like fungus and spreading over the hard machine that carries me.

I could be an F-15. Instead I'm a C-130. Just a big-ass cargo plane. Doing the grunt work while everyone else barrel-rolls across the wild blue yonder.

The Warthogs are laughing, loud and boisterous. A roar close and low like the engines of their planes. Rodney comes in and looks at them and then sits down next to me. "That was some shit today," he says as Bob brings him a beer. "Pretty fucking cool. You know how long everyone's wanted to stand up and say something like that?"

"It didn't come out like I wanted it to."

"You don't have to be elegant. You said it true. None of us gives a fuck anymore. Why should we? World's still ending, just not as quick as before."

In the mirror his face is young and fresh and angry, and I'm sagging beside him and I see us for a second as two climbers on a mountain. He's strong on the upward slope, powering over the obstacles with his eyes on the summit, and I'm already on the other side. I've got my skis on. The peak's in the rearview and there's nothing to do but coast to the bottom.

"I might quit," Rodney says. "That place. We're part of the problem. Every single product we sell is one more cup of gasoline on this big-ass fire that's burning up the world."

"Don't quit. You need the job."

"We're enablers. We make it so easy for them. Easier to throw something away and buy more than it is to reuse a single thing. Unsustainable. I can't do it another day. Another year—thirty years? I'm supposed to just sit there helping fill the world up with plastic and CO2 and whatever else for thirty fucking years?"

"They'd move you before then, anyway. Place is going to shut down in a year, guarantee it. You'll end up in Nebraska or something."

"World's not going to make it thirty years. Not at this rate. We'll be lucky to get half that."

"You're a couple of fucking downers," Bob says. He's been sitting at the end of the bar, going through his notebook. Now he puts it down and opens a beer and leans on the bar in front of us. "All this bitching. White-people problems."

"Who you think you're talking to about white-people problems?" Rodney says.

"Fine. *American* problems," Bob says. "You know what happened in Jamaica?"

"Do *you* know what happened in Jamaica?"

"'Course I do."

"You're from Kansas."

Bob narrows his eyes. Points at the Jamaican flag that hangs over the bar. "*That's* who I am. That's blood. My blood is in Jamaica. I got family there. Had family." He throws the beer back and drinks half of it in three big swallows. Then he rests the bottle on a Baltika coaster.

"I know, Bob," I say. Truth is, we all know about Jamaica. Every country took its licks—except Russia, of course—but Jamaica got it the worst. The outbreak moved fast there, took over Kingston in the first couple of days, the whole city overrun, downtown and the beaches and the slums, all of Trenchtown heaving with zombies, spreading like plague to Portmore, to Ewarton, and in a week they covered everything from Montego Bay to Duckenfield. Zombies were wandering onto boats and floating out to sea. Hundreds got onto an abandoned cruise ship and somehow loosed it from the dock, and it was drifting, drifting toward the edge of the harbor, and that's when the American government decided things had gone too far. This was early enough that they still thought they could rein it in, the outbreak. Things weren't so bad in Cuba, in Haiti; the Cayman Islands were outbreak-free. A boatload of zombies spilling onto the shore would change that.

So they nuked Jamaica. Two B-61s hurled from a stealth bomber into Kingston, three more warheads chucked up out of the ocean by submarines, the Trident missiles dripping into the sky and arcing over the vacant eyes of the zombies and a flash and fire and shock wave and—

Annihilation.

"I'm sorry, man," Rodney says. "I didn't mean it like that, you know. We all got blood somewhere. Runs deep."

Bob nods. "The point," he says, "is look what we got now. We got beer. We got the bay and the Gulf out there. You can swim if you want. That rain"—he points to the ceiling where the rain is falling harder, like marbles pinging on the roof so heavy you have to raise your voice—"that rain is clean. Not radioactive. We can drink it. The rain in Jamaica, the rivers, beaches, everything; you can't go back there for a thousand years." He finishes his beer. Gives us each a new one. Pours another inch into Mo's whiskey, even though he hasn't stirred for fifteen minutes. "So drink up," Bob says, smiling now. "We got it good."

"Shots!" One of the Warthogs. "Hey, Bob! Shots!"

Bob sighs. "What you want, mon?" He plays it up sometimes when it's not just us, the regulars.

"Tequila!" It's the one with the aviator shades. His buddy is grinning, shaking his head. "Good shit!"

Bob turns back to us and snorts. "They ought to know there's no good shit. Like there are still barrels just sitting around aging in Mexico." He pours a couple of shots of cheap tequila and carries it over to the table. "Maracame," he says. "Best in the house."

"No, no," says Shades. "For all of us! You guys, come on!" He's waving at us. "You too, Bob. Shots for everyone. We're buying."

Rodney shrugs and we go over there. Shades grabs a couple more chairs and we sit down and Bob pours three more shots.

Shades holds up his glass. "Hoo-ha, fuck shit up, get wasted!" he says, and he downs the shot and makes a face, shakes his head like he's just come out of a pool. "Yeeeawh!" He takes his shades off and his eyes are red and wild. "Drink up. Don't leave me hanging!"

We take our shots. The tequila burns going down, but it makes me feel warm in my chest my belly, a good warmth with the bar snug and dim and the rain coming down above us.

The other Warthog stands up. "We ought to get going," he says to his friend. "You got to fly tomorrow."

"I can fly hungover," Shades says. "I can fly in my sleep."

"I'm not covering for you."

"No one asked you to. Like you're my fucking mom." He points at me and Rodney. "These guys aren't pussies. They know how to drink. Right?" He's nodding at us, his eyes darting between the two of us. "Right?"

"I can drink," Rodney says.

Shades slaps him on the shoulder. "Fucking knew you could! More shots!"

"Fine," the other Warthog says. "Find your own way home." And he steps out into the rain.

Bob brings another round and we swallow them and slam the glasses down on the table. The pilot grits his teeth, points at the door. "That's Dodger. That pussy. He can't fly for shit. I've seen him overshoot the runway three times in one afternoon, waste half a tank of gas just to get her on the ground. I'm Duck Duck. I'm the best pilot you've ever seen."

"Duck Duck," I say.

"Yeah. Goose was taken."

"You pick that name just so you could make that joke?" Rodney says.

"Yeah. But it's a good one, right?"

And it is a pretty good one. We laugh loud enough that Mo looks over at us and grunts and puts an arm over his head.

"What's his deal?" Duck Duck says.

"He's a country music song," I say. "Lost his woman. Lost his job. If he had a dog he'd have lost it too."

"Ha!" Duck Duck rubs his nose. "I like you," he says, pointing at me. "I *like* you! Shots!"

Bob brings over a round of beer. "Take a break. That tequila isn't cheap."

Duck Duck takes the beer. "All right. Shorten the leash. I get it." He takes a couple of big sips of beer and leans forward.

He's got on a bomber jacket that's somehow still wet with rain even though he's been inside half an hour. Raindrops dapple his crew-cut hair.

"You fly the A-10s?" I ask.

He grins, and his teeth seem too big and white for his head. "How'd you know?" I tell him my theory about men and their planes, and he nods along. "Yeah," he says, "all those fighter pilots think they're hot shit. Get one bullet hole, though, and they eject. You know how much it costs every time one of them ditches? You make a multimillion-dollar fiery hole in the ground. They love to do it too. Gives them a story. Not us. We get her home." He drinks more of the beer and taps the bottom of the bottle on the table. "Not that it doesn't look fun. Ejecting. Maybe as a bucket-list kind of thing."

"Where you come from?" Rodney says. There were no A-10s here before the outbreak. They flew them in in the middle of summer, right before the Army came rolling into town. Kept them stationed here, patrolling the roads, the shores, making sure there are no stray zombies still wandering out there.

"Moody," Duck Duck says. "Up in Georgia. They got Georgia clear fast, faster than Florida. That's why they moved us down here. More fun here anyway. You ever kill one on the beach?"

"Killed them everywhere," I say.

"So you know. That black blood, the zombie blood, you can't see it when you kill one on the road. But on that white sand, man. Damn! Shows up nice. Like modern art." He finishes his beer and puts his finger in the end of the bottle, works the bottle in a circle on the table. "What do you guys do?"

We tell him about work. I tell him about getting fired.

"Fuck your chips!" he says. He puts the bottle down and jabs his finger into my chest. "*You*. I told you I liked you." He looks over at Bob, who's busy behind the counter, and then he reaches into the pocket of his jacket and pulls out a purple snuff vial of coke and takes a bump. Offers it to me.

"Where'd you even get this?" I say. Like the coffee, the coca fields were all burned up or ransacked.

"Got a stash. Been saving it."

I snort a little bit and it's like my brain is on fire, a bottle of soda all shook up. Can feel the points of my teeth. I hand it to Rodney.

"Nah, man," he says.

Back to Duck Duck, who takes another bump and puts it away. "Fuck your chips."

"Yeah," I say, and now I really am mad at that guy. Emailing me about his Pringles. "*Fuck* his chips."

"Hoo-ha!"

"You see what I'm dealing with?" I say to Duck Duck. Rodney seems to recede now. He's leaning back in his chair and not sharing the coke and Duck Duck is looking at me with those intense red eyes, and for right now I know Rodney's my friend, he's the one who's got my back, but it's Duck Duck who understands me, who's there with me on the fiery edge of this volcano with I don't know what inside. "These people," I say. "All these people, acting like nothing ever happened. What did they do over the summer? Didn't it mean something to them? Anything?"

"Meant something to me," Duck Duck says.

"Sure as fuck it did." I take Santana out and set her in the center of the table.

"Oh, look at her," Duck Duck says. "Can I see?"

"No." I pull her toward me.

"I get it, man." Duck Duck's nodding. "I understand. No worries. You're not getting in my plane either. You getting inside her would be like you getting inside my woman."

"That's Santana for me," I say. I pick her up and turn her, and the blade shines even in the dim nighttime bar. "I'm different with her. When I've got her on my hip. In my hand. Especially when she's in my hand. I'm not the same Rip. I'm different, better."

"Rip," Duck Duck says. "I like it. Rip 'em in half."

The door opens and three women come in, pretty, maybe just out of college. They are laughing, and then the front one stops, sees me with the machete in my hand, Duck Duck with his eyes like headlights streaked with red clay. The two behind her bump into her, and they turn and stare. Then they back out the door.

"Room for more!" Duck Duck says.

The women are gone and the rain sounds loud as the door swings shut.

"Fuck 'em. Can't handle us," Duck Duck says. He notices Rodney as if for the first time. "Hey! I got my jet. Rip here has his machete, his Santana. What do you got?"

"I got some knuckles," Rodney says. He leans in and joins the circle, and now it's three of us again. He holds up his fists. "They fit on me nice and smooth, and they've got these spikes, make me feel like Wolverine. Like the spikes are coming right up out of me. Like I've got the adamantium skeleton and I can punch straight through the zombies. They are bad as fuck."

"Can I see?"

"Nah, man. They're at home. Can't go around wearing my knuckles anymore."

"Why not, though?" Duck Duck puts a hand on each of our shoulders. "Why can't you be Wolverine all the time? Anyone would love to be Wolverine! And you were, and now *they* won't let you. Cops or the mayor or whoever. Say you can't be Wolverine. And Rip, Rip was the better version of Rip. The Rip who carries Santana. They're taking the best parts of you away, and we're just letting them. Letting them take what makes us *us*."

"You've still got your jet, though," Rodney says.

"Yeah, I got the jet. I still fly. But I can't shoot the Avenger. They don't even arm me with Mavericks anymore. The missiles. So it's like if they wouldn't let you take Santana out the sheath, Rip. Or if you just had your regular old knuckles, um—"

"Rodney."

"Your regular knuckles, Rodney. Yeah, you can fight with your knuckles, but you're not Wolverine. And Rip, you're still carrying if Santana's in the sheath, but she doesn't do much good. It's like you're impotent. That's what it's like in an aircraft with no weapons. I'm just a lookout. Might as well be a commercial pilot dragging some fat-ass 747 across the Pacific. Back and forth from Australia every forty-eight hours. Shoot me in the fucking face." Duck Duck seems smaller for a minute. He's just a short man in a wet jacket slouched in a chair in a bar on a rainy night. Then he does another bump and grits his teeth and he's lit up again. "Hey! Greatest hits! Best of! What's your big kill? I go first. Flying over from Moody, few months ago after we'd cleared Valdosta and were heading here. Got the order to run a patrol over Mariana, so we're flying around town, and we pass over this gymnasium and I see them just streaming out. Hundreds of zombies coming out, I guess because they heard the engine, shuffling out into the parking lot looking up at us. So my wingman breaks right and I break left and we come around on another pass with the Avengers blasting. That gun, goddamn. You know it fires forty-two hundred rounds a minute? That's seventy a second. You can't even imagine. And we had them loaded with depleted-uranium bullets. They go right through anything—buildings, tanks, whatever. Go right into the asphalt. So we fly over and cut this path through the zombies, and it's like one second, horde of zombies, next second, pile of body parts and the air full of vaporized blood and guts, this blackish-pink cloud hanging over the ground, and all the while the asphalt spattering up into the air like black mud."

"So the ground's all full of uranium now?" Rodney asks.

"Pshh." Duck Duck says, waving his hand. "I guess. But whatever. Better than being full of zombies, right?"

"For now."

"No one's going back there because, listen, here's the best part. We come around for another pass, and it's hard to see with all the asphalt and zombie dust in the air, but they're still pouring out of that gym, just as fast, and then it hits me. That was a shelter. It was chock-full of refugees, and some zombie got in and spread it to everyone. Whole shelter full up of zombies, and now they're spilling out, going to spread through the woods, and the Army will have to hunt them down one by one, so I say not on my watch. Mavericks away. I put two missiles into the gym, and *boom!* Boom, man. It's a building, and then it's a cloud of dust. Goddamn. And I fly through that dust and smoke and it curls behind me and I swear my cock was rock fucking hard."

Bob's beside us now. "Last call," he says.

Duck Duck blinks, struggles to focus on Bob. Like it's taking him a moment to come up out of the memory. "You got a greatest hit, Bob?"

Rodney and I yell it together: "Four in one shot!" We've heard it a million times. Parking lot full of zombies and Bob blasting with the boomstick, and one of those times when he pulls the trigger, four go down like their strings have been cut. No one to witness it. Might be a lie, but whatever. We let him have it.

"One shot?" Duck Duck says.

Bob grins. "It's a big gun."

"One more round of beer, Bob," I say. "Good ones. These are on me."

Bob comes back with three bottles of pale ale. There's a zombie on the side, some sort of undead king. Winged pauldrons on his shoulders, crown on his head. Warhammer gripped in his skeletal fist. "It's called Zombie Dust," Bob says. "It was hard to find before. Now I see it all over the place."

"Zombie dust!" Duck Duck says. "Perfect. That's what I'm saying. Zombie dust hanging in the air. That's what smells like victory. Not napalm—zombie dust."

We drink the beer. It's light and hoppy and smells like grapefruit, and I wonder where they're getting the grapefruits.

"You go, Rodney," Duck Duck says. "Highlight reel."

Rodney leans back and looks up into the corner of the room. "Just got so many to choose from."

"Ha! Don't we all."

And then Rodney grins and puts his elbows on the table. "I got me a professional wrestler. Fucking huge. Like a bona fide walking mountain. I think that was his name, even. Mount Michaels. Or McKenzie, or something."

"Mount Maddox!" Duck Duck says. "The Murderhorn! You fought the Murderhorn?"

"Yeah! That's the guy! They were having some sort of WWE thing at The Beach the week the outbreak started. I think most of them got out, but he was still hanging around. And I saw him on the actual beach. This was before I met back up with Rip. I'd been walking on the road, but there were too many up there, coming out of the condos and all, so I went down along the water. And there he was, standing on the shore looking out into the Gulf like he can see straight over to the Yucatán. Sun's going down, and I can't go back up to the road at night, so I know it's through him or nothing. And he turns, and he sees me, and I swear to god he fucking *roars*."

Can't tell you how many times I've heard this story, but I sit back and let Rodney tell it again. He's gotten good, like he's a storyteller in ancient Greece, standing high up on some stone staircase regaling the people below. How he and the Murderhorn circled each other on the beach, their footprints disappearing into the waves. How the setting sun lit the points of Rodney's knuckles like they'd been heated in a forge. Mount Maddox ran at him, and Rodney ducked, rolled, leaped on the wrestler from behind, left arm around his neck, the right fist punching holes in the back of his huge head. And when Maddox threw him off and Rodney was on his back in the sand, the wrestler looming over him, all seven feet of him, all three hundred eighty pounds, Rodney was sure he was gone. Done. He threw a handful of sand into the zombie's face, but Maddox didn't even blink, just came on at him with dead eyes full of sand. He grabbed Rodney by the arms and picked him up like he was a child, held him right in front of his face, and he opened his mouth and the smell was like rotting fish and seaweed at low tide.

"He comes at me with those teeth, man, and I know I'm dead," Rodney says. "But I squirm, kick, and then I've got a foot on his shoulder. Then a foot on each shoulder. And I push off, and I still don't know how I did it, but I fucking *backflip* onto the sand. Like a ninja or some shit. And then he's all confused, and I get in a solid uppercut, and he goes down, and then I'm on top of him, *bam bam BAM!*" He swings his fists now, smashing in the invisible face, the huge memory of the skull. He smiles, takes a sip of the beer. "Took his ring. WWE champion. Got it on my shelf back home."

"Who's the champ now?" Duck Duck says.

"Damn straight."

Duck Duck turns to me. "What about you, Rip? You got your championship moment?"

"He's got too many to count," Rodney says. "Rip was the king. Never seen anyone like him. Not when he's got Santana working her magic."

"Give us one," Duck Duck says.

I think back. How many did I kill? A hundred? More? Must be more. The way they came in hordes, and the nights when they were just blurs running at me and falling before me. So many. How do you pick one? How do you single out the best moment when you spent months on top of the world? It's like you climbed Everest and someone asked you, Which part of the summit's the best? It's all best. It's all the top.

"Rip killed six in under a minute," Rodney says. "I saw it."

"Six!" Duck Duck says. "Tell it! How'd you get six in a minute?"

And I don't know why, but I'm feeling shy about it all of a sudden. The coke has fizzled out and my skull is numb, and those six zombies, the hundreds more, they all feel like some other lifetime that I don't want to spoil. So I just say, "I got six because none of them were wrestlers."

And now Duck Duck and Rodney laugh, and Bob brings me a bill that seems like less than I ought to be paying, but he's a good guy like that. Bob switches off the Coors light and now it's even darker, and he rouses Guillermo. Mo shuffles over to us, and we say good-night to Bob and step outside. It's raining still, and we huddle under the eaves of the bar, but the wind is blowing and the rain comes down on us at an angle. The outdoor lights go out and now it's near black, with the distant glow of downtown and the marina reflecting on the bottom of the clouds and other than that just the night and the rain. The waves move against the pilings beneath us, and the drops are a million splatters on the black surface.

Duck Duck points at the water. "That's what the road looked like. When the bullets hit. *Splat, splat, splat.* Like liquid." He lights a cigarette. Mo holds out his hand, and Duck Duck passes him a smoke, lights it for him. "You got a story?" he says to Mo.

"No," Mo says.

"Getting wet," Rodney says. "'Night, fellas." He goes off into the dark, and I hear his car crank and the headlights cut through the wet, solid as two fat lightsabers.

"You want a smoke?" Duck Duck says to me.

I never liked smoking much, but it feels right now, so I take a cigarette and Duck Duck lights it and I breathe in and my lungs are hot and ashy. Makes me think of bonfires in the summer, burning debris on wet concrete. Feels like home.

We smoke our cigarettes and watch the rain.

Duck Duck tosses his into the water and it hisses. The butt floats there a minute and goes under. "Dodger was my ride."

"I got no car," I say.

Mo is leaning on the railing of the porch, staring down into the water. He throws up, and there's a churning below him as the fish fight over the vomit. "You want to hear a story?" he says.

"You got your story?" Duck Duck says.

"It's not my story. It's just a story." He looks down at the fish. "About the squirrels."

"Yeah," Duck Duck says. "Tell us your squirrel story."

"Not a story, really. Just something I noticed. When's the last time you saw a squirrel in the road? Used to be in the road all the time, dead ones but the live ones too, hopping across and dodging out of your way when you drive by. And in the yards, looking for seeds and things. But now they're not in the road. Not in the yards. They're all up in the trees." He's quiet for a while, slumped up against a piling.

"Mo?" I say. "You ready to go home?"

He shakes his head. "Listen. The squirrels. The zombies ate them, remember? I don't know how they caught them. Maybe squirrels didn't smell them or something. But the zombies were eating them like they were popcorn. But zombies don't climb trees."

"This isn't much of a story," Duck Duck says.

"You miss the point. The point. I think the squirrels evolved. Like Darwinism. I think we saw it, even though it was only a few months. Some squirrels were land squirrels. Some squirrels were tree squirrels. And the land squirrels made more land squirrels and the trees more trees, and you get it. But all the land squirrels got eaten, and there's nothing left but tree squirrels. Not two kinds anymore, just the tree kind."

We watch the rain move across the black water.

"Somos las ardillas de árbol," he says. "We're tree squirrels."

Duck Duck looks up at the sky. "I'm no squirrel."

Mo is quiet again, slumped forward on his forearms.

"Want me to drive your truck, Mo?" I say. "Give us all a ride home?"

He sighs. "No. Just let me rest awhile."

Duck Duck sticks his hand out into the rain. "I'm not walking to the base. Take me all night."

I look at the water and then at Duck Duck. He's come down now, his eyes soft and tired looking. Hair plastered against his head with the rain. "I'm ten minutes' walk," I say. "You can crash with me."

He nods. We walk through the rain.

BACK THEN

We're standing in the front yard with three bodies on the ground. Mom and dad and son, all bleeding into my grass, my elephant ears.

"You think we got to report this or something?" I say.

Rodney looks at the zombie he's just killed. The woman's nose used to be delicate, plastic-surgery perfect. Now it's bent and nearly punctured in two, pushed down in a mess of broken bone and shattered teeth. Above her ear is a dent the shape of Rodney's fist. "She doesn't look like a zombie anymore," Rodney says. "How they going to know she was a zombie? How they going to know we didn't just up and kill these people?"

From far off in the distance comes the sound of sirens. The noise rises, closer, then fades away again.

"You're probably already wanted," Rodney says. "Bet they got you killing grocery store girl on the security cameras. I don't want them after me too."

"We can't be the only ones," I say. "There's got to be other people out there killing zombies. Or getting ate."

"You want to risk that? Cops come by?"

I look at the dad's body, bleeding out his stump and onto my driveway. His head bumped up against an elephant ear stalk, staring at the fleshy canopy of leaves. "Guess not. All right. Let's move them."

So we drag them behind the house. Mom first. She's light—all that yoga and kale. Then Dad. Big guy. Rodney's got his legs and I've got him by the arms. Clean cut on the neck, the blood oozing onto my shoes.

"One swing," Rodney says.

"What?"

"One swing and you beheaded him. That was impressive. Magic."

"Yeah." Dad is heavy and I'm breathing hard. "Lucky shot."

"No. You got a gift, man. Samurai shit. That was black magic. That machete. She's in your hand, you got that black magic."

We get the kid last. I pull the car out and he crumples onto the floor, a mess, a pile of parts that used to be a little boy. Dad doesn't bother me, Mom doesn't bother me, but this kid lying in a pile in my carport is too much, and I puke over there among the elephant ears, over where Dad's head left a puddle of blood. I wipe my mouth and go back in, and Rodney's covered the boy with the drop cloth. "No more kids," I say.

Then I'm spraying the blood with the hose, watching it run into the grass. I wonder if it's good fertilizer.

"I'm thinking I got to go check on my mom," Rodney says. He's got his phone out. "Still not answering texts."

"You got the news?"

He fools with the phone a minute, reads. "Mostly Brooklyn Bridge stuff. They're trying to say it's terrorism. Some other headlines on here about outbreaks. Houston. LA. Saying they got it under control."

The blood from Dad's head is thick, and I put my finger over the hose to make a jet and blast it into the mud. "Uh-huh," I say. "Go get your mom."

"I don't know if she can handle this shit. Don't know that my brother can either."

"Go."

"All right." He comes over and is about to fist-bump me, and he sees that he still has his knuckles on. "Ha," he says. And he hugs me.

Never hugged me before. I put my arms around him and slap him on the back. "Keep safe," I say.

"You too. Hey, wash these things off for me."

I turn the hose on his knuckles and wash off the spackling of blood. The brass shines in the streetlamp. "Keep those sharp," I say.

"Yours too. That black-magic woman."

The machete's sitting on the trunk of Rodney's car. I take it, and Rodney backs down the driveway. The headlights come on and reflect off the blade. *Black-magic woman.* And now the song's in my head and everything, and I remember the way the blade felt like a part of my body, the way she sang as she cut through the air and Dad's neck, and it was like I was transformed, like she transformed me into something better, someone bigger. It was magic. Turning my heart to stone. Tryin' to make a devil out of me.

Santana. My girl.

I look at her. She's rough from the battle. Zombie blood is beginning to cake on her, and her blade is nicked and dinged from busting skulls. I wash her in the sink, tracing the sponge along her smooth sides, her fierce edge. The rugged rubber of the grip. Then I turn the sharpener on and give her a twenty-minute treatment until she sings again. Rub olive oil on her blade and slide her into her sheath.

On TV, they're talking solemnly about the Brooklyn Bridge tragedy. The number killed and injured. The boats trolling the East River, spotlights on, fishing out bodies. The bridge is barricaded with police and crowds on either side, pressing against each other like they don't know where they're trying to go.

The news has stopped using the word *outbreak*. They've stopped showing the other cities. They keep the eyes of the world firmly on New York, on the human tragedy.

Don't think about the zombies, they might as well be saying. *Nothing to see here.*

After a while, they switch the feed from New York to the White House. There's a crowd there. They yell. Some have signs. Demanding action.

I watch for a few more minutes, and nothing changes. I turn the TV off and get in bed.

Big day tomorrow, I figure.

* * *

But it's not. I thought I'd wake up and step outside and they'd be swarming in my yard, in the street, coming up out of the bay, dropping down from the low branches of the oaks that line the road. They're not, though. It's clean and cool outside and the sun is happy in a sky blue as painted ceramic.

They've got an Oscar roundtable on TV. Debating which actor's the favorite, what film's the sleeper. Everything normal.

I pick up Santana and go outside. Birds are flitting around in the trees, filling the morning with song. A man and woman ride by on bicycles. A toddler is strapped into a seat on the back of the mom's bike, a pink helmet over her blonde curls. The little girl waves at me, and I wave back.

Aw, fuck, I think. I go to the backyard and they're all there, dead family, mom and dad and little boy piled against the house behind some bushes. A few flies are buzzing around them already. They are crushed and bloody and look like crushed bloody people, not crushed bloody zombies. What am I supposed to do with them? I find a big branch in the corner of the yard and drag it over them and throw some leaves on top. Doesn't do much, but at least they're not quite so obvious.

I call Rodney. "Hey man," he says. "You alive, then."

"Yeah. Your mom okay?"

"She's fine. Didn't hear the phone since she was watching TV." He's silent for a moment. I can hear his breathing, crackling static through the speakers. "Man, what did we do?"

"They were zombies. You saw them."

"Yeah, but who's going to believe that?" He lowers his voice. I can tell his mom's in the other room, and he practically whispers. "They're saying it's rabies. We killed a bunch of people with rabies. I feel sick, man. I beat a woman to death. And you killed that kid."

"They were zombies."

"Cops going to buy that?"

I take the phone outside and stand looking at the pile of leaves and sticks. The boy's shoe sticks out the bottom, and I kick some more leaves over it. "I don't know. I don't know what to do with them. Can you help me with them?"

More static. "I ought to stay with my mom."

"Right. Sure."

"Maybe it will get worse."

"What?"

"Everything," Rodney says. "It gets worse, and then everyone knows they're zombies and we're all right."

"You want it to get worse?"

"Might be the only way we get out."

I nod, even though he can't see me. "Just wait it out, then."

"Wait it out."

"All right."

Back inside, there's basketball on TV. Lakers and Spurs in the Staples Center, like nothing's going on outside. Pay no attention to the fires burning right down the road in Hollywood. Other channels, same thing: painfully normal. Forced normal. CNN doesn't even say anything about what happened to Anderson Cooper; instead they're talking about the Oscars. Covering final preparations at the Dolby Theatre. How brave these men and women of the Academy are, the reporters say, working tirelessly amid such crises. The show must go on.

I walk into town and go to Arnie's. I know this is stupid, returning to the scene of the crime, but I feel like I've got to look. The doors slide open, and I see the first security camera right there pointing at the entryway, and then all the little black domes built into the ceiling where the other ones hide, dozens of them, so many views of all corners of the store, of the checkout line, of everywhere I stood and walked two nights ago.

That one, at least, was self-defense. Right? They'll have it on camera. Girl eating that poor kid. Coming after me.

They've got them both all cleaned up. No blood, nothing where the kid died on the white tile, the grocery conveyor belt black and shiny.

The store is pretty crowded, but it's orderly. One old man has a cart piled high with bottled water. Yeah, that guy gets it. I grab a gallon of water myself and a case of beer and another box of Pop-Tarts. Look around the store at the people of Spanish Shanty, people I've seen but don't know, these men and women my neighbors my peers, living their lives. Alive right now and comfortable, leaning on their carts, slow-walking them down the aisles and playing with their phones while the streets burn in Oulu and the bodies drift down the East River and a family rots in my backyard.

And together we all stand on the edge, and I don't know which way we're going to fall.

* * *

Around five they start up the Oscars pregame stuff. Ryan Seacrest is hustling up and down the red carpet, and the celebrities are glittering and posing and showing off their dresses, suits, hair. Seacrest asks them about their shoes. Necklaces. They smile and bat their eyelashes, thank stylists and publicists, dressmakers and tailors. No one talks about the outbreak. No one says a word about zombies. Just sparkling men and women turning, preening for the cameras.

Jack Nicholson has just arrived, and Seacrest runs up the red carpet to meet him. "The great Jack Nicholson is receiving the Academy Honorary Award tonight," Seacrest says. "What a career he's had. We're thrilled to have you with us." He shoves the microphone in Nicholson's face.

Jack's getting old, I know, but he's looking really rough. His eyes are hidden behind dark sunglasses and his mouth hangs open, not his trademark grin but a slack-jawed yawn. Big bandage on his neck. He's got a handler guiding him by the elbow. Nicholson stares, confused. Sniffs the microphone.

I look out the front window. Sun's going down, and a cop pulls into the neighbors' driveway across the street. He gets out and knocks on their door. Waits. Knocks again, this time with the butt of his flashlight. He walks behind the bushes and peers through the window, says something into his radio. Heads behind the house.

Seacrest is still trying to get an interview out of Nicholson. "Any words for us tonight, sir?"

Nicholson leans into the microphone. *Rrrrraaaag*, he says.

"Rag?"

And then Jack Nicholson tears Ryan Seacrest's throat out. Both hands on Seacrest's neck like claws cinching down and tearing, the blood a geyser, and Seacrest screams and gurgles and collapses and Nicholson is on top of him, biting into him, chewing.

The camera jerks and points at the ground. When it refocuses, Seacrest is on his feet and his eyes are wild and he grabs a photographer by the sides of the head and bites his nose off. The photographer screams and puts his hands on his face and the blood is pouring through them, and then there is screaming and the cameraman is backing away and the audience is writhing, some struggling to get away, some shoving forward to take pictures, and then it's pure chaos.

The camera falls, and they cut to the wide shot. The crowd moves like waves. One body rushes forward and a dozen bend and curve away from it, and one is too slow and is pulled down, and a moment later two bloody shapes, two former celebrities, two zombies rage back into the crowd. It repeats, repeats, exponentially, two four eight sixteen in only a few minutes. The place is littered with camera equipment, sound equipment, huge areas roped off or gated, and the fleeing people bounce against one another as the living give way to the dead.

They never cut the feed.

In ten minutes every one of them is a zombie. Nicholson and Seacrest and George Clooney and Meryl Streep and all the rest of them. Zombie Kurt Russell and zombie Goldie Hawn. Jay-Z and Beyoncé. Ving Fucking Rhames.

At last the camera cuts, and a technical-difficulties message appears on the screen.

There's a knock at my door. I look out the window, and there are two police cars in front of the neighbors' house. One in my own driveway, lights whirling.

Shit.

I open the door. He's oldish, overweight. His radio is buzzing with static and a dozen frantic voices, and he shuts it off. "Evening, sir," he says.

Sun's just gone down over the bay, and the orange lingers on the horizon and stretches up into red purple black. "Evening," I say.

"You seen your neighbors around?"

"Those neighbors?" I point across the street.

"Yes. The neighbors with police cars in the front yard. Those are the neighbors to which I'm referring. Have you seen them?"

"Nah."

The cop gives me the up and down with his eyes. He looks past me, sees Santana on the coffee table. "What's the machete for?"

"Elephant ears," I say. I point at them, although who knows why, since they're growing all around and over him.

He looks at them, nods. "Big ones. Didn't die down this winter?"

"Didn't freeze."

"Right." He toes the ground where Dad's head landed. Soil's a bit torn up, still muddyish from the hose. Behind him the other cops are searching the outside of the neighbors' house. One goes down the hill in back, down toward the water. "Mind if I look around?" my cop says.

I shrug. "Go for it." I know this is probably stupid, but what else am I supposed to say? *Nope, bodies in the back,* or *Yeah, search away, just don't go near the bushes!* I try to picture the bodies, bring them up photographic-memory style. Clothes showing? Hair? Hands fingers elbows? I can't remember. I think they are covered. I think.

The cop heads around the house while I follow. He stops in front of the carport. "Came in hot, huh?" he says, pointing at the stuff crunched up against the wall, scattered where the kid was smashed. Still a bit of water pooled in the corner.

"My buddy," I say. "Came over drunk. Told him he shouldn't be driving, but he showed up anyway. Overshot her."

"Whoops." He follows along the edge of the house. It's not full dark yet but it's getting hard to see, and he takes his flashlight out and shines along the path in front of him, in the tall grass along the chain-link fence, at the base of the vinyl-paneled side of the house. He stops when he gets to the backyard and looks around, paints the flashlight beam across the space. Things are overgrown back there. I haven't mowed all winter, so now the weeds are sticking up knee-high and wrapping around the bushes, coming up over the patio. The cop chuckles. "Kind of let it get away from you, huh?"

"Yeah, I know. Been trying to get around to cleaning it up."

"I know how it is. My wife's on me all the time." He's scanning the yard as he talks, moving the white light along the patio, the house. "She's all, 'Larry, I want to enjoy my yard! How can I enjoy my yard when it looks like a jungle?' And she's afraid of snakes. Never seen a single snake." He stops talking as the beam hits the bushes where I've got the family.

"I saw one out front once," I say. "Rat snake."

"What you got here?"

"It was a big one too. Want me to show you where I saw it?" I follow the flashlight, and he's got it on the kid's shoe. I know I covered it up. Fuck. Wind blew the leaves away or something.

"Stay put," Officer Larry says, and he takes a couple of steps and nudges the shoe with his boot. Kicks some leaves off of it, reveals the leg. Then he whirls around, pulls his gun. He holds the gun and the flashlight close together, both pointed at my face. "Don't move!"

"Look," I say. "They were dead when they got here."

He's talking into his radio. "Backup. Backup needed." He gives the address. Then he's calling to the guys across the street, first into the radio and then just yelling into the growing night. "Reynolds! Gonzales! Get over here!"

"They were zombies," I say. "You've seen TV, right? The outbreak. New York and Finland. They're turning into zombies."

"There's no fucking zombies."

"The Oscars! Didn't you just see that?" And then I remember that of course he didn't just see that because he was outside snooping around the neighbors' house, around my house.

"Get on the ground." He's gesturing with the gun and then the other two cops are there, guns drawn, all of them yelling at me.

"All right." I get on my knees. "All right. But I'm serious. Zombies."

Reynolds and Gonzales hold their guns on me while Officer Larry yanks my hands behind my back, cinches them together with a zip tie. He stands me up and leads me around the house. Puts his hand on top of my head and loads me into the back seat of the cop car. Smells like sweat in there. The seat's made out of some sort of hard black plastic, and the roof's so low I have to hunch. There's a sheet of bulletproof glass between me and the front seat.

The three cops stand in front of the car talking to each other, talking into their radios. They point down the street, away from town. Reynolds and Gonzales head back to their cars and haul ass that way. Officer Larry talks into his radio a minute longer, then gets in the front seat.

"Where they going?" I say.

He doesn't answer.

"What about us?" I look over my shoulder at my house as he pulls out of the driveway. Wonder if I'm going to see it again.

"We're going to the station."

"Figured."

We're only a half a mile from my house when we see her. There, in the middle of the road, her skin turning blue red blue in the lights. I recognize her; the woman lives four houses down from me. Big woman in a tracksuit. She's listing to the right like a signpost that's been clipped by a car.

Officer Larry sounds the siren for a second. *Whiiiirp.*

She looks up at us. Mouth open. Those eyes, whirlpools in a poisoned river.

"Zombie!" I say. "See? She's a zombie."

"You stay put," the cop says.

"I'm telling you, dude. Don't go out there. She's going to eat you or something."

He ignores me and opens the door. "Ma'am," he says. "Ma'am, are you okay?" He shuts the door behind him, walks around the front of the car with his hands held out in front of him, like she's a stray cat and he's trying not to startle her. "Are you hurt?" She stares at him, takes a step. "Ma'am?" Officer Larry says, and then she lunges, falls full-weight on him and pulls him down, clawing at his face. The cop gets his gun up under her and fires five shots into her middle and rolls her off, but she's right back up, bleeding from the bullet holes. Officer Larry runs back to the car, tries to get in the front door, but she tackles him from behind, and now his hands are on the window beside me streaking it with blood, and he pulls my door open and tries to drag himself inside but he's yanked from behind and he screams and his eyes are wild with terror and then he's gone.

I look out the window. The zombie's got Officer Larry's stomach torn open, and she's eating the slithery brown-and-yellow stuff inside him. He tries feebly to push her away, and then he goes limp.

I open the door wider and scoot out. It's hard to worm my way through the crack with my hands behind my back, but if I open it any more I'll hit her, and she's got her head down in all that gore and I want her to keep it there. Left foot down. Right foot. Balance. The ripe smell of death thick in the air and the blue and red lights turning the night into a rave. No sound but frantic voices from the cop's radio and the worming slick of the feeding zombie.

I'm out. I turn toward home. And then her hand's on my ankle and I go down right on top of Officer Larry, my elbow splatting in his open gut, hot and slippery like spaghetti draining in a colander. The zombie pounces on me, but I manage to get my feet up under her, and I'm on my back and she's right there, nothing keeping her from me but whatever strength I've got in my legs. Her hands are on me, cold hands on my shoulders. Bite wounds on her arms still oozing through her track jacket. She pauses, breathing in raspy gasps. Staring into me through me. Her eyes are galaxies rushing to the outer edges of the universe, red-shifted and shrunken, outrunning the speed of light on their way to darkness. A weird mix going on in there: that emptiness mixed with a sort of frenzy. A cow gone mad. A rabid squirrel. She stares right into me unblinking, and in her eyes there's something of the woman that she used to be but mostly she's rage, blind kinetic rage. Then she lunges again, mouth open wide teeth exposed, and I can see the fillings in her lower molars.

I'm trying to keep her held off and squirm away, and my hands end up on the cop's utility belt, and then I'm fumbling around blind trying to grab a gun or a knife, anything, and I get my fingers around something with a trigger and pull it from its holster. Kick hard, throw the zombie off. Roll around and point the thing as best I can with my fingers cinched behind my back and fire.

It's not a gun. It's a taser. The prongs fly into her, dragging the coiled wires with them, and she goes down rigid and quivering. Grunting.

I manage to get on my knees and start digging through the belt looking for something to cut the zip tie with, but already the shock is over and the zombie's trying to get up, so I pull the trigger again. She looks at me as the electricity flows through her. Her eyes hold the same blank fury as before. The taser doesn't hurt. Just shuts her body down. She's looking at me like she's thinking, *How many more charges you think you got in that thing? Do you know what I'm going to do to you when you run out?*

I don't want to know. I zap her again and open a pouch on the cop's belt and find a black metal multitool. Flip the blade out and go to work on the zip tie, and then there's another hand on me.

Officer Larry. He's not dead anymore—not exactly. Now he's a zombie, or at least a bunch of zombie body parts. His head isn't attached right, and he tries to lift it but his neck is in tatters and I can see the tendons going in there as he twists toward me.

"Shit!" I say, and I scoot away from him, and now the zombie woman is getting up and I fire the taser but nothing happens. Pull the trigger again, again, but it's out of juice. "Fuuuuuck," I say, and I saw at the zip tie and the zombie woman said *grrrruuuuuug!* and comes for me and then *snap* my hands are free. I'm on my feet, and I dodge her, jump over Officer Larry, run a few feet up the street to where he dropped his gun. Snag it and whirl around and she's right there running at me, and I pull the trigger and the night explodes with the sound. Her head snaps back, then forward. She looks at me. Hole in the middle of her forehead. And then she collapses.

Breathe. Ears ringing from the gunshot. Epileptic lights rocking my vision.

I go back over to Officer Larry. His arms are moving but his torso is just one big mess and he can't get up. One foot is tap-tapping like he's keeping time. He looks up at me, his eyes inhuman but his face creased with the lines of age, thin wrinkles near his lips from all the times he smiled, a heavy furrow across his brow. His life etched in his skin. I wonder if he has kids. Grandkids.

"I told you," I say. "Zombies." And then I finish him off with the pistol.

I kneel beside him and go through his belt. I take his extra magazines. His retractable baton. I pick up the pepper spray and put it back. That woman's eyes, the cold wild stars deep inside them—pepper's not going to do it.

His radio's still going crazy, so I flip it off, and now the silence is complete and the background fills in with the other noises of the night. Waves on the beach. Somewhere, far away, a car's engine roaring, tires screeching. A dog barking. A siren that whines louder louder and fades away. Distant yelling, *no, no, noooo!* that becomes a high-pitched wail.

I leave the car and head back down the road. Get home and shut the door behind me, lock it, put the refrigerator in front of it. Close the blinds, turn off the lights, because I don't know what's going on in the zombies' heads, what's attracting them. Noise, light, movement? I shut it all down. Bend over the kitchen sink and wash Officer Larry off my arms.

The TV has finally cut away from the Oscars, and they've got a split screen up again. There's a concerned-looking anchor on the left, and she's talking to a woman in a black suit with colorful military bars on the chest. On the right of the screen, the image changes every few seconds, new city new city tick tick tick. LA, New York, DC, on and on. In each shot people are running, cars racing. Zombies are in the shot now and then, stalking around. Three of them eating someone in St. Louis, the big arch rising into the sky behind them. Across the bottom of the screen a ticker is running. It says *The following cities have enforced curfews*, and it's streaming through an alphabetical list of pretty much every city in America. Tallahassee is there, and Pensacola. Dothan in Alabama. So that's east, west, and north of Spanish Shanty. Nothing but Gulf to the south of us. So yeah, that's where we are.

"We're still studying the disease," the woman is saying. Words on the screen label her as acting director of the CDC. "Based on its geographical spread, we believe it originated in the Arctic. It's likely been dormant, frozen in permafrost. We've had an unusually warm spring, which may have thawed the disease and allowed it to become communicable once again."

"Like the Russian anthrax outbreak of 2016," the anchor says.

"Exactly. And this disease is extremely fast acting. We believe it may be a prion disease, perhaps related to bovine spongiform encephalopathy."

"Mad cow disease."

"Yes, but unlike mad cow disease, it appears that only humans are affected. As best we can tell, it has a longer incubation period when subjects are exposed to a contaminant indirectly, for example, if they have come into indirect contact with the bodily fluids of an infected person—saliva, mucus, and so on. Contagion is not likely in this case if precautions are taken. If you come in contact with an infected person, do not touch your face or any mucous membranes. Wash any exposed areas immediately."

I turn the volume up loud as I strip and climb in the shower.

"Indirect infection may have an incubation time of several hours. We believe that's why we're seeing this resurgence in the outbreak. Individuals who were indirectly infected are now entering the late stages of the disease."

"Where we see these zombielike symptoms," the anchor says.

I stick my head out of the shower. The director chews her lip, clicks her tongue. "The infected individuals show signs of decreased mental activity, yes."

"Like zombies."

She sighs. "The disease has a long incubation period through indirect contact. You may even be able to treat it. When the prion enters the bloodstream directly, however—"

"Like through a bite."

She chews her lip again. "Yes. Like through a bite. When it enters the bloodstream, it migrates rapidly to the brain, and the infected begins to exhibit late-stage behavior within a few minutes, sometimes almost immediately."

"In other words," the anchor says, "they turn into zombies."

The director glares at the anchor.

"Director, let me ask you this. When you say the disease lay dormant in the Arctic, do you mean the prion itself? Or do you mean the zombies?"

"Okay, we're done. If you're not going to take this seriously, we're done."

"Thank you, Director." The anchor turns to the camera. "We'll keep you updated on the zombie outbreak as more details emerge." And then dramatic music plays *dum dum DUM* and she's replaced by a graphic: the blood-spattered words *ZOMBIES! In America!* Then it cuts to the Charmin commercial where the bears have toilet paper stuck on their asses.

I scrub the blood off my skin, out from under my fingernails, wash it from my hair. I look myself up and down for scratches, bites, and I'm clean.

Out of the shower and dressed, I pack a go bag. I throw the extra ammo and the baton into my backpack. A couple of bottles of water and some food, the soup and the Pop-Tarts. Get a can opener too, a chef's knife. A spoon. Don't know how long I'll be out, what I'll need.

Santana in her sheath on my hip. The cop's gun in the back of my pants. Go bag by the door. I stand and wait while the distant noises outside get louder.

The TV's got protesters in front of the White House with smoke drifting past them. Their signs say *Respect Their Rights!* and *The Living-Challenged are People Too!* and stuff like that. A reporter gets one in front of the camera, a skinny guy with horn-rimmed glasses and hair swept over half his face. "Why are you here today?" the reporter says.

"These were our friends yesterday," the guy says. "They're sick, but they're still human beings. And people are just murdering them. Murdering them!"

"You believe the zombies have rights?"

"Don't use the Z-word," the guy says. "It's hurtful." And then a zombie wanders into the shot and chomps into the guy's arm.

The screen cuts to a montage of YouTube videos and Facebook Live feeds. People standing in front of groups of zombies, filming themselves with their phones. Backing up, closer, closer, finally tapping the zombie on the shoulder and then sprinting away, laughing. The anchor talks over the footage. "The Zombie Tap Challenge has gone viral, and we urge you, do not attempt this. Do not let your children attempt this. The results can be devastating." And they show some more videos: tapping the zombie, trying to run, getting caught. Some of the phones still filming as the teeth dig in.

Then the screen goes blue.

Outside, the sirens are louder, the screams closer.

WEDNESDAY, OCTOBER 23

Duck Duck and I sit on the couch, and on TV is *Ultimate Zombie Challenge*. These Japanese people are trying to traverse crazy obstacles like giant seesaws or spinning platforms over the water or whatever, and people in zombie makeup are chasing them, knocking them down, eating their brains in a twisted pantomime while the announcers mock their progress in deliberately poorly dubbed voice-overs.

"I could do that," Duck Duck says. He's pointing at a wall-climb obstacle. Up twenty feet while zombies grab at your ankles. "Had a wall like that in basic."

The guy makes it over the wall and starts hopping along a series of floating stepping stones. He's halfway across when a zombie pops out of the water and grabs his legs, pulls him in. They show the replay half a dozen times. They add in zombie roars, dramatic music, inane commentary.

"That's bullshit, though," Duck Duck says. "They don't like the water. Listen to this shit. This one time, we saw about fifty of them while we were flying over Whitehead Bay. Floating there a hundred yards offshore. We tore them apart, turned the water red. Ha." Then he's quiet, and he stares right through the TV, doesn't blink for a long time. "Wasn't till later we found out zombies don't go in the water," he says. Then he shakes his head. Looks around the house, at the low window, the thin wood doors. "You made it through in here?"

"Nah. I got out early. I knew the place wouldn't hold if shit got bad enough."

"Where'd you go?"

"Water park."

"Lazy River?"

"Yeah."

"Smart man. Like you've got a moat."

For a moment I'm back there, up in the pirate ship, looking down on the pools, the slides, the people. My people. The river itself meandering all around us. Thing's 4,900 feet long, second longest in the world, but damned if Texas doesn't have a longer one. The owner of our water park wound that river back in on itself so many times, going for the record. Thought he had it too, named the whole park after it—Lazy River Fun Park. But he measured wrong, along the outside edge. Measurement's got to be on the inside. The thing's still huge, and the zombies wouldn't cross it. They'd just shuffle along the edge, lap after lap after lap, looking in at us and groaning, like starving Somali kids at the windows of a Golden Corral. "It was a pretty sweet place," I say.

"You ride the rides?"

"When it rained."

"Fun. We didn't have rides. Just the jets."

"They never got in? Never got past the fences at the base?"

He shakes his head. "No zombies on base. Not during the outbreak, anyway." He lets that hang in the air a moment. Then he says, "How many of you were there? At Lazy River?"

"Just like five of us at first. But more came. Probably thirty by the end."

"Like a big family."

"Yeah. We had a Fourth of July barbecue and everything. That was a good day."

They go to commercial, and it's a new propaganda one I've never seen. Big logo that says *Earth: Alive*. We've already had *America: Alive* and *Europe: Alive* and all that, so I guess they had this one in the can waiting for the last zombie in Asia to go down. Now they've done it, so the commercial plays celebratory music and shows piles of dead zombies burning interspersed with couples holding hands and children playing on the beach. A woman's soothing voice narrates the whole thing, talking about how we all came together. The camera zooms out and the planet is there against the black, clouds swirled over the ocean and auroras flashing at the poles, and she says, "The zombies are gone. Enjoy Earth—alive."

And I feel a spark inside of me go out. Something that buoyed me after the Army came in, after the all-clear, after Davia left and I went back to work. The spark that kept my eyes wide and Santana on my hip. I was waiting for another one, for that groan that growl and the dragging footsteps on the asphalt behind me. Just waiting for the cold hands on my arms, Santana singing in my fist. And now the last one's dead.

I remember how on the Fourth of July the air was hot and still. The moon was a sickle dangling just above the trees.

Someone had found some fireworks, and they lit the sky white and red and green; sparklers in the kids' hands tracing their hallucinatory patterns, reflecting in the water; bottle rockets whistling swishing popping; and some big boomers, *thud screeee BOOM!* the flower of color and fire raining down and the zombies staring from the other side of the river, their faces ravenous and bored. Davia and I sit in lawn chairs on the pirate ship, watching it all, and she climbs from her chair to mine and curls up, her head on my chest, my arm around her, my fingers in her hair, the long loose spikes of her Mohawk, the downy fuzz on the sides of her skull. "Happy Fourth," I say to her, and she says, "Fuck your stupid American holiday."

I smile. "Sometimes I miss it."

"Yeah?" Duck Duck says. The show's back on now, and he grabs the remote and turns down the volume.

"Yeah. I miss it. I miss *them.*"

"The zombies?"

"Well, maybe not the zombies. I miss the way they made me feel. The way they changed the world. I miss that." I watch another idiot try to cross the stepping stones and get pulled down by the same fake zombie. He splashes into the pool, stands up. He's laughing, the zombie's laughing. They shake hands. "You know what? Fuck it. I do miss the zombies. They make you real. Because they're real. Everything's full of so much fakeness, everybody all day every day putting on an act to be who they think they're supposed to be. Not them, though. The zombies don't give a fuck. They're just out there all day, being zombies, whether you like it or not. They're real. And if you're not real, you don't make it out."

"I feel you," Duck Duck says. "I feel you, man. We're out flying patrols all day. Up and down looking for zombies that aren't there, or running drills, fake strafing runs on zombies that aren't fucking there."

"They make you real. They made the world real. This—" I gesture at the TV, at the open beers on the coffee table, at the cheap food in the kitchen, the walls windows the whole house. "This isn't real. This is bullshit."

"Listen." Duck Duck turns off the TV. The rain has stopped outside and there's a slow drip from the trees. Soft pattering on the grass, the elephant ears. Duck Duck's eyes are sober now, clear and calm. "What if it doesn't have to be bullshit?"

"It's bullshit from here on out," I say.

"But it doesn't have to be." Santana is on the table, and Duck Duck reaches for her and taps her with one finger. "We could have that. Again. We can have it if we want it."

"The fuck you talking about? They're dead."

"Not all of them." He's smirking now.

"What, you got some hidden away?"

The smirk turns into a grin.

And it shouldn't be like this, I know. I shouldn't feel this way about monsters that killed and killed and ate and turned people against one another and started wars and burned the world halfway to the ground. I shouldn't feel the spark inside me flare back up into a miniature star burning in my chest. I shouldn't feel my dick move. But I do. Duck Duck's still grinning at me and I'm grinning back like a fucking moron and I say, "You've got some hidden away. You son of a bitch. Where you hiding them?"

"At the base. They've got a few. My buddy works in the lab, and he told me. They're keeping them and doing research on them. I bet they've got them at all the bases. I bet there's hundreds alive."

"And we could kill them." I pick Santana up and she seems to vibrate in my hands.

"Are you crazy?" Duck Duck says. "Kill them and then there's really none left."

"So what, then?"

Duck Duck's grin is wider now, madder. He says, "We set them free."

THURSDAY, OCTOBER 24

I wait for Rodney outside the call center. The rain is gone, but it's still cloudy, wet, water coming from the sky in a heavy mist. I huddle close to the building, under the eaves.

Around noon a few of my other coworkers come out. They look at me, go quiet. Then they walk off in the other direction. Rodney comes out alone and stands next to me. "You made it home all right, then," he says.

"Yeah."

"And the pilot?"

"Duck Duck? He crashed at my place."

Rodney nods. "Something's not right about him. Screw loose."

"He's a good guy. When you get to know him."

"So you know him now?"

"Enough."

Rodney puts his hands in his pockets, looks up and down the street. "We just going to stand here, Rip? I got forty-five minutes. You know that. What you want?"

"Let's go eat. We can talk."

So we walk through the mist to McDonald's, and in a few minutes we're sitting in the molded plastic booths with burgers and fries and Cokes. Coke tastes different now—a sweeter taste, but not in a good way. Like they ran out of regular sugar and replaced it with something else. Which is maybe exactly what they did. Coffee fields, coca fields, sugar fields, so much of it trampled and burned. Get one zombie loose out there and they'd burn a mountainside down rather than risk contaminated food.

"You got some plan, then," Rodney says.

"Ha."

"No, I can see it on you, Rip. I know you. You got some plan. You're waiting to tell me about whatever plan you've got. So just spill it. We don't got time for bullshit."

"All right." I dip some fries in barbecue sauce and shove them in my mouth. "We had a good time this summer, right?"

"Eating canned food all day? Sleeping in a water slide? Such fun."

"Admit it. It was fun. I saw you talking about Maddox last night. You know you liked it."

Rodney gets this wistful look in his eyes. "It had its moments."

I push my burger aside and look around the room. The same girl that laughed at me is behind the counter again, but she's not paying any attention. Nobody's paying attention. All focused on their food or their phones. I say to Rodney, "You can have it again."

"Have what?"

"Those moments. That thrill. That life."

"Huh." He sips his Coke, and the straw makes a slurping sound. "What makes you think I'd want that again?"

"I've seen you at work. I know how you talk about it. 'Spreadsheets spreadsheets durp de durp' like you're some kind of robot nerd. You hate that shit. You know you hate that shit."

"Everyone hates their job."

"I didn't! Not when my job was killing zombies! And neither did you."

Rodney sighs. He shakes the ice around in his cup. "This Coke is cold, Rip. It's *cold*. And this burger is hot. It's delicious, and I got both of them, and the fries, for ten bucks. They pay me twice that every hour. So I work thirty minutes and I've got this meal with hot food and cold drink. In the summer we had times we fought *all day* for less."

I look at my burger. It's half eaten and limp on the paper place mat. Cooling in the air conditioning. "So the burger's worth the spreadsheets?"

"Eating is worth working."

"I know that, but get what I'm saying. You're making a choice. You've got scales, right?" I put my hands up, weigh them side to side. "On one side you've got your stuff. Your food and your car and whatever else." I push my burger and the fries and the Coke all over to the right side of the table. Take my phone out and add to the pile. "All your stuff—the things you need *and* the things you want—they're all over here. But all by themselves, they weigh the scale down. It's out of balance. No one's just going to give you the things you want. You got to work for them. You with me?"

He's looking at the pile of stuff. "I get it, Rip. You want more, you work more."

"That's not the point, though!" I point to the left side of the table, heft my left hand in the air. "This side of the scale, that's the time you put in to get the other side. That's work, sitting behind your spreadsheets or answering their emails. *Or*, or, it's killing zombies. Climbing through the ruins of abandoned condos. It's bonfires and smoke in the sky. Those things have to weigh down the left side until it balances the right."

"Okay." He takes out his phone and starts looking at Twitter.

I snatch the phone from him and put it in the pile on the right side of the scales. "Rodney," I say, "is that worth it? That phone, Twitter? Is it worth pouring your life into the left side of the scale day after day doing something you *fucking hate*? Look at the scales. That's your life—your whole life. The things you do and the things you have. That's all you are. And you're filling half the scale with hours in that building looking at spreadsheets."

Rodney takes his phone off the pile. "It keeps the other half full."

"At what cost?" He doesn't look up from the phone. Those fucking phones. When the service went out a week into the outbreak, people lost it. Couldn't follow their friends or the celebrities, couldn't tell Instagram stories about whatever they were doing. They cared so much. And then they didn't. Just kind of all at once, everyone stopped giving a shit, and the phones all went into a drawer in the margarita hut. We ate and drank and talked to each other at night. We were humans with other humans. No one missed the virtual world. Everyone said so. And then service went back up after the all-clear, and people were like, *No, I don't need it anymore*, until they said, *I'll just look at my email* or *I'll just check Twitter real quick*, and then that was that. They turn the world back on and the phones come on with it, and another thing that makes life real goes out.

He's still looking at the phone, but I keep talking. "We had the scales balanced this summer, Rodney. We did. Maybe we didn't have as much in the right pile. There were no burgers, and the Cokes—if we even had any—were warm. I'll give you that. But the left side of the scales!" I look at that empty side of the table like it's holding all the world's mysteries. "That side of the scales was the shit. That was *life*, man. That was wake up with the air sparking with energy and burn through the day on the razor's edge, killing when you had to kill and fighting for every scrap on that right side of the scale. Fighting together. All of us."

He sits back in his chair and stares at me.

"We were a family." I can feel tears forming in my eyes. "All of us together at Lazy River. You were my family. The people you love," I say, pointing to the left side of the table, "they're over here too. They're part of your life. And you're not with them when you're with your spreadsheets."

"They go on the right side," Rodney says. "You work so you can provide for them."

"But we've got it backwards! We shouldn't leave them to provide for them. We could live *with* them, work with them. Fight with them. We did that. Think of how we were."

He gets the faraway look again. "I do miss that."

"And when are we ever going to have that again? That, that *camaraderie?*"

"Okay," he says. "You've got me listening. What's your plan? How we going to get that again? We going on some sort of retreat?"

"No. We're going to bring back the zombies."

His eyes narrow. "The fuck you talking about, Rip?"

"We can start the outbreak again."

"They're dead. They killed the last one the other day. In China."

"And you believe them? You really think they'd kill every single zombie? The government, the military? You know they've kept some. You know they're studying them. Probably trying to figure out how to reverse-engineer the disease or something. Make a weapon out of it. Maybe even make the zombies into weapons."

"You think so."

"I know so." I tell him about what Duck Duck said, the zombies in the lab at the Air Force base. How he could bribe people, since no one gives a shit anymore anyway. He'd create a distraction; we'd sneak on, steal a zombie. I watch Rodney's eyes get wide, his mouth open and close as I talk.

When I'm done, he scrunches his eyebrows and shakes his head. "What you're talking about is crazy, Rip."

"Is it, though? All I'm doing is getting our life back."

"But people are going to die. If you let them loose, start it all over again, thousands of people are going to die. Millions, maybe."

"But not us. Not the strong."

He just stares at me, shaking his head.

"The strong will be fine. We made it through before, we'll make it through again. Maybe it's evolution, even. Natural selection. We're tree squirrels."

"What?"

"Nothing." We're quiet for a long time while we finish our food.

Rodney looks at his phone again. "I got to get back to work."

"We'd need money," I say. "For the bribes. I got a little. I bet Mo's got some. He's got to be paying for that liquor somehow. But not enough. We'd need a few thousand at least. So if you've got any extra, you can bring it. We're meeting at my house tonight. To talk about it, and plan, and—"

"You're serious about this."

"Rodney." I put my hands up like the scales, and I turn my left hand over, let it flop to my side. "I got nothing, man."

"You can get another job."

"Not just the job. Our family. Davia. Santana. All of it. I miss it all. Shit, man, I even miss the zombies. The way they sounded, the way they smelled. And the way we were when they were around. We were kings. Now we're nothing. But back then we were kings."

"*You* were a king."

"Well, you were at least a duke. Don't you want to be a duke again?"

"I'm going back to work," he says, standing.

"Rodney."

He pauses.

"After work. What are you going home to?"

"That's low, Rip."

"You know the answer, though. Your brother's not waiting for you. You mom's not waiting for you."

"Fuck you," he says, and he's out the door. I watch him through the windows, the mist forming drops on his skin, dampening his clothes as he heads down the street, waits for a light to change. A car comes by and splashes him. I can hear him cursing from inside the restaurant.

* * *

Seven o'clock, Duck Duck rolls up on his motorcycle. It's a chopper, handlebars way up in a stupidly awkward position to hold. The engine *braaaaps* like a metallic fart as he putters up the driveway. He revs it a couple of times and the roar fills the neighborhood, and then he kills it and comes to the door. He doesn't knock, just walks in. It's twilight outside but he's got his shades on anyway, and he takes them off in the doorway and says, "What's up, fuckers?"

Mo is on the couch. He stares at Duck Duck for a long moment, and then he goes back to watching TV.

Took nothing to convince Mo. I found him in the bar earlier in the afternoon, bought him a whiskey. Gave him the whole your-life-is-scales spiel.

He threw the whiskey back in one gulp. "Fuck it. I'm in."

Nothing left to lose, I figured. He's already lost it all: first Lupita, then his livelihood, and now Gabriela. He fought like a hero and came out the other side ruined. The world didn't give him what it owed him, and now he wants revenge. Burn it to the ground. It's that or drink himself into oblivion every day until finally he passes out and doesn't wake up. Whiskey or fire. Mo chose fire.

Now I'm in the kitchen, and I get beers out of the fridge and bring them over.

Duck Duck cracks his beer and tilts his head back and drinks it all. Then he burps and crunches the can and tosses it into the trash. Walks to the fridge and grabs another. "Where's your other friend?"

"I don't know that he's coming," I say.

"You didn't talk to him?"

"I did. I just don't know if I convinced him."

Duck Duck's face scrunches up. "Fuck, man! How are we supposed to do it, then? You going to do it with just Mo? And the money. What about the money? Guys aren't just going to let us in because we ask nicely."

"I talked to him. What else do you want me to do?"

"Convince him! God, it's not that fucking hard."

"So get one of your friends to do it!"

"Not my job! My job is the distraction, remember? I'm going to do my job. I'm going to do my job so fucking solid. Because I get shit done." He's standing in the kitchen, waving his beer around, spilling it onto the floor. "I get shit *done*! And you can't even convince your friend to help you out with a little cash."

Then it hits me. I don't know why it didn't hit me last night. The beer, maybe, or the coke, or the sting of getting fired. But now I see it: Duck Duck is an asshole. Maybe the biggest asshole I've ever met. And now I'm thinking, *Fuck this guy*. "All right," I say. "We're done."

"Done? We haven't even started."

"No. We're done. Me and you. Give me my beer. And go."

"Can't do it without me," Duck Duck says. "I know where the zombies are. I got the inside men. I'm your chance, Rip. You kick me out, you'll never see another zombie as long as you live."

"Don't matter." I point at the door. "Out."

He comes out of the kitchen, puts his finger in my face. "You know what you're giving up? You know—"

Mo stands up, sets down his beer. Sober, he seems bigger. He stands straight, tall, his arms thick from years of carrying shovels and weed trimmers and fat squares of sod.

Duck Duck nods. "Okay. Can't say I didn't try." He goes to the door and opens it and Rodney is standing there. "Aha!" Duck Duck says. He grips Rodney in a bear hug, lifts him off the ground, a weird sight with Duck Duck so much shorter than Rodney. "My man. Here after all! Come on in, bud. We're just getting started."

Rodney comes inside and Duck Duck offers him one of my beers, but Rodney shakes his head. He points to the back door. "I talk to you a minute, Rip?"

We go out back. In the near dark it feels like we're in a clearing in some wild rain forest. I was gone all summer, and I haven't trimmed or tended the plants, the grass, anything in the yard since I've been back. Weeds grow tall among the blades of St. Augustine, up between the bricks on the patio, along the edges of the house. Vines snake through the chain-link fence. The elephant ears are massive, their fat fleshy faces reaching above the roof, sheltering us like a canopy. Tree frogs whir all around us and crickets chirp in the dusk.

I can barely make out Rodney's face, a silhouette against an indigo sky. "So you're in?" I say.

He shrugs. "I'm not out."

"But you're not in."

"We'll see how it goes." He walks over to the bushes where we hid the bodies, the neighbors, the first zombies we killed all those months ago. They were still there when I came back after the all-clear, rotted messes by then, and I dragged what I could out to the curb to be picked up by the disposal truck. There's traces of them still on the ground, brown and black fluids sunk deep into the dirt. New weeds are growing thick there, and it hits me that they're in those weeds too. The kid and his parents are in the weeds, the shrubs, the earthworms beneath the soil. Rodney toes the dirt with his tennis shoe. "I don't know what I want, man," he says. "I don't know that I want what we had in the summer."

"It was a good summer."

"I guess. I mean, that shit was fun. Yeah. I don't know that it's what I want. But I don't want this." He gestures into the night. "Just nothing. Work and food and sleep. I went back to work after we ate, you know. And I sat there and I stared at the spreadsheets and I couldn't get anything done. And then I went home and ate a ham sandwich that wasn't any better than the stuff we scavenged in the summer, but I ate it all alone in my house and watched *Wheel of Fortune*. And those puzzles were so easy. It's not even a game."

"I like *Jeopardy* better."

"Because you're not an idiot. We're smart, me and you. But we're not going on *Jeopardy*. We're wasted doing what we're doing. That's all I felt at work today. Waste. Like, what am I doing this for? Mom and Trey are gone. Not getting them back. So I don't know what family I got except for you and Mo. Family we had this summer."

"That's our family." I put my hand on his shoulder. "You're my brother."

He nods, puts his hand on my shoulder, and we lean our foreheads against each other. Stand like that while the tree frogs scream all around us. Then he breaks away. "I don't know that the zombies are the answer," he says. "But they're something. Got to have something, else I'll just be nothing for the rest of my life."

We go back inside. Duck Duck is leaning over the couch, laughing at the TV with Mo, and the room feels bright and full of warmth.

"Oh, hey Rip," Rodney says. He's behind me in the doorway. He reaches into his pocket and pulls out a wad of cash. "I got some money."

"Shit, Rodney. How much is that?"

"Enough." He turns the money over in his hands, riffles through the hundred-dollar bills.

"Where'd you get all that?"

"It's Mom's life insurance. What they gave me, anyway. It was supposed to be ten times this, but they gave me a bunch of shit about not having zombie coverage, and I said how was I supposed to know I needed zombie coverage, and . . ." He sighs. "This is what I got."

Duck Duck looks past me, sees the money in Rodney's hands. "Aww, shit!" he says. "Time to kick the tires and light the fires!"

"Why's everything got to be about *Top Gun* with you?" Mo says.

Duck Duck shrugs. "Cool movie."

BACK THEN

You know what that first day was like? It was like holding a fire-cracker in your mouth and watching the fuse burn down and spitting it out at the last second. The tension of the sizzle ticking down to explosion and knowing that it's all on you, it's on you to act or get your head blown off. Hot damn, it was a rush. There would be more exciting days, more fun days, more fulfilling days, but nothing like that first day. Like the first time you have sex: it's not going to be the best time, but it's going to be electric and you're going to remember.

By the time the sun starts to come up, the smell of smoke is in the air, seeping through the cracks beneath the doors, coming in at the edges of the windows. All night the sounds of chaos drift on the breeze. Sometimes it's close: panicked voices just up the road. Other times far away: honking horns downtown or gunfire popping and echoing against the flat backdrop of the night. Once I hear another zombie outside. It stands in my front yard for fifteen minutes, lowing like a wounded cow. I peek out at it. It's an old man, hobbled and hunched, tinted orange by the streetlamp. He sways like he's listening to a slow big-band number. Maybe he is. Maybe his brain is on a loop, remembering something he did seventy years ago. I don't know what's going on in there. I watch him, Santana in one hand and the dead cop's gun in the other, until the zombie wanders off toward downtown.

The TV signal comes back intermittently. It's always the same: news anchors reading government warnings and lists of infected areas, or footage of cities spiraling out of control. Half a million people sprinting east on I-10, out of LA. It looks like the start of a marathon, except people are trampled, left in the middle of the interstate. Some in the crowd move differently, herky-jerky, and they grab their fellow runners and pull them to the ground.

In Miami, all along the southern coast of Florida, people are setting to sea. The harbor is full of boats, everything from giant motor yachts to Sunfish and Hobie Cats. Some people are floating on rafts, inner tubes. They're headed for Cuba, the anchor says, or for the Bahamas. She knows what they don't, reports it in a grave voice: all those places are infected too.

The camera lingers on infected celebrities. Actors are still clustered near the theater in LA, and that original feed from the Oscars is running. Meryl Streep is alone amid the carnage, on her knees in the center of the screen, feeding placidly on a cameraman. In Texas, Willie Nelson stands among a crowd of zombies on the banks of Lake Travis, reaching out over the water for the people who tread there, bobbing for who knows how long. Willie's toes are right on the edge of the water, but not in. None of the zombies are in the water.

And then LeBron. The zombie to end all zombies. Waves of police in riot gear crumbling like they're trying to bring down a Tyrannosaurus.

The feed is out again as the sun's coming up, and I hear the birds outside and smell the smoke, and then there's an image on the screen, one more time before it cuts off for good. A golf course. The sun higher because it's in South Florida, and that's a bit east of where I am up in the Panhandle. The grass dewy and gold-tinted in the morning light. And then there's Trump. Zombie Trump trudging across the green in his presidential pajamas. He looks around, bewildered. He stops at the hole and touches the flag. He says *uuuurg?* and from off-screen comes the sound of a gunshot, and then blood is coming out of his head and he falls. A Secret Service guy comes on-screen and walks up to the body. He fires fourteen more times, empties all the bullets into the zombie president's motionless body. He looks up smiling, and then he sees the cameraman. "Aw, shit," he says, and he makes the cutting motion, hand across his neck. The blue screen comes back, and then there's nothing else.

I call Rodney. "Where you at?" he says. He sounds out of breath.

"At home. You?"

"Fuck. Hang on." There's some scuffling and Rodney yelling and then a crunching sound. More crunching. And then Rodney's back on the phone. "I'm at work."

"What you doing at work?"

"Thought it might be safer here. Home wasn't no good. Mom and Trey, they . . ." He pauses, catches his breath. "Home wasn't no good."

I grab my go bag. Stuff the gun into my pants, Santana on my hip. "Stay put, man. I'm coming to you."

"No," Rodney says. "No, no. Don't come down here. It's a mess."

"Not just going to leave you there."

"Rip, just—" and then some groaning sounds and Rodney cursing and the phone cuts out.

Outside the air is cool, but I can tell it's warming up; something about the difference in temperature between sun and shade says the sun's going to do its job today. Right now it's just sliding up over the horizon, and its honeyed-orange colors come between the leaves in the trees and cast hazy dancing shadows on the grass, in the road. The smoke gives everything a smudged feel, like looking at the world through sunglasses covered in fingerprints. The air stings my nostrils and sits acrid in the back of my throat. I head to the end of the driveway and look up and down the street. It's empty except for the mess I left last night.

Officer Larry's car is where I left it—lights running, door hanging open. The zombies are starting to dry up in the sun. I pass them and go up the road to where there's a gap between the houses and I can see the water. There are a handful of boats in the bay—three motorboats with the engines wide open and five sailboats struggling to move in the shifty morning breeze. They are all headed for the pass, toward the Gulf. Some boats are already beached on the island. Across the pass from them, at The Beach, a line of smoke drifts from one of the condos. To my right is the Spanish Shanty marina, and a few boats are pulling out of the slips down there. More smoke is coming from the direction of downtown, and I walk toward it.

The smoke smell becomes stronger and the noises from downtown are like a riot—glass breaking and horns sounding loud and long and screaming and yelling—and then a little red pickup truck comes careening up the road, leaving black tire marks in its wake. It makes big jerking arcs because the driver is trying to dislodge a zombie from the bed of the truck. The zombie has its hands through the sunroof, and its legs fly up behind it and slam against the sides of the truck as the driver swerves, but this is a strong zombie, young and fit and tough, and he clings tight, and I jump out of the road as the truck flies past me and headlong into a tree. The zombie sails over the cab of the truck and lands in someone's front lawn fifty feet away, and then it stands up—crooked now, one of its legs broken at the femur—and limps toward the truck. The driver's struggling to open the door, but it won't budge since it's all warped from the wreck, and he sees me and yells for help. I pull Santana from her sheath, but then I see the other zombies, five of them, coming from a house and two more coming up the road where I came from, and I think, *Sorry, buddy*, and turn and head downtown. His yelling turns to screaming behind me.

Downtown, where the street shifts from pavement to cobble, the windows of the coffee shop are busted out, and two zombies are standing inside. They're regulars; I see them sitting at the outdoor tables most mornings. Now they're fighting with the vintage cappuccino machine, apparently still determined to get their morning fix. The machine is a big brass mess of pipes and spouts, and they've turned it on somehow. It's hissing and gurgling, and they hiss and gurgle back at it. One has a hold of the big central canister and is rocking it, *clank clank*, side to side. It gets enough momentum going and falls off the counter, jangle-crashes to the floor. Now there's water everywhere and the zombies slip and lie on the floor, turning in slow circles as they try to regain their footing. I leave them and step onto Main Street.

The sun is above the buildings and coming down yellow and warm, burning the winter away, dissolving the low-hanging scrim of smoke. Down the road near my work, a car has crashed into the building, and it flames heavy, and thick black clouds belch from the interior and drift out toward the bay. Two zombies stand near it, watching. East of me, up near McDonald's, several more are crouched on the sidewalk, eating someone. I can see body parts in the zombies' hands, the glistening slick skin of internal organs.

I heft Santana in my right hand, let the light slide all over her blade. Check the chamber of the pistol. Deep breath. Smile. And turn east.

One of the zombies hears me coming and looks up from its meal. I've seen him before: a lawyer, works in one of the law offices down here. He eats lunch at McDonald's, on his phone, briefcase open in front of him. He's in his fifties, balding, and he's wearing the same suit he always wears, fraying brown with a brown-and-tan-checked tie, thin round glasses bent but still somehow on his face. He drops a piece of liver and steps toward me, trips over the body. Stands up again, one foot planted in the body's open torso. He drags a fat cord of intestines with him as he steps out, and he says *urgle urgle urgle*.

I swing Santana at an angle, and she comes down fast and clean. I cut his head in half, ear to jaw, and he drops.

Three more zombies stand up, advance.

And then I'm lost in the smoldering depths of the kill, that hallucinatory calm that comes over you when the blade is singing in your hand and the bodies fall around you. It's a dance that you know all of the moves to even though you've never practiced. I turn, I duck and dip and spin, and Santana is alive in my hand and she snicks into the zombies and out again, trailing blood and sunlight, and I feel hands cold on my arm, cold as the bare sand beneath your feet on a hungover morning, cold as the stones you pull from the ground when you turn the earth with your fingers to plant an elephant-ear bulb. The bones in the wrists are thinner than you'd think, thinner with lots of empty space where ligaments stretch and hold things together, and Santana comes down like wrath and severs those hands, and the blood is in the air on my face.

Three are down and I look for the fourth, but she's gotten behind me somehow, jumps on my back and her teeth are scraping my skull, trying to bite in, but it's like I'm one of those giant jaw-breakers too big for her to get her mouth around. I duck and hurl her over the top of me, toss her flipping onto the cobbles, and as she starts to regain her footing I pull Officer Larry's gun from my pants and fire and she's knocked flat, her legs bent under her, the hole in her skull bleeding down into the cracks between the stones.

I catch my breath. The sun hits the windows of the store across the street from me, and I see my reflection. Santana dripping gore in my right hand, the pistol in my left exhaling a wisp of white smoke. My clothes blood spattered, a tear in my shirt near my belly, skin showing through.

I look cool as fuck.

* * *

Inside the office, the lights are on, but the place is deserted. A body on the floor in the lobby—the building's receptionist, Keith or Kyle or something—with knuckle-shaped holes in his face. Another at the bottom of the stairs, her head crushed under a big laser printer. *Good one, Rodney*, I think, and I go upstairs to the call center and all the cubicles sit empty.

The boss is in her office at the back, talking on the phone. She sees me and beckons me over. "Thanks for coming in, Rip. Knew I could count on you." Her kids are sitting in a stroller in the corner of the room. Each has an iPad, and they're immersed in some game. Eyes glazed, kind of like the zombies'. The boss sees me looking at them and says, "Day care was closed, and I couldn't get a babysitter." She rolls her eyes. "Some people, huh? How hard is it to do your job, seriously?"

"You stuck in here?" I say. I'm not crazy about the thought of dragging her and her kids around with me, but it feels like I've got to ask. "Where you trying to go? We can go together."

She blinks. "It's nine o'clock, Rip. I'm exactly where I'm supposed to be. I don't know what everyone else thinks they're doing."

I look at the empty call center. "You want people working?"

"It's not a holiday."

"There's zombies."

"Zombies aren't going to answer the phones. They're not going to respond to emails. We have customers, Rip. We have responsibilities. The world doesn't stop turning just because a few people get sick." She looks me up and down. "You're sort of . . . dirty. Do you have a change of clothes?"

"No. I don't have a change of clothes."

"Well, go to the bathroom and wash your face off, at least. We have standards."

I shrug and go to the bathroom. I scrub my hands and my arms and look at my face in the mirror. There's blood on it, but it's not in my eyes, my mouth, my nose. I remember what they said—mucous membranes and all—and I scrub all the shit off my face and make a note to try to be more careful. Get a mask or some goggles or something. Can't have zombie bits flying into my mouth when I'm cutting them up. My face is clean and my eyes are bright. In the mirror I'm grinning. Grinning back at myself. I don't know why, but I just can't stop grinning, the gun warm against my back and Santana humming a quiet tune in her sheath.

Back in the boss's office. "You seen Rodney?" I say.

The boss is on her computer. She's going through the troubleshooting protocol with the wireless internet. "Internet's not working," she says. "You're going to have to work the phones if you can't get online to do email."

"Rodney. You seen him?"

"He was on his way out when I got here. I told him it was going to cost him if he left. He just looked at me and left anyway." She turns to me, shaking her head. "I swear, Rip, some people have no respect for the job."

I leave her and go to Rodney's desk. There's a note on it:

Rip, waited as long as I could. Too many out there. Not sure if town's going to make it through. Going to go out to Beach, looks slower out there maybe. Meet up if you can.

The Beach. Why is he going to The Beach? There's nothing out there but plastic and noise. And the people out there: What are they going to think of him? Of any of us who go out there? Everyone knows what they think of us who live in Spanish Shanty. We are the hicks. We might as well be southern

Alabama. Eating KFC and drinking Natty Light in lawn chairs parked in three inches of water in the bay. And yeah—maybe some of us do that. But is it really so much better to drink a nine-dollar frozen margarita next to the Gulf? Or to live among the spring breakers for six weeks a year while they show their tits for a string of plastic beads or funnel vodka shots up each other's asses? No. Fuck The Beach.

"I've got the internet working," the boss calls from her office. "You can get back to email, Rip. You can—dang. It's out again."

The fluorescent lights cut out for a second, then flicker back on.

"Oh, foo. Now it's got to reboot."

I leave her and go back outside. The car that crashed into the building has burned down to a low glow, and the two zombies that were watching the fire are trying to get inside. One is reaching through the driver's side window, grabbing at the charred head of the driver's body. The zombie's sleeves are on fire. The other one is tearing at a melted front tire. I take Santana out and dispatch them both, the flames as hot on my skin as an open oven.

Now there's nothing moving downtown. It's just me and the dead zombies I've left scattered up and down the road. *That's right*, I think. *Trail of destruction in my wake.*

I walk westward, toward the marina, and stand at its entrance and look out at the water. Most of the boats have made it to the pass by now and the bay is empty, bright blue with ripples kicked up by the shifty breeze. Up and down the road— back toward my house or out away from town, out toward The Beach—things are quiet. Palm trees rattle their blades.

A car comes creeping up the road, right down the center of the street. The driver's buckled in, but he's straining against the seat belt, pulling first toward the passenger side, then out the driver's window. He thrashes in the seat. Closer still and I can see his face, and he can see me. Zombie. I step out of the road, and the car passes me at idle speed. The zombie reaches out the window, grunts as he passes, and continues down the road. I take the pistol out and aim and put a bullet in its head. It collapses forward onto the wheel, slumping to the left, turning the car off the road, over the shoulder and into the parking lot of the library. The car keeps slow-crawling right up to the side of the building, crunching through the big picture windows and knocking over a few bookcases before coming to a stop.

The glass tinks on the ground while the engine rumbles. A moment later, there's groaning from inside the library. A single zombie comes out. She looks like she was probably the librarian. Old woman with glasses. She sees me and starts to shuffle my direction, and I get Santana out, but another appears behind her. I switch to the pistol, take aim, and already there's another zombie, another, another, spilling out of the library like ants when you kick their hill. Ten, fifteen, twenty. Too many to count. They're not all shuffling. Some of them have better control of their bodies than others. They power-walk, they jog. And then one comes out, big guy with a mullet, and he's running. Flat-out *running*, straight at me, eyes dead and ravening. I aim at him, fire, miss, and all the zombies turn at once, swivel swivel *click*, focused on me, only on me, and they are coming.

"Shit," I say. And I run. I run toward The Beach.

Like I said, I'm not in the best shape. I don't run for fun. I don't exercise. So this shit is hard. I can hear the big zombie behind me, footsteps clunking on the pavement, and I know he's gaining on me. I'm embarrassed—he's dead and he's still faster than me. But I keep running even though my legs are already heavy and my lungs aren't pulling in the air I need. My bag weighs me down; Santana bangs on my hip, bruising me.

I look behind me, and the big zombie has almost caught up, so I shoot. I get him in the leg, and he slows, hobbled now, but he's still so close and he lunges at me, grabs me by the ankle as I turn to run again. I jerk my leg, but I can't get loose. Take Santana out and crack him in the head and he lets go, but another one has caught me; a kid in a school uniform grabs my Santana arm, so I have to shoot him, the report loud and the zombies frothing at the sound.

I'm loose, and I run a few more steps, and they are gaining, gaining. There is nothing but road ahead of me and miles to go before The Beach.

I turn and look at the horde. Fifty of them taking up the whole road, their dead voices filling the morning, and I hold Santana in one hand and the pistol in the other and yes, I'm going to die here probably, but glory, glory, what a hell of a way to die.

There's movement at the back of the pack. A zombie flies into the air, tumbling end over end. Then another. One is knocked sideways, sprawls on the edge of the road. The sound of an engine thunders over the noise of the zombies, and then I see the truck, the zombies going down before it, pulled under the tires, smashed and rolled over the windshield, crushed beneath the heavy trailer full of landscaping supplies. The truck barrels through them all and comes to a stop beside me. Mo gets out and looks back at the carnage. A few zombies are still shuffling our way. The rest lie broken on the road, the sidewalk.

One zombie is caught in the wheel well. His leg is wrapped up in the axle. His upper body dangles out the side of the truck, and he gnashes his teeth and reaches for Mo. Mo pulls a pair of work goggles and a face mask from his pocket, puts them on. Then he steps past the zombie, reaches into the bed of the truck, and pulls out a blade that looks like it could be a helicopter rotor. He lifts the huge hunk of metal above his head and brings it down on the zombie and cuts it in half below the shoulders. "Going to fuck up my truck," he says, sighing. The zombie is still alive, even though it's nothing but shoulders and arms and a head. It reaches for him as Mo digs beneath the truck and frees the leg from the axle. He tosses the mangled leg into the bushes and wipes his hands on his jeans. Then he kicks the zombie in the head with his steel-toed boot until the skull is bashed in and the thing stops moving. Finally, he looks at me. "Hey, Rip," he says. "You need a ride?"

* * *

I've seen Mo a million times at Bungalow, but this is the first time I've been in his truck. It smells like cut grass and gasoline. Empty paper cups scattered on the floor and across the back seat represent all the fast-food chains. A crumpled pair of leather work gloves rest in the center console. I crank the window down, and the fresh smoke from outside mixes with the stale smoke that clings to the seats, the dash—saturated from years of cigarettes and two-stroke engines. The trailer clatters over the road behind us, some of the stuff shifting around at every pothole, the bigger things strapped securely. I see chainsaws, weed trimmers, three types of lawn mower. "You got an arsenal back there," I say.

Mo glances in the rearview mirror. His long brown arms are thick and roped with muscle. One arm dangles out the window; the other grips the wheel with two fingers as he leans back in his seat. "Nah," he says. "Too loud. Too messy."

"Even the chainsaw?" I grin at him. "Come on. You don't want to do *Evil Dead*?"

"Blood would go everywhere. It would be in your mouth, in your eyes. You'd end up catching it, and then you'd be a zombie." He shakes his head. "No. It should be blades. Still a splat, but just one." He puts his fists together, then spreads his fingers. "*Splat*. You can wear protection. But with the chainsaw, man, it would be a fountain." He looks over at me. "You don't have goggles?"

"Haven't had a chance to get any."

"But you killed some zombies?"

"A bunch, yeah."

He pulls the truck over. We're on Beachfront Lane, where the old colonial-style houses line up end to end, overlooking the bay, the million-dollar sunsets. Fat white columns and well-tended yards. Mo grabs my face, turns it in the sunlight. Pulls my eyelids up and stares into my eyeballs. He puts one thumb under my nose and the other on my chin and stretches my lips apart, examining my teeth like I'm a dog at the vet. After a moment, he lets go and says, "I think you're okay. Go in the glove box. I got some more stuff you can wear."

In the glove box I find another mask and goggles. I fold the mask and stuff it in my pocket, put the goggles on the top of my head. "I was using a blade anyway. Call her Santana." I show him the machete. "You got a name for yours yet?"

He thinks a moment. "El decapitador. It means—"

"Oh, no. I get it."

We stare down the empty road. A car sits half submerged in the bay a couple hundred yards ahead. Across from it, a zombie wanders into a yard, trailing salt water. Mo points. "I'm supposed to cut that house today. I don't think I'm going to get around to it."

"Where's your crew?"

"Zombies."

I nod. "They turned into zombies? Or the zombies ate them?"

"Both."

Three guys worked for Mo. I met them a couple times at the bar. Nice enough, but quiet, the work-hard-get-paid-go-home type. Still, Mo worked with them every day for years. "I'm sorry, Mo."

He shrugs. "Sea lo que sea."

The wet zombie has noticed us and is coming up the road in an awkward jog. It's a middle-aged woman in expensive-looking clothes. Jewelry in her ears, on her fingers, around her neck. "Señora Jacobs," Mo says. He puts the car in gear. "Her yard's on my route." She raises her arms as the truck gets close and she says *aaaaaag*, this high-pitched howl, and then Mo swerves toward her and she goes under the wheels. The car jerks, and the trailer bounces behind us and she's spit out twisted on the asphalt.

At the sound of her yell, other zombies emerge from the houses. Mo speeds up.

"We're overrun, man," I say. I watch the sideview mirror. Zombies reach the road, walking stumbling running after us. Smoke is forming in thick clouds over downtown. It's a mess back there. "Shit, I should have got more stuff from my house." I open my bag and look in at the sad pile of Pop-Tarts and whatever else I threw in there. "I had all night. And this is what I put together."

"I got some shit." Mo jerks his finger toward the bed of the truck. "We'll share."

Beachfront ends and we pull up to the highway, the busy stretch lined with businesses and restaurants. Right takes us back into town. Left goes to the bridge, to The Beach. Mo looks off in that direction.

"Where we going?"

"The Beach."

"I don't want to go to The fucking Beach, Mo."

"Gabriela and Lupita are out there. You don't want to go to The Beach, you got to find another ride."

There are cars burning in the road to our right. Two zombies crouch in a parking lot, pulling a body apart. The body sits up and pushes them away, and then the three of them amble together into the road. An RV comes flying around the corner, swerves to miss them. Its tires squeal and it comes up on two wheels, wobbling, then crashes on its side and drags scraping along the asphalt before slamming to a stop against a telephone pole. The driver tries to climb out of his window, but he's old, and he struggles. The three zombies scale the side of the RV, and the driver ducks back inside. The zombies slip one by one into the window behind him.

To the left, the road is clear. "Rodney went to The Beach," I say. "Everyone's at The Beach."

"All right, then," Mo says, and we drive.

The stores get kitschier as the oak trees give way to palms. Fast-food joints and bait shops are replaced by sunglass huts, snow cone stands, souvenir shops with baskets of foam pool noodles in front. Then the shore is ahead of us, the quiet beach that marks the border of Spanish Shanty, and the bridge looms gray against the sky. A flat concrete monster they built fifteen years ago as The Beach was really taking off, a faster way to get the tourists from the highway to the other side of the channel, keep them from having to stop in Spanish Shanty. They blew the old bridge up. Sank it, the ruins left to sit sixty feet below the water, staring up through the shimmering surface at the sleek replacement.

A couple of zombies are standing at the foot of the bridge, looking toward The Beach. Mo runs them over, and the truck bounces like we're on a rain-gutted dirt road.

"Can't that mess the truck up?" I say.

Mo shrugs. "Tough truck."

We make our way up the bridge. It's by far the biggest hill in Spanish Shanty. The land falls away and the water sparks in the rising sun. Down below us, a cargo ship is steaming westward, but it's off course. Mo and I stop at the top of the bridge and watch. The ship is a hundred yards long and full of colorful shipping containers. It veers to port, clocking the green channel marker and knocking its piling to a forty-five-degree angle. Then the ship runs aground with a thump and a scrape, and several of the containers splash into the bay. The stern of the ship drifts counterclockwise in the tide, the engines still forcing the bow forward, farther up into the shallows, forming a pivot point for the ship to swing like the hand of a clock. Finally the ship is sideways in the channel, and we can see the deck well. Zombies mill about down there, walking to one edge of the ship, looking into the water, then walking to the other edge. Ten of them, dressed in the blue-and-gray jumpsuits of commercial shippers. Back and forth, back and forth. One sees us. It raises its arms and opens its mouth. We're a quarter of a mile away, but I can hear its moan. Then the tide wins out; the ship comes loose from the sand and drifts. It moves landward, crunching docks and day sailors as it nears the shore. It gets lodged against a peninsula and is still.

Behind us, Spanish Shanty burns. The town is spread out on a knobby bit of land that sticks into the bay in a sprawl of bulbous peninsulas. The low houses and trailers are mostly obscured by trees. Smoke gushes skyward from dozens of different fires. Three fires downtown. Looks like the paper mill might be on fire. It always belches clouds of smoke, but that smoke is white and stinks of sulfur. This smoke is a thick black, and it glows orange near the ground. More smoke on the horizon, plumes east west and north, a big one up north at the edge of vision, up around Dothan.

"I thought we might head out of town after I find my girls," Mo says. "To Pensacola, or go north." He points up toward Dothan. "Now I don't know."

I shake my head. "I think they got it worse than us. Saw it on the news. Outbreaks in Pensacola and Dothan big enough they were getting reported on CNN."

"Tallahassee?"

"Same deal."

He walks to the other side of the bridge and looks out toward the Gulf. "So what? We're stuck here?"

I stand next to him. "We're surrounded," I say. At the edge of the bay, the barrier island sits pristine, the Gulf green behind it. A few sailboats are anchored close to shore. "We could go to the island."

Mo shakes his head. "No food out there. Hardly any fresh water."

East of the island is the Air Force base. A couple of jets take off, rising up into the sky like luminous bugs; they turn north and their engines flame orange as they blast over Spanish Shanty and vanish into the smoky horizon.

On the other side of the bridge The Beach seems quiet. "Where is everybody?" Mo says.

It's a good question. There are five times as many people living at The Beach as in Spanish Shanty. It ought to be a mess of zombies and chaos. Instead, it looks like a ghost town. "Maybe they had an evacuation," I say. "In fact, I bet that's exactly what they did. They got the fuck out of Dodge and left us to get eaten. That's exactly the kind of thing they'd do."

"Pendejos."

"Exacto."

Mo smiles. "Close enough."

We get back into the truck and follow the bridge down, down the hill to The Beach.

* * *

The Beach seems like an oasis after the chaos in Spanish Shanty. There are some zombies, sure. Mo steers around them but ends up clipping a few with the trailer anyway. The trailer clangs and the zombies bounce off, somersault across the asphalt.

No one's alive that we can see.

"I told Gabriela to go," Mo says. "She said she was staying. She didn't want to scare Lupita." He's gripping the wheel tight now, his knuckles white, his eyes focused on the road as he dodges zombies. The condos loom ahead of us, smoke streaming from some of them. We turn onto Beach Boulevard. "They should have left."

We head west down the empty road. Scattered zombies wander in the parking lots of the condos, the hotels. One is trapped out on a balcony, way up in a peach-colored tower, the room on fire behind her. An old woman. She walks, bumps into the railing, takes a few more steps. Back and forth. And then she hits the rail hard, tumbles forward, over. Her legs are still going like she's walking in midair as she falls twenty stories to the pavement. She lands behind some bushes, so I can't see her, but I hear it. Like a garbage bag full of meat splatting on stone. Which is, I guess, essentially what it is. "Which one is she in?"

"Down near the end. Mahimahi."

Mo's wife always worked out at The Beach, a maid in one of the big hotels. When she left him, she moved out there for good, took their daughter with her. They don't talk much, as far as I can tell. But Mo doesn't talk about Gabriela much either, so I don't know. He *does* talk about Lupita. So I guess we're going for her.

There's a putt-putt golf course up on the right. It's dinosaur themed, with a T. rex out by the entrance and a brontosaurus sticking its neck way up in the back. It's called Triassic Park, which is either a good joke or one step away from copyright infringement. In the middle is a volcano that squirts water in the air every few minutes. On top of it are two people: a woman and a child.

Mo squints. "Not them."

"Why would it be?"

"I don't know. I'm just looking, okay?"

The people see us coming and start waving. The woman is black with hair cut close to her head, and the girl is a miniature version of her—obviously her daughter—but her hair is long and wild, a storm cloud around her head, her shoulders. They're both wearing bright sundresses like they're ready for church.

Mo keeps driving.

"Help!" We can hear them now, both of them, frantic. "Help! Hey! Help us!"

Then we're close enough that I can see inside the park to the bottom of the volcano. There are probably ten zombies there, scrambling to get up to the woman and her daughter. Most of them in church clothes too. The volcano is steep and made out of some hard ceramic-like stuff, and the zombies are not exactly dexterous, so they climb a few feet before losing their grips and sliding back down. Then they get up, try again.

"We should stop," I say. I take the gun from my pants and rest it on my leg.

"No," Mo says. "I need to find my girls."

"Mo. Look at them."

He stops the truck and looks. We're right next to the T. rex, and its head hangs over the truck, its teeth casting long shadows on the ground in front of us. The volcano is a hundred feet away behind some palms. The girl is screaming at us, jumping up and down, and her mom is holding on to the back of her dress to keep her from falling.

"She's a daughter too," I say.

He looks up at the volcano, then down the road. Sighs. "Okay. We make it quick, though."

We get out, and Mo pulls el decapitador from the bed of the truck. He walks ahead of me, the blade over his shoulder, and he crosses the bridge over the fake lava river and goes right up to the nearest zombie—a big one, like a former football player— and swings the heavy metal at its neck, takes its head off. The other zombies turn, shuffle toward him, and Mo cuts another one in half, shoulder to hip.

I don't want to miss it, so I take Santana out and jump into the fight. She sings her song, and Mo and I turn and dodge and cut, and in a few moments there are eight zombies on the ground. Only a couple remain, over on the other side of the volcano, still trying to make their way up. The woman up top looks down at them and pulls a big chef's knife from somewhere inside her dress and slides down the side of the volcano. She puts that momentum into the knife and drives it into the skull of one of the zombies right as she reaches the bottom. Then she yanks it free, squares off against the other one—a middle-aged guy in a T-shirt with the Triassic Park logo on it. He dives at her, and she dips to the left, and then she comes up strong and shoves the tip of the knife through the underside of the zombie's jaw. The point of the blade juts out the back of its head. The zombie falls down, and the woman steps on him and drags the knife out and wipes it on her pants. Then she looks up at her daughter, beckons, and the girl slides down the volcano.

There's a fake real river next to the fake lava river, and Mo takes his blade over there and starts to wash it off. I dip Santana in and wipe her on the fake grass of the putt-putt green.

The woman and her daughter come over. "Thanks for stopping," she says. She's my age, with an angular face and fierce eyes. A thick scar wraps around her throat. "I'm Xan," she says. "This is Rain."

The girl stands slightly behind her mother. Ten years old or so. "Hey," she says.

"Hey," I say, and then we hear them. Already the sound has a Pavlovian effect. The zombies groan, and your hand automatically goes for your weapon. Your pulse quickens, your senses sharpen. You key in on them, gauge distance, number. They're on the road, coming this way. At least twenty. Must have heard the ones we just killed, heard them clamoring for food and come toward us like the dinner bell had been rung. They fill the street, moving fast.

Xan flips her knife in her hand. Mo joins us, his blade over his shoulder. I pull the pistol from my pants and grip Santana tight.

"Too many?" Xan says.

"I don't know," I say, and as we watch, they see us. They get louder, speed up. I look around, and there's no good way out other than the way we came in. "I don't think we got a choice."

And then there she is. Where she came from, I don't know—hidden in the trees or crouched in a parking lot or out beneath the water past the beach, I don't know—but she's suddenly there behind the pack of zombies. She's small, lissome, but she moves in a way that screams power and speed and strength. Like a gazelle. Like a shooting star. Like an armor-piercing bullet. Her skin glows olive in the sunlight. Her legs are long and smooth, like they're rubbed with oil, smooth all the way up to her cutoff jeans, and her ribbed black wifebeater clings to her thin frame. Her arms are compact with muscle, and in her hands is a home-made poleaxe.

She stands in the road behind the zombies, looks them up and down, taps the saw blade on the asphalt. Then she looks past them, at us, at me. Her eyes are dark, dark. Her hair shaved close on the sides with a long loose Mohawk of dark hair in the middle. She blinks at me. Pushes her hair back. And then she goes to work.

The woman leaps, her poleaxe held high, and she comes down with all her weight and all her strength and crushes the skull of the nearest zombie. Before it's even hit the ground, she's pulled her blade free and swung it into another one. The zombies still come toward us, and she is a flurry of skin and speed and metal in their rear, biting into them with the saw blade's curved teeth. She's got half of them down before the ones at the front notice her, and they turn, advance on her, but she skirts the outside of them, leaping, dancing almost, circling them, picking them off one by one.

In two minutes she's killed them all.

She stands in the middle of the carnage. Her chest rises and falls and she pushes her hair back again. Then she looks at me.

I try to look cool, but I'm grinning like an idiot.

Her eyes narrow but the corner of her lip turns up, just a bit. The smirk to end all smirks.

And then she's off the road, heading toward the beach.

"Hey!" I say.

But she's between the condos, a silhouette against the sand and green water, and then she's gone.

"Dios mío," Mo says.

"Yeah," is what I say, but I'm thinking, *I'm fucking in love.*

THURSDAY, OCTOBER 24

"All right," Duck Duck says. "So I'm the zombie. I'm over here in my cage or whatever."

"Is it a cage?" Rodney says.

"Well, it's locked up in something, don't you think?"

"They could be chained up. Or just in a room. What makes you think it's a cage?"

"Look, you'll see when you get there."

"But don't you think we ought to know?" Rodney's been getting more frustrated as the night's gone on. Twice already he's threatened to pull out, and Mo and I have talked him back in.

This is supposed to be a practice run. We've moved the furniture around in my house, and we come through the door with our imaginary key cards and Duck Duck the zombie is waiting for us, and we're supposed to figure out the best way to get him out of there.

"Can you ask your guy?" I say. "If he's getting us a key card, he's probably been in there. Seen them."

"He hasn't, though," Duck Duck says. "He works security. He can get the cards since he knows where they keep them, but he's not authorized to use them. He's just supposed to keep people like us from getting into the buildings. Keep us from even getting on the base. Him and all the others."

"We're bribing them all?" Mo says.

"No. I told you. I'm going to Create a Diversion." He says it like it's a grand event. "Once I Create a Diversion, everyone's going to be diverted. So you can just get in. You'll have to be quick, though. What I'm going to do, I can only do it once."

"Why can't you tell us what you're going to do?" Rodney says.

"Because it's a surprise!" Duck Duck has an unhinged look in his eyes. He brought some coke with him tonight, and he's offered it to me, but no, not tonight, not when we're supposed to be planning. He's high, though. "You're gonna love it," Duck Duck says. "It's gonna be badass."

"Fine," I say. "Let's try another run. You're in your cage."

"Right." Duck Duck puts his hands up on imaginary bars. He lets his head droop and wobbles on his feet. "Raaaar!"

Rodney, Mo, and I go outside. The air has that heavy late-summer stillness about it even though it's supposed to be fall. The elephant ears are turning yellow at the edges from the heat, and the bay smells of dead seaweed.

"This isn't going to work," Rodney says.

"That's why we're practicing."

"There's too much we don't know. How are we supposed to open a cage? Or if he's in another room with another key card? Duck Duck's going to do his big diversion or whatever, and we're going to get in there, and we're just going to be stuck with our thumbs up our asses. And what if there's a guard inside? Or even some lab guys who just call security?" Rodney shakes his head. "There's a million ways it can fuck up. There's a million wrong ways and only one right way. What makes you think we're going to get the right way?"

"Practice," I say.

Mo has brought his whiskey outside with him. He takes a sip. "You never know what's going to happen until it happens," he says. "We made it the whole summer, figuring it out along the way. We can do it now too."

Rodney sighs. He looks through the window, where Duck Duck is still pretending to be a zombie, even though we're all outside. "All right. More practice, though. We practice until we get it right."

Mo slides his credit card through an invisible scanner next to my front door. "Beep," he says, and he opens the door.

Duck Duck rattles the bars of his cage. "Roar!" he says. "Goddle goddle giddle goddle!"

"They don't sound like that," Rodney says.

"Just play along," Duck Duck says. "Rooooog!"

"All right," I say. "So he's in a cage this time. And we've got to find a key."

"Ruuuur," says Duck Duck. "Ruur—heylookherecomes-ascientist—arrrg!"

"So I guess if we can find a scientist, he'll have a key," I say.

"We get the key from the scientist." Rodney says it like he's making a move in Dungeons and Dragons.

Duck Duck breaks character. "How?"

"I'll grab him," Mo says, "and I'll threaten to feed him to the zombie."

Duck Duck grins. "Now you're thinking." Then he's a zombie again. "Roar! I'm going to eat this scientist!"

"And he gives us the key," I say. I take the key and open Duck Duck's cage. He lurches out and goes straight for Rodney. He grabs him by the shoulders and bites him on the biceps.

"Dude! Don't fucking bite me!"

"Zombie's going to bite you!" Duck Duck says. "And look. I just left a little mark. If the zombie bites you, it's over. You're dead." He looks at Rodney. "I mean, I guess the plan would still work. Just you'd be the zombie restarting the apocalypse instead of whatever zombie we steal. It would still work, but that's not what we want, right? We want to be the good guys again."

"Right," I say.

"So don't get bit."

"You get one arm," Mo says to me. "I get the other. Get back in your cage."

Duck Duck goes back inside the imaginary cage and pulls the invisible door closed behind him. "Rar," he says, and we open the door and each grab him by the arm. He shakes and wrestles against us and we hold tight. Duck Duck tosses his head and leans over and bites Mo on the shoulder.

"Ay, cabrón!"

"See?" Duck Duck says. "Still dead. You need something to grab him with."

We try again a few minutes later. Get him wrapped up in a bedsheet. Duck Duck struggles, worms his way loose, bites me on the ankle.

Then it's rope. We slip a lasso around him, but we can't get it tight fast enough with him coming at us, and we're bitten.

Turns out it's a lot harder to catch zombies than it is to kill them.

"We need one of those dog things," Rodney says.

"Ah!" Duck Duck points at Rodney. "Ahhh! Smart man!"

"What are you talking about?" Mo says.

"Mo, you be the zombie," Duck Duck says. He gets a broom out of the kitchen and comes back. "Be the zombie."

"Grr," Mo says.

"Okay, so like this." Duck Duck takes the broom and presses it against Mo's throat. "You get the collar around him, right? And this part is rigid"—he's pointing at the broomstick—"so you can hold him away. Like, come at me, Mo. And you've got a collar on, remember."

"Grr." Mo reaches for Duck Duck, but Duck Duck holds the broom out, and Mo's sweeping arms fall short; his teeth snap three feet away from Duck Duck's face. Duck Duck moves in a slow circle, holding Mo at the end of the broom, and he guides him out the door. Then they both come back inside and Mo's not a zombie anymore.

"Easy!" Duck Duck says.

"It's a good idea," I say. "Where do we get one of those?"

"I don't know. Amazon?"

I get online and look. There's a four-foot catch pole for eighty-five dollars and a six-foot for a hundred. "You think four feet will do it?"

Rodney looks at the screen. "You're not willing to pay fifteen dollars for two extra feet?"

"I don't know. Fifteen bucks."

"What if he's big? What if he's got long arms?"

"But if we can do it cheaper."

"Shit, man," Rodney says. "I got your fifteen bucks. Jesus."

"I'll get two. That gets us next-day delivery."

Rodney shakes his head. "Unsustainable."

* * *

When we're done with practice, Duck Duck leaves and the rest of us get in Rodney's car and go to Bungalow. It's sort of crowded tonight, a dozen people inside, so we go out back and sit with our beers, looking at the black water. The moon is bright and full overhead, and it casts a reflection that sparkles like a disco ball in the center of the bayou. The voices are loud inside, boisterous, bragging voices and laughter.

Bob comes outside with another round. He sits down at our table, his own beer in his hand. He raises the bottle and we silently toast the night, the moon, I don't know what.

"How's business, Bob?" I say.

He shrugs. "Better. Getting better, I guess."

Mo is cracking peanuts, eating the insides and tossing the shells into the water. The surface roils with whiskers and fins as fat black catfish slurp up to eat them.

"It's a different crowd," Bob says. "I've got you guys. Love you guys. But everyone else. They're different than before."

I know what he's talking about. I can't put my finger on it, but the world has a different feel. The people carry themselves differently. Not better, not worse—just different.

Bob drinks his beer. "So many people died, and everyone who comes here, they're the people who didn't die. And they know it. And I thought that would make them grateful. We ought to be all walking around every day giving thanks to Jah that we're still alive. We ought to be doing the carpe diem thing, or treating each other better because we learned a lesson. Something."

"No one learned shit," Mo says.

"But they changed. Can't you see it? They're different. We're different."

And he's right, about me at least. I am different. I'm worse than I was before it started. I was bad before. I was asleep back then. The world was there and life was there but it was all hanging just out of reach, like it was behind a dirty pane of glass. Everything was distant, blurred, because the only things in focus were work and TV and food and all the stuff that fills up every minute of every day. And then there were the zombies and I was awake, like I'd been turbocharged with electricity, like there was nitrous in the tank, afterburners pouring fuel directly into the turbine. The edges of life were sharp. Every word and every movement was heavy with meaning. Life had weight, fat fruits bending the sapling branches and waiting to be plucked, eaten, the sweet juice wet on your lips. Alive. Alive.

And now it's all over and I'm still awake. It's like making out with the beautiful girl at the bar at closing time, and then they turn the lights on and cut the music and suddenly you're stone-cold sober and you can see the hair on her upper lip and the blue veins in her legs and the grease in her hair. Awake when you want to be asleep. "I know what you're saying, Bob."

Bob points at me with his beer. "I know you do. I can see it on you. Every time you walk in here. You too, Mo. Rodney—you're all right. I'm not sure how you're hanging in there."

"You just get by, man," Rodney says. "Day by day."

Bob opens his mouth to say something else, but the noise picks up inside, people shouting, "Shots! Shots! Shots!" so Bob sighs and gets up. "Take your time, guys," he says. And he goes inside.

A cat walks out to the end of the porch. Puffy Himalayan with gray fur all over, but bald in three thick lines down its left hindquarters. Scars. Scars like claw marks. It finds a chicken-wing bone under a table and begins to gnaw on it.

"I thought they all got eaten," Rodney says.

"Like the tree squirrels." Mo points at the cat. "That's one of the smart ones. He outran evolution."

The cat picks the bone clean and sits up. It licks its paw, runs it over its head a few times. Then it flops on its back beside Rodney. Rodney rubs its belly with the toe of his shoe, and the cat purrs loud enough to vibrate the planks beneath it. "You ever thought maybe you just need a pet, Rip?"

"I don't want the responsibility."

"But maybe you're just lonely." He picks up the cat and puts it in his lap. Runs his fingers over the scars. "I know we don't like to talk about it. Maybe it makes me less manly, or whatever, but I don't care. I'm lonely. I miss my brother. My mom. I got no one but you guys left."

Mo shifts in his chair, looks up at the moon.

"And you don't want to admit it, but you're both as lonely as I am. I know you miss Gabriela, Mo, and of course Lupita. And Rip, you don't even have to start in on Davia. I saw the two of you. I know what she meant to you. I know what it all meant to you—not just Davia but all of us that lived out at Lazy River.

We really were a family. A big old family." The cat sits up in Rodney's lap and twitches its ears as it looks at something none of us can see. It jumps down, skitters out of sight. Rodney holds his hands in front of him for a moment, hovering as if he's saving space for the cat to come back. Then he lets them rest on his thighs. "I miss that family too, but I've been thinking on it. Bringing the zombies back isn't going to bring that back. Not that family, or that feeling. It's not bringing back Gabriela and Lupita. And it's not going to bring Davia back, Rip."

"So what are you saying, then?" I say.

"I'm saying I'm out."

"Damn it, Rodney. We spent all night practicing with you. You were in an hour ago."

"And now I'm out. I'm allowed to change my mind."

"You're out, you're in, you're out. You change it every goddamn fifteen minutes."

"It's a crazy idea, Rip," Rodney says. "It sounded all right in principle. Especially when I was sitting at home all lonely, or when I was at work all bored. But then tonight, when we were practicing, I was thinking to myself, 'We're practicing murder. We're practicing the end of the world.' You see what we're doing, right, guys? And how fucking crazy it is? You're listening to that lunatic Duck Duck. He's an asshole and a cokehead, and you're just letting him put the plan together."

"He knows the base," I say.

"But he doesn't! He flies a jet. He doesn't know what's in that fucking lab. Maybe nothing. And we're going to break into a government military base, an experimental science lab full of classified shit at an American Air Force base. If they catch us, we'll go to prison forever. This might be treason. In fact, I take it back. We probably won't even go to jail. They'll just shoot us right there. Is that what you want, Rip? To die? Because you had plenty of chances to die this summer and you never did. Why you aching to die now?"

I look out over the water. "But aren't we already dead?"

"No! You sound like a goth teenager. We're not dead. Millions of people are, Rip, and we're not. You get to stay alive and enjoy all this." He waves at the water, the moon, the beer. Then he looks at me again. "So quit whining." He starts to leave.

"So you're out?" I say.

"I'm out."

"And the money?"

"Money goes with me." His feet clomp on the planks as he heads for the door.

"Rodney," Mo says.

Rodney stops. "Yeah?"

"This is the answer, you know."

"To what?"

"You've said it. You've gone on about it at the bar. There are too many people using too many resources. I don't know how many times I've heard you say *unsustainable*. It's your catch-phrase." He drinks his beer and looks up at the moon. "You say millions of people are going to die if we do what we do. You're right. But there will be millions left. If we do nothing, we kill the planet. Then everyone dies."

"It's still crazy."

"Is it as crazy as doing nothing?"

Rodney's lips twitch. His hand rests on the door.

"You're right," Mo says. "The zombies are the ones who can save us."

Rodney looks at us for a long time. Then he pushes through the door, and the bar noise seeps out onto the porch. The door swings shut behind him and it's quiet again.

Mo's still looking up at the moon. "Can't do it without his money," he says after a while.

"I know." I look up too. The moon is so white it hurts the eyes. The craters sprawl gray-black across the surface. People like to say it looks like a face, like the man in the moon, but I always see a woman. She's got long hair, a long dress, and she's running to the left, her hair and her dress flying out behind her, tossed in the wind. She's been running forever, and I've never known if she's running to something, something out there in space that only she can see, or if she's running away. And looking at her tonight, I know for certain that it's the latter. She is fleeing. There's something on the other side of the moon. Something dark from the dark side of the moon has risen and is coming for her, and she runs, she runs. She ran until the moon stopped turning, and she'll run until its orbit creeps close enough to Earth that tidal forces pull it apart, turn the moon into a scattered and rocky ring, a miniature Saturn. Still she'll run from the darkness that rises in the shadows we cannot see.

FRIDAY, OCTOBER 25

"So what's left? No money, no plan." Duck Duck is furious. He comes over all coked up and raves for an hour about how this has to happen, it has to happen *now*, that everything's all set up and I've got to get the money somewhere.

I say, "Can't you get the money?"

And he looks at me like I'm the crazy one.

When he's gone, there's nothing to do, and this is where most people would move on or end it. I'm not good with either of those. Moving on—another job, another bunch of coworkers, another boss. Another desk to sit behind eight hours a day, 480 minutes just tick-ticking away, minutes of my life going going while I sit there and do whatever it is I'm supposed to do. I can't. I can't do that again. And I can't end it, because the only thing worse than wasting a life by being half alive is wasting a life by being dead.

At some point it occurs to me that Davia might be the answer. When I think about the summer and the way life simmered and flared at the edges, three things stick out. Killing zombies was one, obviously—their black blood on my skin and Santana's music in my fist.

Then there was the camaraderie, the kinship, the family. Waking early in the water park with the sunlight stretching through the spindly pines, cooking breakfast over propane stoves while new-arrival zombies paced the outer banks of the lazy river. Or setting out with Rodney or Mo or some of the others, wandering the ransacked buildings, the empty streets where the pavement sizzled. Returning home at night, gathering again, all of us around the fire, the food, to talk and laugh while the stars careened overhead. The stars—so many and so bright with the city lights gone. We gave them new names, new constellations to tell new stories. Our family of starwatchers beneath an infinite night, and we crept to bed, one by one or two by two, couples and families, me and Davia, and we slept in peace under those endless stars.

Davia, the third thing, the molten core of my world.

I go to the coffee shop. The kid behind the counter recognizes me and pours me a coffee-flavored coffee. Good on him. "You seen a woman in here?" I say.

"Lots of women in here."

"Yeah, but this one's different. She was here the other day." I don't know how to describe her. It's like trying to describe an orgasm or a burn. You can't. You've just got to feel it. "She's *Davia*."

The kid shrugs.

I take my coffee and sit at a table near the back. The owner has mounted his wife's baseball bat above it; the wood is stained, blackened by zombie insides. The nails driven into the bat and sharpened have started to rust.

I look up at the chalk-written list on the blackboard behind the wall. Lattes and mochas, cappuccinos and espressos. Coffee like a milkshake and coffee like a brown slushie. Arabica beans from Columbia, Peru, Brazil, from Tanzania, from India, and Robusta beans from Madagascar, Thailand, Vietnam. All those years the world turned, seeds sprouted in the soil, grew into bushy plants with quivering, shiny leaves, branches lined with the green and red fruit. Farmers plucked the cherries and dried them in the sun, separated the bean from the meat. Fermented the beans and dried them, milled them, shipped them off to be roasted. And then these shiny black and brown beans were shipped around the world, to America, to Spanish Shanty, to this coffee shop so that the kid behind the counter could grind them up and put them in my cup. A web of impossible complexity behind something so simple.

Now those fields are burned and the farmers are buried. We're mere months removed from a zombie-strewn hellscape, but still the people want their coffee. So we've got Arabica chemicals and Robusta chemicals tweaked just right to taste like something that sprang from the earth in Honduras or Ethiopia or Papua New Guinea. Capitalism finds a way.

The coffee is good. But I'd trade it all to have the hellscape back.

I watch the door and wait for Davia, but she never comes in.

* * *

I show up at Bungalow at three and Mo's waiting outside. Bob lets us in and we hit it heavy and fast. I drink until the room is swimming and my eyes are heavy. Bob keeps pouring me glasses of water, pushing them under my nose, and I keep dumping them in the sink behind the bar when he's not looking. I don't want to dilute this. I want to be gone.

But then Rodney's here, seated beside me at the bar. "All right," he says.

I sit up. Hard to hold my head straight.

His face is angry, his eyes dark. Bob brings him a beer, and Rodney sips it, sets the bottle down on a napkin, lines it up perfectly in the center. He folds his hands in front of him. Waits. Then he says, "I'm back in."

"Back in?"

"Back in."

My brain is swirly, so it takes a minute for it to click, and when it does the endorphins and adrenaline come rushing in and shove the alcohol out of the way. Things sharpen at the edges, and Rodney clenches his fists on the bar and I can see them again the way they were, with spiked knuckles dripping blood, and even though she's far away back at my house I can hear Santana tuning up, her voice carrying like harp strings across the still night waters. I grin at Rodney. "The plan?"

He nods.

I elbow Mo. "Mo. Hey, Mo!"

"Déjame en paz."

"Rodney's in. He's back in."

Mo lifts his head off the bar and looks past me to Rodney. His lips curl up, and I can see his teeth, somehow so white even after all the cigarettes and whiskey. "All right. Things are happening. Things are happening." Then he puts his head back down.

I turn to Rodney. "We couldn't do it without you."

"I know. I got the money."

"Not just that. We need you. I need you." I put my hand on his shoulder. "You're my friend, man. My best friend."

"Turning this into a real bromance," he says, but he's smiling now too.

"Beers, Bob," I say. And we're drinking and talking and laughing like it's before. After a while, I ask him, "What changed, Rodney?"

He puts his beer down, looks at the bar. "Mo's right. What he said last night. It's dark. It's fucked up. But it's math, man. That's all it comes down to. Numbers. We keep going like this—overpopulated, overconsuming—every single one of us dies, and we leave the earth a lifeless broiler. We lose a few billion to the zombies, we just might make it."

"So you're Thanos?"

"I guess so."

"He's supposed to be the bad guy in *Avengers*," I say. "I don't know. I thought his plan kind of made sense."

"That's not the only thing," Rodney says. "It's the main thing. But it wasn't the tipping point. The boss called a meeting today. Call center's shutting down. They're moving it."

"You knew they were going to eventually."

"I know. I just thought they might not, after the outbreak and all. But no, they're moving up to North Dakota. Dickinson. Never heard of the place, and now they want me to move there."

"It's like in *Fargo*?"

"You mean all the snow? And people talking weird? I don't know, man. Probably. It's practically in Canada. I can't go up there. I can't take that kind of cold."

I shake my head. "Nah, fuck that. When they moving?"

"End of the year."

Now I'm wired, revved up. "Let's not even give them the chance. Let's get those fucking zombies. We can turn them loose in the call center if we want. Oh, man. North Dakota. Fuck North Dakota."

Rodney nods. "Fuck North Dakota."

"Let's set the world on fire again. Let's burn this motherfucker down."

BACK THEN

Mahimahi is on fire. We sit in the parking lot and watch through the windshield of Mo's truck. Me and Mo and Xan and Rain, all smashed together while the truck's engine vibrates the bench. Rain's hair a mushroom cloud that seems to fill the cab.

The hotel is longer than it is tall—ten stories up but maybe thirty units long, stretching out over a hundred yards of beach. The fire is burning in the bottom right corner; looks like four or five units hit already, but it's spreading. A couple of zombies on the second floor looking at the flames.

"She wouldn't be at home?" I say.

"At the apartment?" Mo says. "I don't know. It's small. One story. She might think she'd be safer here."

"So which room?"

"Could be any of them." He honks the horn, waits, honks again. The zombies are fifty yards away, but still they reach over the guardrail at us, mouths open. The fire licks upward, tongues of flame dancing their way to the third floor.

"You think they know it's on fire?" Xan says. She found a whetstone in the trailer and she's running it over her knife, a methodical shushing scrape that blends with the crackling of the fire and the rumble of the engine to make a soothing kind of music. Apocalypse in C minor.

"Not if they're on the other side. If they're hiding." He cuts the engine. "We've got to check."

"We got to check the apartment first, Mo," I say. "We're going to feel really stupid if we search this whole building and they're just sitting at home."

"But what if they're not at home? Look at the fire." It's already lit a room on the third floor, and now it's reaching sideways too, orange arms working to encircle the whole building. "I'm going." He gets out and grabs el decapitador. "You check the apartment, Rip. Quickly. And come back and help." He heads for the hotel.

Xan scoots behind the wheel and drives west. Everything's empty and quiet.

"Why didn't you leave?" I say.

"With what money?" Xan says. "It's just like when a hurricane comes. They tell you to get out like we've all got cars and money for a hotel up in Montgomery or whatever. Not that easy."

"They told you to leave?"

"They told some people. Didn't tell *us*."

"My friend told me she was leaving," Rain says. "Didn't know why, though. Her parents said she was going on vacation. That's all she told me."

"Word gets around," Xan says. "But you poor, you get left. That's the way it goes." There's a gaggle of zombies in the road ahead of us: two guys in board shorts and a girl in a bikini. One of the guys is dragging a surfboard by the leash. "Look at that," Xan says. "If they're dead, why they carrying their stuff?"

I shrug. "Muscle memory?"

Xan swerves around them. "We went to the church last night," she continues. "That's where we go when there's a hurricane. We prayed and slept in the pews. This morning, a zombie got in. I don't know how, but there he was when we woke up, standing next to the altar. Preacher tried to pray him away." She's got the chef's knife balanced on her leg, and she rests her hand on the hilt.

"Praying didn't work," Rain says. Her mother puts her hand on the girl's head, sinks it deep in the curls, pulls her close.

The apartment's a couple of miles from Mahimahi, a weathered string of a dozen units built in the seventies. Probably had a view of the Gulf back then, but now they're looking across the street at another stucco behemoth. We check the rooms. All empty.

By the time we get back to Mahimahi, the place is flaming up good. The right side is burning almost up to the tenth floor, and smoke's coming out of units nearly halfway down the length of the building. All the doors on the first floor are open, a couple on the second floor. Looks like Mo has taken care of the zombies; one of them is lying in two pieces in the parking lot. We wait, and after a moment Mo comes out of a door on the second floor and walks to the next one, kicks it a few times until it busts open, and goes inside.

"All right then," I say. "Wait here."

"I'll come with you," Xan says. "He helped us. We help him." She gives the knife to Rain. "Lock the doors, keep the windows up. Don't let them in. But if they do get in, tear them up, girl."

"I'll get them, Mama," Rain says.

Xan digs an axe out of the trailer and we head to the hotel. We run into Mo as he's coming out of the last room on the second floor. He points at Xan. "Three," he says. "Rip, four. I've got five." And we head up the stairs.

The doors come open way easier than they ought to, and it makes me wonder why they've got locks on them at all. Some illusion of security, I guess, but a couple of solid kicks just below the doorknob splinters the cheap wood of the frame and sends the door swinging inward, banging a hole in the Sheetrock behind it. Each room is the same: cool gray tile and baby-blue wallpaper with shells on it. A bed with a sand-dollar–print bedspread and a Paul Brent watercolor on the wall, a pelican or a sandpiper or some other beachy cliché. Big sliding glass doors opening to a balcony that looks out over fifty yards of sand to the green water beyond. I open the door in the first room and stand on the balcony. There's a cool breeze coming off the Gulf, and the palm trees rustle like paper wind chimes, and it seems like it's just a nice day at the beach. A zombie is down there eating a lifeguard, but other than that, a real nice day.

I can get to only half the rooms on the fourth floor. Beyond that, the smoke is too thick, the air too hot. It's like there's a dragon perched at the edge of the building, asleep, and he's letting out a wash of flame with every dozing breath. Each breath pushes the fire another inch down the beach, another floor upward. Bit by bit, the building is being devoured.

We meet in the stairwell on the sixth floor. Xan's arms are covered in blood. "Two of them in the bathroom," she says. "Snowbirds. Old Canadian people. Easy."

I feel it before I hear it, before I see it. It starts in my stomach way deep inside me, a twisting sickness that creeps down my spine and into my hamstrings, and I can see on Mo's and Xan's faces that they feel it too. Something off, something horrible building and growing, and I know what it is before I know what it is, I know what's going to happen. I touch the railing that runs along the stairs. It's vibrating. The concrete trembles beneath my feet.

"It's going to go," Xan says.

Mo looks up. "Five more floors. They could be up there."

There's a groan from the other side of the building, the sound of the dragon waking up. A bang as something heavy hits the concrete.

"It's going." Xan starts down the stairs. "It's going now."

And then the groan is a roar. It's a rocket taking off, an eight-lane interstate full of semis, a dinosaur in your fucking ear, and the tremble is a full-on shake, and down at the other end of the building a chunk of the walkway along the front breaks off and then the unit behind it and the one beside it and now it's coming down, it's all coming down. There's no time to yell or argue and Mo's hauling ass behind Xan, taking the stairs three at a time, and I'm behind him, the dust and smoke already blowing our way, making every breath like your mouth's on the exhaust pipe of a race car. We get to the bottom and out into the middle of the parking lot and look back, and the building crumbles like a sand castle with the tide coming in. The right side with all the fire comes down and leaves a cloud of dust where it stood, a shadow, an afterimage, and the force of the collapse pushes the dust over us, a wall that envelopes us entirely and turns the world into a blind mess of gray. We crouch behind the pickup truck and wait, and for what feels like forever there's nothing but that gray wall and the endless sound of chaos.

Then it's quiet. The dust clears enough that I can see Xan. She is as gray as the sky, her skin plastered with the ruin of Mahimahi. She goes around the truck and knocks, and Rain opens it up, and Xan takes her daughter into her arms and holds her.

Mo looks back at the building. The fire is mostly out, just some smoke seeping out of the fifty-foot-tall pile of rubble.

I stand beside him. "They weren't in there."

"They might have been."

"They would have come out."

"We don't know that." He crosses the parking lot and climbs up on the loose concrete. Throws aside a couple of the smaller pieces.

"Mo."

"I've got to look." He digs a mattress out, throws it into the parking lot. "I've got to find them."

The dust is clearing but it's still hard to see, and I realize it's because the sun's going down. "It's going to be dark soon, Mo. We need to get out of here."

"You the boss now?" He climbs up higher on the pile. "You the zombie expert?"

"You don't have to be an expert. It's going to be worse at night."

Mo crouches beside an overturned bathtub and lifts. It rolls a few feet down the pile and breaks in half on a chunk of concrete. A couple of zombie legs are sticking out of the mess where the tub was. They're walking, walking upside down on an invisible path. Mo moves some more concrete, swings el decapitador, and then the legs are still. He keeps digging.

There's nothing more to say. He's not leaving. So I climb up on the pile with him and help him work. It gets dark and Xan turns the headlights on, and after a while she and Rain come over and help.

The dust clears and the moon comes out and shines on us, and it's like everything has been painted with silver. Long fine shadows narrow as bones stretch from the ruin of Mahimahi into the sand, and the Gulf rolls on, shushing at the shore, the waves speaking in their whispers, every wave carrying some sand away and putting new sand in its place, on and on destroying rebuilding, the ancient sound of the inner workings of the earth.

It's the middle of the night when we see something coming up the beach. We stop our work and wait, weapons in hand. It's a person, but it moves smoother than a zombie. It doesn't shuffle; it strides. When it gets closer, it waves. We wave back.

"Who's that?" it says.

And now I'm laughing, because I know it's him. Rodney's climbing up the rubble from the beach, and I make my way across the broken bits of building like a mountain goat, and we meet on top of what must have been the gym because there's a treadmill sitting there like it's waiting for one of us to hop on, and Rodney hugs me like he wants to lift me off the ground and I hug him back and there's tears in my eyes but maybe it's just from the dust. Yeah, the dust.

"So you're still alive, then," Rodney says.

"'Course I am."

"Ving Fucking Rhames."

"You're goddamn right." I look at his fists, at his knuckles, those spiked knuckles spattered in blood black in the moonlight. He's got a ring now too. Big-ass ring like something from the Super Bowl. "What's that?"

"Spoils of war," Rodney says. "Zombie messed with the wrong motherfucker."

Mo looks up from the rubble, his face streaked with dust. He nods to Rodney and goes back to work. We all do. We dig.

* * *

The moon sets and the night is blacker than black. I hear Mo and Rodney and Xan and Rain, hear them breathing, coughing, hear the chunks of concrete knocking against each other like stone ice cubes in a glass. Every now and then someone digs up a zombie, or still-moving pieces of one, and takes it out. My ears are full of the noise of work and waves on the shore.

We don't hear the horde until they're almost on top of us.

A growl. Xan cursing, fighting. The heavy *whurp* of el decapitador splitting the night in half. Rain's feet on the concrete, tapping like—well, like rain.

Then I see them. Two nurses, a man and a woman, still in their scrubs. Shadows moving behind them, dozens. They come into view: orderlies, secretaries, doctors, janitors, patients in gowns with their asses hanging out the open back. It's a whole fucking hospital coming for us, climbing up the rubble.

"Too many," Rodney says. "Go. Go!"

We run. We scramble back to the parking lot, and the zombies follow. Some of the fast ones are mixed in there with them, hopping over the gaps in the rocks with what looks like dexterity but can only be blind luck. Xan picks Rain up, sprints ahead of us. Down into a drainage ditch with a foot of stagnant water at the bottom and up the other side. Rodney and Mo and I follow her through, the water sour and rank with runoff. Gets all on my jeans, soaks my shoes. Going to be wet all night.

I'm up the other side and waiting to hear them in the water and up the hill and their feet scraping the pavement, but now it's quiet behind me. I look back. "Guys," I say. "Hey, look."

We all stand at the edge of the street, right on the grassy divider between ditch and pavement. The zombies stand on the other side. The ditch is maybe ten feet across, if that. Feels like I could reach out and hold hands with one of them. But they all just stand there. Fifty of them or more, like the whole hospital got infected and everyone wandered out at once. They pace back and forth, look down at the water, across at us. Reach for us, growl in a dejected way.

Rain walks a few feet up the road. The zombies move with her, mirroring her, but they don't take another step forward. And I remember that news footage of Willie Nelson, his toes at the edge of the lake while people floated a dozen yards offshore.

"Don't like the water, huh?" Rodney says. He points toward the Gulf. "Wrong city!"

"How long's the ditch?" Mo says.

Xan looks up and down the street. "Just the length of the hotel. It's like this in front of most of them. The ditch goes under the parking lot at the entrances. They'll figure it out."

I nod. "So we've got to go where there's no bridge."

"We've got to go back to the hotel," Mo says. He's leaning on el decapitador, staring past the zombies, back toward the pile. "They might be in there."

"We can come back tomorrow. The sun will be up. The zombies might leave."

"And my truck's in there. All of our stuff."

Rain sits down on the edge of the ditch. She rests her head in her hands.

Rodney puts his hand on Mo's shoulder. "We got to rest, man. We got to get somewhere safe and rest."

Mo wipes the blade on his pant leg. Watches the zombies. "Tomorrow. First thing tomorrow." He rests the blade on his shoulder, holds it loosely with one hand. "Where we going, then?"

Rain stands up. "I know."

* * *

We hop the fence at Lazy River and walk through the empty park.

I've never been there, but I've seen the commercials. Sunburned kids and overweight moms and wave pools crammed shoulder to shoulder with tourists swimming in T-shirts. I don't know why they got to swim with their shirts on. You get your jeans wet, your shoes, your shirt—ruins your day. And they're doing it on purpose. Dumbasses.

On TV, the place looks miserable. Tonight, it's got an eerie kind of beauty about it. The slides cut dark whirling patterns against the sky. The kiddie pool with its giant smiling ocean creatures and its Wonderland toadstools and its wild array of buckets and sprinklers and squirt guns and whatever other ways to get you wet, it's all like some psychedelic fever dream, some trip through a haunted memory. Looming in the distance, at the center of the park, is the pirate ship—built to be a wreck, its hull lilting sternward and to port, its mast cracked in two, the bowsprit like a dagger piercing the night. The water is everywhere and infuses the air with chlorine, the chemical smell of summer. The lazy river itself shimmers in its slow, dark revolutions.

There are two wooden bridges over the river. We clog them both with beach chairs and garbage cans and whatever else we can find. For now, we're safe. A fence around the park, a moat inside the fence. Our weapons and each other. The citizens of our own small kingdom.

We have everything we need.

* * *

Mo finds his girls on the third day.

He does it all alone. We wanted to help him, were ready to help him the second day, but already things were shifting, the new order of life was setting in, and we had shit to do to get the park ready. Other people were showing up—a family of four, this old couple, a handful of maids from one of the other hotels—and we had to get them across the lazy river and find places to put them. Had to go get food, me and Rodney hiking down to the Publix a block away, breaking through the automatic doors and helping ourselves to the fruit and bread and the other stuff that would go bad soon. Save the canned goods for later, we figured.

And to be honest, we all thought Gabriela and Lupita were gone. We hoped they'd left town, that they had never been in the hotel to begin with. And if they were in the hotel—still gone.

Mo didn't care. He was out all that second day, came back covered in dust and blood, his or zombies' I don't know. Bathed in the wave pool and drank a six-pack of beer alone in the margarita hut and went to sleep. He was gone before sunup on the third day.

The fence came down a little after dawn. The zombies had been congregating along the southern edge of the park, watching us through the chain-link, leaning their bodies against it in big pulsing shoves that got stronger the more of them showed up, and finally they reached some critical mass and pushed the whole thing over. Swarmed in, but only twenty feet until they hit the moat. They stood on one side and we stood on the other, and we looked at each other, and they groaned and reached for us with those cold fingers and there was this helplessness in their eyes. Even dead, their frustration was obvious. I almost felt bad for them. But the moat held, and we shrugged and went back to work.

Mo comes back near sunset. We hear his truck in the parking lot, and then he's out, Gabriela limping beside him, her arm around his shoulder, leaning heavy on him, and Lupita in his arms, gray and matted with concrete powder but awake, alert.

We throw the stuff off the bridges and the zombies start to head our way, but Rodney and Xan and a few of the others who turned out to be half-decent zombie killers take them out, and we lead Mo and his family across to safety.

"We were in the kitchen," Gabriela says later. We're all sitting around the fire eating peanut-butter-and-banana-sandwiches. About fifteen of us now. "We had to get in the walk-in refrigerator to get away from them. It's got that heavy door, you know? To keep the cold in. And the zombies couldn't get us, and there was food. We didn't even know about the fire until the building came down."

Lupita has a fever, and we've given her some ibuprofen we found in one of the lifeguard towers. She's ten but seems smaller than that, her dark hair falling all around her face over her eyes. She sweats and shivers, leans against her dad. He puts his heavy arms around her. She drifts in and out of sleep.

Gabriela takes a second sandwich. She's just a larger version of Lupita, like someone took the kid to Kinko's and blew her up to 150 percent. "The concrete smashed half of the walk-in. We were in the other half, but we couldn't open the door. There was only a tiny bit of light coming through. And then this morning, more light. And a little more. And then he was there." She looks at Mo with a kind of awe, like he's a celebrity she's seeing in the flesh. "He came for me."

"Por supuesto lo hice, cariño," Mo says.

We sleep. In the morning a heavy rain is falling. There is no wind, no thunder. The Gulf is green-black glass, and the rain comes across its surface in waves of froth and foam. It drenches Lazy River, fills the pools with the spattering voice of a million raindrops. The zombies are hidden behind the veil. We hear them *ruuuurg?* at the rain, at the wetness that soaks their clothes their hair their skin.

I'm up on the pirate ship, crouched beneath the helm where I can stay kind of dry but still see most of the park. I can see Rodney beneath the big mushroom in the kiddie area, Xan and Rain huddled under the arms of the octopus. Mo's family slept in the margarita hut. Lupita comes to the door and looks out at the rain. She's clean now, her time in the rubble scrubbed away by chlorine water and food and sleep. Her eyes are wide and her face fresh, smiling. She points, says, "The slides are on!"

And I look. The rain is falling the length of the slides, water flowing fast and heavy as it would if you turned them on.

Lupita laughs and strips down to her underwear, and she sprints to the kiddie pool. Gabriela is at the door, about to yell for her, but then Mo is behind her, his hand on her shoulder, speaking quietly in her ear. Gabriela relaxes, smiles.

Lupita is already soaked by the time she reaches the slide, a big hippo with its mouth open wide, its thick pink tongue stretching down into the water and slick with rain. She climbs up the ladder on the hippo's tail and stands astride its back. She looks back at her parents, makes a muscleman pose. "Raaaah!" she yells, and then she goes down the slide and splashes into the pool, and her laughter is like birdsong slipping through the beams of light that arc through the trees at sunrise, like wind chimes outside a cottage tucked far up in the Alps. It cuts through the downpour and the complaints of the zombies and wakes us from whatever haze we were in that kept us hidden from the rain.

We leave our shelters, step into the storm. Why the hell not?

And then all of us are playing. Rain and Xan and Gabriela join Lupita in the kiddie pool. Mo and Rodney and I take our shirts off and let the rain pelt us. It prickles your skin where it hits you because it's cold like rain is always cold, but it's a good cold, a clean sting that washes something off of you that you didn't know you were coated in. It washes away the life that was and the worry that came with it, the time clock and the emails from customers and the boss and coffee breaks that weren't long enough and McDonald's food that didn't look like the picture on the menu. The house that you don't clean as often as you ought to and the chores you said you were going to do and never got around to. Politics and climate change and war and everything else, all the things that hang over you all day every day, all of them washed away in this torrent, flowing over the concrete in heavy runnels and pooling in the lazy river while the zombies march on the other side.

It leaves you clean. Fresh. Ready.

We climb the Super Slide. A long ramp takes us halfway up, planks like decking with a rubber mat stretched across it, bumpy black rubber tickling our feet like the nubby arms of a thousand anemones. Then stairs, four more flights of stairs, and we're at the top of the tower. If it wasn't raining we could see everything from here, all of The Beach, and I know I'll come up here again and again, that this will become a watchtower, that there will be hard days and there will be fights and there will be hunger, but for now the rain hangs a gray scrim around us so that there is nothing of the world outside our water park. Just Lazy River and me and my friends, old and new. My family.

Mo goes first. He sits at the top of the slide and the rain pools around him.

"You going or what?" Rodney says. He's shouting over the rain, but there's joy in that voice, the voice of a kid. A kid at a water park.

"Hang on," Mo says, but Rodney puts his foot square in the center of Mo's back and shoves, and Mo goes, "Ayyyiiii!" and is lost in the spray as he hurtles toward the bottom.

"Got to arch your back," Rodney says. "Fewer points of contact. It's faster. No friction. Like this." He crosses his arms over his chest, crosses his legs, so he's standing there like a mummy in a sarcophagus. "Just one heel and your shoulder blades." Then he gets in the slide and goes, and you know what, he is going faster than Mo did. Really hauling ass.

And I'm alone. I can barely see the bottom of the slide. Rodney splashes into the pool, comes up shaking his head. He says something to Mo, and Mo lunges, dunks Rodney, and then they're both wrestling, laughing. The rain is on my shoulders and I smile, and I run and I leap, and then the plastic is hard beneath me and the water is flowing rushing and I flow with it, and I slide.

SATURDAY, OCTOBER 26

When the jets fly over, they vibrate the hood of the truck. Mo and Rodney and me, we're sitting there on Mo's truck at the end of the runway in the middle of the night, and the A-10s are doing touch-and-go drills above us. We watch the heavy machines approaching from our rear, lights blinking against the blackness behind them, and then they pass fifty feet overhead, not soaring like birds but scraping through the sky, monsters tearing the air in half. The heat of the exhaust washes over us. The moon is out high overhead, and the spectral shadow of the jet follows it along the runway until the wheels touch the pavement with the hiss of hot rubber. The engine roars and flares orange, and the jet noses up and grunts its way back into the sky. There are three A-10s running the drill. Round and round.

"Which one's Duck Duck?" Rodney says. He's already got his ski mask on, and it turns his whole head into this black silhouette against the sky.

"Don't know," I say. "One of them."

Mo is smoking a cigarette. The smell of tar and fire mixes with jet fuel.

In the lull between the jets, the night noises come back. Crickets in the tall grass along the chain-link fence. Tree frogs whining back in the woods on the other side of the road.

Mo tosses the cigarette into the grass, and it glows there, smoking. "What time is it?"

Rodney looks at his phone. "Little after midnight."

"Vámonos."

We get in the truck, Mo driving and Rodney at the window with me in the middle. Mo backs onto the road, careful to keep the trailer straight. We've got the big enclosed trailer this time. Twenty feet long and ten feet tall, metal sides, heavy door that slides up and down and locks with a padlock. Mo uses it to carry delicate plants—orchids or soft-limbed saplings, things that will fall apart in the wind on the roads.

Tonight, we're using it to carry zombies.

We follow the fence for a mile. It's fifteen feet tall, topped with vicious coiled razor wire. Something's stuck in it up ahead. A pelican. Twisted, torn, its neck bent and its head back at a weird angle. Feathers in the wire around it, on the ground. We drive past it.

Mo pulls over when we see the gate. The clock on the dash-board reads 12:27.

"How do we know it's the right one?" Rodney says.

"Twelve thirty," I say. "That's what Duck Duck said. Shift change, and then it's our guy."

A small pickup truck approaches the gate. Someone comes out of the guardhouse as the truck's door opens. The two guards stand in front of the pickup and light cigarettes. One leans against the truck. A laugh carries on the breeze, but it's drowned out by an approaching jet. The men watch the jet fly over, and then the guardhouse one stomps his cigarette out, shakes the other man's hand, and gets in the truck. He drives away and the new guard assumes duty.

"So that's our guy," I say.

"We sure?" Rodney says.

Mo puts the car in gear. "Look, it's him or it's not. Sitting here arguing about it won't change that." The truck bumps back onto the road and the tires hum on the asphalt. "If it's not him, we say we're lost."

The guard approaches as we pull up. A heavy metal gate rests across the road in front of us, and beyond it a series of concrete pilings. To get through, you have to drive like you're following a slalom course. Can't do it more than a few miles an hour without hitting a piling. Not sure we can do it at all with the trailer.

Mo rolls down the window. "Got your willows here."

The guard looks at the trailer. He's young, probably twenty-five, but he has a tired look about him that makes him seem older. Bags under his eyes, dark circles too, like he's been punched. "Weeping or white?"

"Weeping. Always weeping."

That's the code. Mo came up with it. Pretty good, I think.

We made the final plans last night. Called Duck Duck to Bungalow once Rodney was back in, and we sat outside, drinking and talking with our voices low, even though the porch was empty and the people inside were noisy and oblivious. The three of us were quiet, anyway; Duck Duck is never quiet. He was so excited that things were a go that he'd hardly sit down.

He stood there, drumming his hands on the table, or he paced around looking into the water. Mo came up with the code, and Duck Duck thought it was the greatest thing he'd ever heard.

"Like we're fucking spies!" he said. "But the deeper meaning, you know? Always weeping. It's dark. Badass."

"And you know you can buy this guy?" Rodney said.

"I told you, man, he's cool. I talked to him already. Why you keep asking?"

"Because it's my money."

"Money well spent. He's cool. I know this guy. He's like us. He said *fuck it* long ago. And five thousand bucks gets him on our side no problem. Other guy too, at the lab. He was harder to convince, but the money got him. We got them both."

"I just don't know. Everyone else on that base. It's a big base."

"Goddamn, Rodney. So many questions. Stop being a fucking pussy and let's get on with it."

Rodney stands up so fast it sends his chair clattering across the porch behind him, and then he's in Duck Duck's face. "The fuck you calling a pussy?" He's a good eight inches taller than Duck Duck, looking down on him like he's a child.

Duck Duck stands on his tiptoes. Narrows his eyes.

Rodney clenches his fist. "Think careful before you talk."

"Tranquilo, amigos." Mo's not even looking at them. Just leaning back in his chair, looking out over the water, his whiskey dangling from two fingers. "Tranquilo."

Duck Duck nods, sits down. Rodney watches him a moment, and then he sits too.

I lean forward, look Rodney in the eyes. His eyes, dark and twitching. Angry, nervous. Lots of stuff swirling around in there. "Rodney. Are you cool? You cool with this?"

He looks at his beer. "Yeah. I'm cool."

"You got to be cool. You're in, you're out, you're back in. We can't half-ass this."

"We cool."

I turn to Duck Duck, who's smiling this dickhead sneer. "Rodney's right. It's a big base. What are we going to do if we run into someone else?"

"Security's light at night," Duck Duck says. "Light all the time, really, since half of us are dead. But especially light at night. And I'm Creating a Diversion."

"What kind of diversion?" Rodney says.

Duck Duck grins. "Big Diversion."

So now we're at the gate right on time, and we've got fifteen minutes before Duck Duck's Big Diversion.

"Weeping willows," the guard says. He points in the direction of the runway, where an A-10 is just roaring back into the sky. "They go down that way. Quarter mile on your left."

"Gracias," Mo says. The guard goes into the guardhouse and pushes a button, and the gate rattles as it slides open. Mo pulls forward, around the first piling. He watches in the rearview mirror as the trailer follows us. Slowly, slowly. He clears the first piling and rounds the second. The trailer follows like the tail of a clumsy snake. Round the second one, the third. Past the fourth one and the truck is in the clear, the trailer almost there. Mo slows, inch by inch. We turn around to watch. Clears it by a millimeter.

"Nice," Rodney says.

Mo turns onto the main road through the base. The buildings are dark, the roads and parking lots empty. In the distance down one of the side roads, a security car drives by, its light blinking. Up ahead is the lab, right where it's supposed to be, a big hangar as gray and featureless as an overcast sky. The guard stands out front, an M16 slung across his chest. Mo pulls into the parking lot. The guard nods at us but remains at his post.

"So we wait for the diversion?" Rodney says.

I nod. "That's what he said."

We wait. The windows are down and the night is cool, the breeze moving the fall air through the cab of the truck. I close my eyes. Feel the warmth of the bodies on either side of me. Listen to their breathing. And you know what? This isn't so bad. Quiet night with good weather and friends. Maybe this is enough. Maybe what we're doing really is crazy. We ought to turn around, go to Bungalow, have a beer. Call it off.

"That must be him," Mo says.

I open my eyes. The runway is a half mile ahead of us, and one of the A-10s is on approach. It's coming in fast, too fast, and too high. Angle way too steep. It passes the fence where we were sitting a few minutes ago, waggles its wings.

The breeze picks up, a wind now, rushing through the windows and shaking the car.

The jet is coming down at a thirty-degree angle. It looks like it's careening down a ski slope. There's a roar as the engines go full throttle, and the nose of the plane comes up, arcing, the bottom of a giant capital _U_.

The guard turns, watches.

More roaring engine as the jet pulls through the arc, misses the ground by a few yards. It ramps skyward, nose up, up, the exhaust flaming bright in the night as the sound drowns out everything else, and then the jet loses momentum, stalls. It hangs in the air a moment, motionless, like a feeding humming-bird beside a flower. And then gravity wins. The plane is no longer an instrument of flight; it's fifty thousand pounds of metal hanging in the air. It has no business being there. In this moment it is so obvious. Flight is not for man. The sky is not for man. Metal and fire can't hold you up there forever. Gravity wins, always. It pulls the jet back to Earth.

There's a pop, and a rocket blasts from the cockpit. The parachute unfurls, and Duck Duck hangs in the sky a hundred feet above the falling A-10.

The jet hits the runway in a fireball. The initial flash is blinding in the dark, and it leaves behind the roiling flames of burning jet fuel.

Duck Duck is the weight at the bottom of a pendulum. He swings gently in the night. I think I can see him waving at us.

And then the wind picks up again and blows him straight into the fireball.

"Fuck," Mo says.

Rodney scoffs. "Whoops."

The parachute crumples in the fire. The smoke turns white for an instant as it burns, and then it's gone. All trace of Duck Duck sucked into the belly of the flame.

Sirens. The security car rushes by. Lights come on in a few of the buildings closer to the runway. Fire trucks appear, more flashing lights. Everyone hurrying to the crash.

"Hey!" The voice comes from the lab. The guard is beckoning us. He looks over at the runway, waves to us again. "Come on! Now or never!"

We pull our ski masks over our faces. Mine's hot, itchy, like a tube sock dragged through dead grass. We grab the catch poles from the back of the truck. Mo carries one, I carry the other. I've got Santana on my belt. Rodney slips his knuckles over his fingers.

The guard scans a key card. Heavy dead bolts slide back, and he pulls open the door. We go inside.

It's dark except for some runner lights along the floorboards. They put off a shadowy half-light that makes it look like creeping things are moving in every corner. The guard shuts the door behind us, and we stand blinking, waiting for our eyes to adjust. Then Mo flicks the light switch, and everything is lit with humming fluorescents. Blinding.

"Shit, Mo," Rodney says. "They'll see us."

"No windows," Mo says. He puts his mask in his pocket.

We look around. He's right: windowless. The room is as workmanlike as the call center. Cubicles with gray cloth on the partitions. No personal touches, though—no family photos, no bobblehead dolls, no tacky cat posters or calendars with pictures of chocolate labs. Just empty chairs and blank computer screens.

Also, no zombies.

"We in the right place?" Rodney says.

I pull my mask off and breathe, head down the hallway, looking into the cubicles as I pass. Open a drawer. Regular paperwork. I'm beginning to think we've been screwed.

"They've fucked us," Mo says. "Took our money and fucked us."

"We should go," Rodney says.

"Hang on," I say. There's a door at the far end of the room. It has no knob, just a card scanner mounted beside it. I cross the room and put my ear against the door. Inside, there's a knocking sound. A low hum. "We need to get in here."

"Locked," Mo says.

"So we find the key."

It takes five minutes of rooting through drawers, but Rodney finds a key card in a desk in the corner. He runs it through the scanner, and the door slides open like something out of *Star Trek*. Even makes that mechanical hissing sound. Very cool.

On the other side are the zombies.

I hear them before I see them. That sound comes back to me, their voices, low and grating. The zombie song like music, the sound of the summer, of fire and life and the water park and Davia.

Grrrooooooooaaag, says one of them, a voice from the back of the room.

Raaagaaagaaa, says another.

The room has no overhead lighting, but a green glow permeates the darkness. The light comes from countless tanks that line the walls. They're filled with zombie parts. Smaller tanks hold feet, hands, a shriveled-up zombie dick. One has a heart, another a brain. In one corner of the room are heads—half a dozen zombie heads looking out at us through green liquid. Formaldehyde? I don't know. The heads float in it, their eyes moving in their sockets, their mouths opening and closing.

I thought they died when you decapitated them. How many heads did I leave lying around, blinking and biting at the sky?

I go over to the heads and look closely. One is at eye level with me, a black man a few years younger than me, probably good-looking when he was still attached to his body. He sees me and his eyes open wide, his mouth agape in a silent groan. The cut at his neck is surgical. Several inches of vertebrae visible, sticking out below the skin and muscle. This guy wasn't decapitated; his body was removed. Different. They wanted to keep him alive. Alive-ish.

Farther into the room, the tanks get bigger. Torsos. Legs still attached to hips, a whole lower body floating in a green fish tank. Beyond the tanks, a Plexiglas enclosure. Clear, thick walls with metal frames, another door locked with a key card. And inside, three zombies, shuffling and moaning, just like they're supposed to.

"Three!" Mo says. "I thought we'd be lucky to get one."

I recognize one of them. It's the Asian guy from the day of the all-clear, the one that caught the bullet that the mayor fired from his golden gun. He's standing with his hands on the Plexiglas, his eyes empty but fixed on us. He's dressed in some sort of scrubs, loose blue shorts and shirt that cover him mostly but leave his legs and arms visible. The bullet wound is there in his leg, a bloodless hole, the bone around it caved in. The wound is clean. His whole body is clean. All the zombies I saw during the summer were covered in blood and filth, but these have been taken care of. He just looks like a man—a pale, sickly man with dead eyes, but a man nonetheless.

Behind him are another man and a woman, dressed in the same blue scrubs. The man is old, frail. He could be someone's grandpa. His hair wispy and white across his gray scalp. The woman is Latina. She's voluptuous, big lips, long shiny black hair.

"Holy shit," Mo says. "It's Tiffany Tetas."

"Who?" Rodney says.

"The weather girl. Tiffany, uh, I think Rodriguez. But she's Tiffany Tetas. I mean, look at her."

She would be gorgeous if she was alive. Now, she looks deader than the other two, much deader than a weather girl ought to look. While the men are clean and well preserved, Tiffany is coming apart. She's missing an eye. Something's wrong with her jaw, and her mouth hangs open in a crooked frown. One arm is black, as if rot has set in. Worst, she can barely walk. She hobbles, her left leg dragging, bent at a weird angle. Something's broken in there, but still she tries to keep moving. She spots us, presses against the glass. Pounds. *Bang. Bang.*

"Which one are we taking?" Rodney says.

I look at the three of them. "Maybe we should take two. In case we lose one of them or something."

"Isn't that the point? To lose one? Let it out?"

"I mean if we have to kill one."

"Oh." He goes to the glass, puts his hand up against Tiffany's. He moves his hand down, and she slides her hand with him. He moves his palm back up, and she follows. He squints, looks into her one eye.

She cocks her head as she looks back. She says *urrrrrg*.

"Urg," Rodney says. Then he turns to us. "All right. Which two?"

"Not Tiffany," I say. "Look at her. She can hardly walk. It'll take forever to drag her out of here. We probably can't even get her in the truck."

"So the other two. Okay then." Rodney gets the key card out and stands next to the scanner. "You guys ready?"

I get in position beside the door, holding the catch pole out in front of me like it's a weapon. "Just open it a little. Let one out. The Asian guy. Just him."

Rodney scans the card, and the door beeps and the locks slide open. "Too easy. Same card. Why'd they make it so easy?"

"I don't know. Let's just do it. Open the door a little."

Rodney cracks the door, and immediately the zombie is pushing on it, reaching his arm through the opening. Rodney leans against the Plexiglas. "Shit. Get him."

I work to get the collar around the zombie's neck. The moaning is frantic, all three of them louder, higher in pitch now that they see the opening. Tiffany and the old man both scrambling behind the Asian guy, all three of them pushing on the door, trying to get out.

"Mo," Rodney says. "Shit, help me, Mo."

Mo leans against the door with Rodney as the zombies grasp at us, their arms reaching, bending around the glass, clawing at Rodney and Mo.

I get the collar around the zombie's neck and tighten it. "Okay. Let him out."

Rodney and Mo ease off a little, and the zombie comes barreling out. I grip the pole and hold him at arm's length. He reaches for me, his eyes dark, his mouth like a snake's, so far open it's like his jaw has come unhinged. I pin him against the tanks behind him. Lean against him with all my weight to keep him stuck. "Get the old guy," I say to Mo.

Mo lets his weight off the door, and it starts to swing open.

"Shit," Rodney says. He's straining, his shoulder pressed against the door. "Do it fast!"

Mo handles the catch pole like an expert. He reaches past Tiffany and snags the old man, drags him around, pins him beside my zombie.

Rodney slams the door on Tiffany's arm a couple of times, and she retracts it and the door clicks shut. The locks slide back into place. She's alone in the cage, and she looks around kind of forlornly.

For a second, I feel sorry for her, like we took away her friends.

Rodney's catching his breath. "All right." He smiles. "Got them. You guys ready?"

And then the room is full of light. The door to the office part of the lab is open, and someone stands in it, a rifle in his hands. "You guys fucked up *big time,*" he says.

"Oh, goddamn it," I say.

The figure approaches. He's no longer a backlit silhouette, and I can see his uniform. Another Air Force security officer, different from the one we bribed. Big guy. M16 at his shoulder, the barrel moving from Mo to me to Rodney. "You with the machete. You got any other weapons? Or did you bring a knife to a gunfight?"

"Just Santana."

"Santana. I like it. I'm going to introduce her to Beatrice." He lifts the gun. "Rifle's Beatrice, pistol's Benedick."

"Cute."

"Most people don't get it," he says. "Like, read a little. Anyway, put her on the ground."

I've still got the zombie pinned against the tanks. I'm holding him there with both hands, and he's writhing, reaching for me, his teeth gnashing, clicking together. "I can't let go of this."

"You better figure it out."

"Rodney," I say. "Take the machete."

"Nope," the guard says. He turns the gun on Rodney. "No one moves." He takes one hand off the gun, reaches for his radio.

"Then how do you want me to do this?" I say. "You want me to just drop the fucking zombie?"

Mo turns to me. He's between me and the guard, his zombie pinned, frantic, squawking a high *reeehhg reeehg* again and again. "Yeah," Mo says. "That's exactly what you should do."

"What?"

But he's already moving. Mo spins, swinging the catch pole like a baseball bat. His zombie practically becomes airborne, and Mo hurls him down the aisle of tanks, straight at the guard. The guard drops the radio and tries to get his gun up, but the old man rushes him, hands clawing, dead fingers on the barrel. The guard gets a shot off and the bullet blows straight through the zombie, thuds as it ricochets off the Plexiglas cage. It crashes through a tank, and a head rolls out of it along with a bunch of formaldehyde. The head lands on the floor and spins, the mouth open, eyes wide. The chemical smell fills the room.

The guard is screaming because the old man's on him now, tearing into the guard's throat with his teeth.

Mo tries to get the collar on him. The zombie dodges it and leaps to his feet.

Fast. I forgot how fast they are. Not like the George Romero slouchers; they're *28 Days Later* sprinters. This zombie is quicker and stronger than the man could have ever been in real life. He lunges at Mo. Mo shoves him away, tries again with the collar, but the old man ducks it, comes at me. I've still got my zombie pinned against the wall, and I try to get at Santana with one hand and hold him still with the other but he's squirming, reaching for me, and I can't let the pressure off, and here comes the old man and I say, "Oh fuck oh fuck."

And then Rodney steps forward, catches him midstride. The zombie goes full speed, face first into the punch, into those spiked knuckles, and there's a crunching sound as his face gives way. He falls on his back, still writhing, but his limbs are out of sync with each other. Rodney stands astride him, brings his fist down again, and the zombie's still.

Rodney stands up smiling and out of breath.

"Fun?" I say.

He nods. "Just like you remember it."

"Hold this one," I say to Mo, and he takes the catch pole from me and leans my zombie against the tanks. I take Santana from her sheath and cross the room to where the guard lies in a pool of blood. He's not breathing, not moving. His eyes are open, a terrified look frozen in them. Then the moisture seeps out of them, draining the eyes of color, giving them that glassy dead look that the zombies have. His right hand twitches. It closes into a fist and opens again. He blinks, turns his head, looks at me with new sight.

I swing Santana over my head and bring her down in the center of zombie guard's skull, and he is still, back to being dead in the normal way.

I close my eyes. Feel Santana's song flow up my arms, into my core. Through my blood my body my heart. Oh, how she sets me afire.

"Get your zombie," Mo says.

I blink. Shake the rapture away. Then I take the pole from Mo. He picks up his own pole and returns to the cage. Rodney opens it for him, and Mo slips the collar around Tiffany Tetas. He half leads, half carries her from the cage and into the hall. It's slow going; she's about to collapse with every step. Her leg is a barely-functional mess. Mo pins her against the tanks next to the Asian man.

"He needs a name," I say. "My zombie."

"Why?" Rodney says.

"We've got Tiffany. Makes me feel like I know her. And she's important to us, so we ought to know her. Ought to know this guy too."

"So, like, a Chinese name?"

"He's Cambodian," Mo says.

We both look at him. "How you know that?" I say.

"Look at him." Mo waves toward the zombie. "Look at his skin. His eyes. He's obviously Cambodian. They look nothing like Chinese people. You think they all look the same?"

"No. I just didn't know."

"Just like you don't speak Mexican."

I sigh. "Just give him a name."

"His name is Thu," Mo says. "Cambodian guy I knew. He was named Thu."

"Fine. Thu."

"We should go," Rodney says. He's looking at his watch. "How much longer they going to watch that plane burn, anyway?" He goes past us and stands in the door to the office. He looks around, beckons. "Yeah. Time to move."

I turn Thu at the end of his pole and head toward the open door. The zombie keeps facing me, reaching for me, hacking and groaning. He shuffles backward as I push. It's hard to keep him upright, but he won't turn around and walk like a normal person. Pain in my ass.

"Go," Mo says. He's got Tiffany held right behind me, and she is facing forward, trying to eat me.

Zombies on either side of me. Just like old times.

We guide the zombies through the office space and out the front door. I stick my head back inside my mask and look out through the eyeholes. Sirens howl in the distance, and the runway is lit by the smoldering fire. A dozen vehicles are around the wreckage, a couple of them spraying it with fire hoses, but still it burns.

The guard who let us in is outside. "Whoa," he says when he sees us. He backs away. "Look at those fuckers! I knew they had stuff in there. Not whole zombies, though. Goddamn."

"Why'd you let that guard in?" Mo says.

"He's my superior. Had to."

Mo pushes Tiffany toward the guard. She reaches for him and the guard jumps back, pulls his gun. "Get that thing away from me," he says.

"You almost fucked us up," Mo says. He's shoving Tiffany at the guard, and the guard keeps backpedaling until he hits the wall. Mo lets Tiffany hang right in front of him, her long finger-nails cutting the air just in front of his face. "Your superior is dead," Mo says. "You let him in, and now he's dead, and we're left with this gimpy zombie."

"Let's go, Mo," I say.

"I should let her eat you," he says to the guard. Mo's not wearing his mask. His face is turning red, his jaw rigid.

"Mo."

Mo looks at me. His eyes are wild and angry. But he leads Tiffany away from the guard, heads toward the trailer. The guard slides down the wall, puts his arms around his knees.

Rodney opens the door to the trailer and pulls out the ramp. Mo and I guide the zombies up one at a time. Push them all the way to the deepest part of the trailer. There are hooks built into the walls, there for hanging power tools and rakes and stuff like that. Mo loops the collar over one and lets go, and Tiffany is stuck, pinned by her neck against the back wall of the trailer. I do the same with Thu, leaving him on a hook beside Tiffany. Then we stand at the door of the trailer and watch. The zombies' arms are outstretched, their feet sliding on the metal floor, heavy clanking sliding footsteps as they keep coming for us. Pinned up or not, they keep trying. They'll hang there forever if we let them, eyes locked on us, mouths open, coming and coming for our skin, our blood.

At the runway, the fire is burning low, the smoke leaving the rubble in thin streams instead of the heavy black cloud it once was. One security car backs away, turns toward the base.

"Time to go," I say, and I slide the door shut.

Back in the truck and on the road, headed for the gate, the zombies clanging around. Even though the engine's running and the trailer's ten feet behind the cab, we can hear them. *Bang, clang, bang.* And their feet sliding, sliding on the floor.

We make it to the pylons, and Mo starts the slow slalom. Halfway through, the gate guard exits the guardhouse. He stands in the middle of the road, holds up his hand.

"That's not our guy," Rodney says. "Not our guy! Fuck! Where's our guy?

The guard adjusts his rifle, takes a step toward us.

Mo speeds up. The trailer clanks against the third pylon as Mo negotiates his way around the last one.

The guard levels the gun at us. "Stop," he says. "Stop!"

Mo floors it. The truck lurches forward then jerks to a stop as a horrible crash sounds behind us. The trailer is hung on the last pylon. Mo stomps on the gas and the engine revs, but nothing happens. We're stuck.

"Out of the car!" the guard says. "Engine off! Then out! Hands up! Now!"

Mo looks at me. Shrugs.

I sigh. Nod at him.

Mo kills the engine and we open the doors. Rodney and I go out the passenger's side; Mo steps out to the left. Outside into the cool night.

And you know the rest. The guard yelling, pointing that rifle, and me and Rodney on the ground, Rodney saying, "This was so stupid. The stupidest goddamn thing," and me trying to talk the guard into just letting us go, and then Mo. Mo and his decapitator and the moon. Then a *whuuuuurp*, and the sound of skin splitting and bone cracking, and the guard's head falls to the ground between me and Rodney.

"The fuck!" Rodney says, leaping to his feet.

Mo is standing over the guard's body, el decapitador over his shoulder, blood running down the black blade.

"Mo," I say. "What the fuck did you just do?"

He steps over the body, tosses the decapitator into the bed of the truck. He goes to the back corner of the trailer, leans against it, lifts. It moves a little, begins to come clear of the pylon. He grunts, catches his breath. "Want to help?"

Sirens are loud across the base now, coming toward us. Rodney and I kneel beside Mo, and we put our shoulders against the metal and lift and push, and in a moment the trailer is clear. We hop into the cab, and Mo cranks the engine. He stomps the gas, and the truck hurtles forward and into the gate. It bends, crunches, comes loose from the fence. We drag it fifty yards down the road as Mo accelerates, and then it clatters off to the side, and we're gone into the dark, flying, flying into the night, the sirens vanishing in the distance and the zombies doing their treadmill walk right behind us.

"What the fuck, man?" Rodney is screaming at Mo. I'm in the middle of the bench, and Rodney is leaning over me, his finger in Mo's face. "You just murdered that guy. You fucking murdered him."

"Like you murdered the old man," Mo says. His voice is barely audible over the engine.

"He was a zombie!"

"Zombie, man. What's the difference?" He stares straight ahead as he follows the highway around the bay, back toward Spanish Shanty. Out there on the water are the shapes of sailboats moored in the shallows, beyond them the green and red lights of others making their way across the quiet black.

"One's alive." Rodney sits back on his side. "Other's dead. You know that."

"Yeah, he's alive now. But he's going to be dead. We're letting the zombies out, remember? He'll get dead, one way or the other. I just saved him a few tough weeks. Saved him a painful death."

"He might have lived. He made it through the first time."

"He's not a tree squirrel."

"The fuck you talking about?"

"Guys," I say. "It's done. Can't do anything about it now." I look over at Mo and he's expressionless, as if he's driving to work in the morning. He's bigger than me, not just heavier but thicker, his muscles dense from all those days moving the earth around in people's lawns. Doesn't matter if they're covered with fat now. He's still a beast. I'd be lying if I said I wasn't a little afraid of him. So I want to quiet him down, quiet Rodney down. Get settled and figure out what to do next. I say, "Let's just get them home."

"I'm hungry," Mo says.

"We'll order a pizza."

"Don't want pizza. Let's get burgers." He points up ahead. We're on the outskirts of town now, and there's a couple of gas stations and a Wendy's at the intersection. He heads into the drive-through.

"Mo, we need to get off the road. They're after us."

He ignores me and pulls up to the speaker. "Um," he says, looking at the menu. "Two junior bacon cheeseburgers. And a Frosty. What you guys want?"

I shake my head. "Not hungry."

"Nuggets," Rodney says.

"And some nuggets," Mo says.

The girl at the window smiles when we pull up, but her face goes cold when she sees Mo. I look at him in the light of the drive-through. There's blood all over the front of his shirt. I hold my hands up, and they're spattered as well with blood from the guard. Rodney's covered in old-man-zombie bits.

The zombies bang on the walls of the trailer, and the girl looks back. Then at us again. Her eyes take us in, all of us, our faces our builds our clothes, everything she needs to ID us later. "Ten-fifty," she says. Mo pays her, and we take the food and go.

I see her in the rearview. Writing down the license plate number. Making a mental note: Guillermo's Gardens, written huge across the side of the trailer.

Rodney shoves a whole nugget in his mouth, chews. "We going to jail, man. We going to jail forever."

"Nah," says Mo. "We're fine."

"We're fucked is what we are."

I watch the streetlights go by as we head back into town. A zombie groans, its voice carrying over the rumble of the engine. Behind them are all the witnesses. The girl at Wendy's and whoever else was watching—coworkers, customers, the glass eyes of the security cameras. And more cameras, all over the Air Force base for sure. How many? How many staring at me at Rodney at Mo as we stumble around with top-secret government-property zombies? As Mo cuts off someone's head like he's Attila the Hun? Wasn't even wearing his mask.

Rodney's on his last nugget. He upends the box, pours the little crunchy fried bits onto his palm, eats them. "I'm gonna miss nuggets," he says. "You think they got nuggets in jail?"

"We're not going to jail," Mo says.

"Why not, Mo? How you think we're getting away with this? We didn't plan it out for shit. They'll be at your house in an hour. Might be there now. Got your fucking name written on the side of the trailer."

"So we don't go to my house."

"Where we going, then?"

They keep going back and forth, louder every second, and I'm trying to think. Trying to focus as we drive through downtown past the call center, the salty smell of the bay coming through the windows. I see the world as it might be, a world through bars, fifty more years in a box lined with bars with nothing to look forward to, no Davia, no Bungalow, certainly no zombies, no Santana.

"Ought to turn you in," Rodney's saying. "You a fucking murderer."

"And what are you?" Mo says. "You and Rip and me, we're all going to be murderers. Setting the zombies free. Like I said, he was dead already. Just didn't know it."

And then I've got it. He's right—if we set the zombies loose, if the plan works, then we're murderers, but everyone who's after us is already dead. The military police? Dead. Cops? Dead. Girl at Wendy's, customers, anyone who might watch the security footage? Dead. Dead. Dead. "That's our way out."

Rodney turns to me. "What's your plan then, King Rip?"

"Same plan as always. Zombies are going to save us. Restart the apocalypse. Everyone's a murderer when the world's ending."

*　*　*

So we take Thu and Tiffany to my house. Where else are we supposed to take them? It's the middle of the night right now. Can't let them go yet—not until people are out and about, until there's plenty of people to bite, to turn, new zombies to run amok. If we let them go now when everyone's shut up in bed, there's a good chance the cops will find them first make it all for naught. So we've got to hold them.

Can't keep them in the trailer, either. The big Guillermo's Gardens sign might as well be a flashing arrow at this point.

Mo pulls past my driveway and backs up, swings the trailer around, edges it right into the carport. We get out and open the doors and the zombies are both looking at us. Quiet. Calm.

"Why they acting like this?" Rodney says.

"It was a big night," Mo says. "Maybe they're tired." He pulls Tiffany down from her hook, passes the catch pole to Rodney. He gives Thu to me. They both come along amicably, like horses being led to feed. Thu grunts, claws at me with a half-hearted wave of his hand.

"Okay," Mo says. "I'm going to go hide the trailer. You two can watch them?"

I don't know how it happened. How Mo has taken over. But suddenly we're listening to him, me and Rodney. We're nodding along.

"Hasta luego," he says, and he gets in the truck and takes off through the sleeping neighborhood. Rodney and I are left standing in the driveway with two zombies on poles.

"You ever really look at one?" Rodney says.

"Seen hundreds, dude. You know that."

"No, I mean look at her. When she's not trying to kill you. Look at her eye."

I lean over and look at Tiffany. Maybe see what he's talking about. Something swirling around back there behind that dilated pupil, that bloodshot rotting white. Some process, cognition—something. Something in there.

"She's looking at me," Rodney says. "Like, she's really looking."

"She's not in there. I don't know what's in there, but it's not her."

Rodney leans closer, and Tiffany lunges against the pole, snaps her teeth at him. Rolls her head in a wobbly circle, a bobblehead toy with some springs loose, neck bones cracking like Bubble Wrap. Rodney sighs. "Maybe I want something to be in there. Something else, you know? Like something there after they're dead."

"There's nothing there. This is all there is."

We stand in the driveway, and there's a breeze coming from the north that is almost cold, and the elephant ears shush against each other as they bow in the moonlight. Out past the empty house where the zombie neighbors used to live is the bay, still and black, and from the bone-bleached shores the heron calls long and mournful, like a song, like a bell, tolling something, I don't know what. At the edge of the bay, the lights of The Beach are on, bright as they've always been, and beyond them is the Gulf. That Gulf a bottomless well, a billion gallons of water and salt and the blood of those who sank, those who sank in the outbreak and before, the merchants the pirates the travelers, the spring breakers pulled loose from the world by ravaging riptide, the divers lost to tangled anchor lines and the bends and the blurry bliss of nitrogen narcosis, the shark-bit surfers and the toddlers who waded too deep, the refugees and their failed flotillas, and the dead, the dead, all of them lost out there in the blackness where the dark things rollick and roil.

"What we going to do with them, then?" Rodney says.

My house is small and the walls are thin. There's the living room with the kitchen attached, the bedroom and the bathroom, and then the junk room—a spare bedroom I started off calling an office, but I gave it up when the desk was so piled with random shit that there was no way anything could get done in there. It's the room where I throw my junk. So I guess that's where we throw the zombies. "Let's take them inside. We'll figure it out."

The plan feels stupider by the minute.

* * *

An hour later Rodney and I are on the couch with beers and Tiffany and Thu are locked in the junk room. I closed up the hurricane shutters outside the window. Rigged a lock on the door, wound some rope around the doorknob and fed it through the living room into the bathroom, knotted it around the heavy porcelain base of the toilet. Tight, tight.

"Where you think he's going to hide the trailer?" Rodney asks after a while.

"Don't know."

"He's fucked. Not even wearing his mask. Truck with his name on the side. He can't show his face here again. Ever."

"Unless the plan works."

"Yeah," Rodney says. "I guess."

The zombies slouch around in the junk room, banging into furniture, knocking stuff off the desks, the shelves. Moaning and scratching and the usual zombie stuff.

I finish my beer, stand up. "You want to crash here?"

"Don't know how I'm supposed to sleep with them back and forth all night." He takes one more swig of beer and lies down on the couch anyway.

I go into my room and shut the door. Look at the unmade bed, at my reflection in the darkened window. I stand there a long time. Then I sleep.

BACK THEN

Mo wants some whiskey.

It's been a week, and there's twenty of us now. We've been back and forth to Publix every day, eating up whatever we can. The meat has gone rancid, most of the fruit and vegetables turned moldy. We've moved on to Little Debbie stuff and canned food. Beer. Wine. But Publix has no liquor. There's a Walmart a mile farther down the beach, and it's got a liquor store tacked onto the side of the building. Mo and Rodney and I pile into the truck and drive.

There are still fires burning, and a couple of the other hotels have gone down completely. I don't know who keeps setting the fires. Zombies? Are they wandering into electrical stuff? Lighting themselves up and rambling around like giant propane torches?

But I like the fires. The smoke in every breath, it reminds you you're breathing. The glow on the horizons at night reminds you that civilization is still out there. It's burning, but it's out there.

There are some cars in the Walmart parking lot, but the building looks deserted. Big metal garage doors over the entrances like hurricane shutters. We park the truck and get out and try to lift one. Bang on it a bit. It reverberates, this hollow wobble of metal like a sound an airplane might make right before it goes into a tailspin.

The liquor store is shuttered too.

"Damn it," Mo says.

And then there's the sliding sound of metal on metal behind us, that unmistakable *chk-chk* that you've heard in a million movies. A pump shotgun. A shell in the chamber.

"Time to go," she says.

We turn around. She's forty, probably, thin, long blonde hair. Pretty hot. She holds the gun like she knows what to do with it.

"We just wanted some whiskey," Rodney says. He's got his knuckles on, and he slips them off and puts them in his pocket.

"It's our whiskey," she says.

The wind blows a Cheetos bag across the parking lot. It scrapes on the asphalt, the loudest sound in the bright morning. The woman's hair blows out around her shoulders.

"You staying in the Walmart?" I ask.

"I said go."

"You can come stay with us. Got plenty of room."

"We got plenty of room too." She looks at the building. It's huge, a concrete behemoth stretching a hundred yards on every side in the center of the great square of asphalt. The power's off, everywhere, I guess—it's off in the offices and food shacks at the water park. Probably dark in Walmart. And now I wonder how they ever lit the whole thing. How did they air-condition it? Thousands and thousands of cubic feet kept a crisp seventy degrees while the Florida summer sweltered outside. I ought to ask Rodney about it. He'll sigh. He'll say *unsustainable*.

"So I guess you're not inviting us in."

She shakes her head.

"How many of you in there?" Mo says. He takes a step toward her, and she raises the gun.

"Time to go."

We put our hands up and walk backward to the truck. She stands there with the gun until we drive away, leaving her alone in front of Walmart, this small shape against that huge building but a small shape that takes up so much space, a cowboy, the gun in her hand while the tumbleweed garbage skitters around her.

"There's an ABC up that way," Rodney says, and we go.

The liquor store's windows are intact. We cup our hands around our faces and look in. There's a single zombie standing behind the counter like he's waiting for a customer. He sways, staring off between the aisles. Middle-aged guy, red apron on. Don't know how he ended up zombified all alone in there. Like he got bit outside and ran in, put the apron on, and died behind the counter. Dedicated to the job.

There's a pile of cinder blocks beside the building, and Mo picks one up. "Move over." He lifts it above his head and chucks it at the window and it bounces off, breaks in two on the pavement. Leaves a little white scratch on the window. That's all.

I put my hand on the window, push. Some sort of thick plastic. No wonder no one's broken in. "How do we get in there?"

Rodney looks in again. "Oh, ha. I got it. Hang on. Watch him." He walks around the building.

Mo and I wait with our faces against the window. After a minute we hear it: banging coming from the back side of the building. The zombie snaps to attention. It walks straight into the counter, nearly falls over. It keeps scrambling against the counter, back and forth until it finds its way around the end and heads down between the aisles to the back door.

"Ah," Mo says. "Smart man."

The door is one of those with the big bar you push to open from the inside. Rodney's outside, banging on it with something. The zombie gets to the door and scratches at it, pushes randomly. Eventually it stumbles upon the bar and shoves the door open, and Rodney is waiting for it. He catches the zombie square in the face with his spiked knuckles, and the zombie falls backward like a felled tree. Rodney props the door open with a cinder block and waves us around.

Inside it's cool and smells of disinfectant. The rows of liquor are orderly, organized by type: whiskeys and rums and vodkas and tequilas. Dozens of varieties of each. Thousands of bottles. Enough to get you fucked up every night for the rest of your life.

Mo and Rodney go behind the counter, where they keep the good stuff. Mo grabs a box of Blue Label from a glass case. "Never had it," he says. He opens the box and takes out the bottle and holds it up to the light, and the sun filters through it like it's resin beaded on the side of an ancient oak. Mo takes a sip, and he closes his eyes, relaxes his face, breathes deep. "Increíble," he whispers.

Rodney grabs the bottle and takes a swig. "Tastes like Scotch."

They start taste-testing the other top-shelf stuff while I walk up and down the aisles. So many bottles in all these different colors and shapes, some of them crazy and beautiful things, liquor stored in glass buildings or Buddhas or naked women. The spirits turned into art. It is excess beyond belief.

"What you think of this, Rodney?" I say. I hold up a bottle of Crystal Head vodka shaped like a skull. "Think of what it takes to make something like this."

"Unsustainable," he says.

"That's what I figured." I turn to put the bottle back on the shelf and she's there. Like she just materialized. I see her first through a bottle of Stolichnaya, her body stretched by the glass and the vodka like a circus mirror, and I step around the corner and it's her, her legs stretching out forever from those shorts and the long lean muscles of her arms hard as they peruse the shelves, her chest rising and falling calmly beneath the black wifebeater and that Mohawk on her head like a blade, like half the saw blade bolted at the end of the broomstick that rests over her shoulder.

She doesn't look at me. Like she's shopping. She looks at the Stoli, puts it back. Settles on Moskovskaya and puts four bottles in her backpack and slings it over one shoulder. Then she turns to me. Those eyes dark as shadows on obsidian. They scan me head to toe. Her face disinterested. "It is you," she says, and her voice is wind in the snow-weighted branches of pines in Siberia. It's blood spilled in the mud of a rutted dirt road in a village of plywood shacks. Quiet but fierce and with the gunmetal accent of the Russians, streaked with boredom, with indifference, with the terrible knowledge of the true weight of the world. It is the sexiest thing I've ever heard. "From volcano putt-putt," she says.

Even *putt-putt* comes out laced with eroticism.

"It's me."

She glances at Santana. "Nice knife."

Rodney and Mo are at the front of the store, leaning on the counter, a bottle in each of their hands. Watching the show.

"I can see?" the woman says.

I take Santana from the sheath. Hold her, feel her song flowing into me. She's mine. No one else has held her. But now I rest her across my palms, hold her out to the Russian.

She takes Santana and flicks her wrist, spins the machete around, makes a couple of experimental cuts through the air. "Is light, but sturdy. Is good blade."

"Her name's Santana." I point to her weapon. "Yours have a name?"

"Putin." She doesn't look at me, spins Santana again like she's some sort of swordmaster.

"Can I see him?"

"No." She hands Santana to me and puts her bag over the other shoulder and walks past me toward the door.

"Hey, hang on," I say. She pauses. "That was badass the other day. You killed like twenty of them. Never seen anything like it."

She shrugs. "You kill zombie. One zombie, twenty zombie, does not matter. You kill until there are zero zombie."

"What's your name?"

She looks back at me. Doesn't say anything. Just looks, like she's categorizing me, deciding where she's going to put me in her brain.

"You want to come with us?" I say. "We're staying—"

"I know where you are," she says. She heads for the door again. She's almost out, and she looks back one more time and says, "Davia." Then she's gone.

It's quiet in the store for a moment, and then Rodney says, "Ooooohhh!" and he and Mo are hooting and laughing and Rodney says, "Rip's got a *girlfriend*!" like he's in sixth grade and you know what, I feel like I'm in sixth grade, that slippery mix of lust and love running up and down every part of my body and making my back tingle and my eyes water and my heart beat fast.

"Davia," I say, and the name tastes like vodka.

* * *

We drag a bunch of wooden beach chairs up the beach and across the road, pile them in the center of the picnic area at Lazy River. Light the bonfire as the sun's going down, and that smoke close in my nose mixes with the smoke from the smoldering hotels and whatever other stuff is wafting through the atmosphere from other cities, those glows just over the horizon.

We drink, and Mo plays guitar, an oversized black acoustic with a rose on the side. He found it in a hotel we raided; zombie was sitting on the edge of the bed holding the guitar, staring at it like he was trying to remember the chords to a song he once knew. Didn't even fight us. Mo grabbed the guitar by the strap and lifted it over the zombie's head, and we left him there, shut the door behind us. Now the guitar is Mo's, and he sings songs in Spanish that only he and Gabriela and Lupita understand, but the music feels like a spring day in the Yucatan when everything is bursting with color and cheer.

Cell phone signals come in now and then, and we catch snippets of what's going on outside our little slice of the world. Major cites evacuated or overrun—New York, London, Beijing. We're already on President Pelosi; no one is saying what happened to Pence. She's apparently trying to bring the military back from all the far-flung bases around the globe, but communication and travel are spotty and troops keep turning into zombies. The National Guard is fighting back, they say. They've retaken large parts of Chicago, they say. Two-thirds of the country is unaffected, they say. They say.

Rumors online tell of horrible things. Nuclear explosions in Lagos, Bangkok, across the entire island of Jamaica. Other cities so overrun with zombies that no one made it out alive.

And somehow we are singing and drinking expensive booze and watching the sky fade from orange to purple to black.

The fire burns low and people retire, one or two at a time, to their places in the park. We've already divvied it up in unspoken agreements: common areas and private spaces for individuals or families. A corner where they keep the dumpsters becomes the latrine, and we pour ash from the bonfires over the shit to keep it from stinking too much. Pile our garbage in some wheelbarrows we found and toss it over the fence every couple of days. We dump zombies over there too, whenever we decide it's time to clear some of the herd that gathers around the river.

After a while I'm the only one left. The fire has burned down to embers and the moon's coming up behind the stand of pines east of the park. I've got a bottle of Crystal Head, and I hold it like I'm mourning Yorick, try to recite the line but I can't remember that shit, so I just throw back a couple of sips and feel the alcohol burn down my throat and fill my chest like a furnace turned on. The wind blows and the trees move and it's all delayed and slurred, stop motion. I'm pretty drunk.

There's some noise on the other side of the river. A zombie's groan cut short. Splitting sounds, like someone chopping wood. Then silence. I take another sip of vodka.

Davia appears out of the darkness like a shadow come to life. She sits across from me and leans Putin against the chair beside her. Blood is thick on the poleaxe's blade and spattered on her skin. She pulls a bottle of Moskovskaya from her bag and drinks, long and deep, the bottle upturned and her head back. She puts the bottle down, licks her lips, watches me across the fire.

"Privet," I say. I looked that shit up.

Her eyes narrow, and then she smiles. More than the smirk I saw the other day. A smile that shows her teeth and makes her eyes spark the firelight back at me, a smile like the open mouth of an anglerfish at the bottom of the Marianas Trench, beckoning me in, turning me into her next meal.

I smile back. "That's all I got."

"Is something." She brings Putin with her and walks around the fire and takes the seat beside me, offers me the Moskovskaya. I give her the skull, and we taste each other's vodka. She scrunches her nose. "American shit."

"I think it's Canadian."

"Is not Russian." She takes the Moskovskaya back and drinks, nods. "Is not Russian, is not vodka."

We watch the fire. There's not much left but the glow. The stars are out above us. All of them visible now with no light but the distant fires. Billions of stars. Like someone has shaken salt across a black tablecloth. The Milky Way like spilled cream.

"I see the ones you killed," Davia says. "Over there. And all over The Beach."

"How can you tell?"

"You kill them clean. With your—Santana. You are good at it."

"Not like you."

"No. But good for an American." She reaches across the space between us and pulls Santana from her sheath. Like she's undressing me, stripping me naked, and I let her do it. She runs her finger along the blade. "You had never killed one, yes?"

The way she looks with Santana in her hand. Like she's holding a part of me. A part of me I desperately want her to touch. "Not before last week."

"I kill one when I was a child."

"There've been outbreaks in Russia?"

"No. We don't let them turn to outbreaks. We have our shit together." She looks at me now, and in her eyes I can see the long nights of the Siberian winter and her first frigid zombie falling beneath her five-year-old fists. So much darkness filling her with fire, like the nuclear edge of a black hole where things are torn apart at the event horizon, set alight by the forces of the universe. "Would you like to hold Putin?"

"Yes." She gives me the poleaxe, and I stand and swing it a couple of times, and for a moment I'm with her on the tundra, tearing down the zombie horde with great swings of the blade. Santana is beauty and song, but Putin is pure death, a thousand years of snow and blood frozen into steel and sharpened into the teeth of fury. "It's pretty cool," I say.

And now she laughs. Low and throaty. If a shark laughed, it would sound like her. "Pretty cool."

We trade weapons again, and I sit down with Santana in my lap. We don't talk for a long time, and it doesn't matter. I'm drunk and I think she is, and I can feel something flowing between us that is below words, something that's been around since before people learned to speak, from the time we first climbed down from the trees and stalked the savannah in silent tribes.

"You going to stay here tonight?" I ask when the last ember fizzles out and my bottle is empty.

"Maybe." Her bottle dangles from two fingers. She's got one long leg crossed over the other, and she waggles her toe like she's directing an orchestra.

"You can pick a spot." I get up, stumble a little, catch myself on the edge of the chair. "I'm up in the pirate ship. There's plenty of places you can crash. But I'm—I'm up in the pirate ship." I wait, but she doesn't say anything, just keeps staring at the pile of ash that used to be the fire and waving her foot *one two one two*. "Okay then," I say.

I'm not sure how long I lie there, the planking of the ship's deck rough on my bare back, the moon spinning dancing a slow circle above me, the stars sailing their blind course across the blackness. But she comes. Finally, she comes. I hear her on the stairs, and then she's looming at the edge of sight, but my head's too heavy to turn. I track her with my peripheral vision. She leans Putin against the transom. Pulls her tank top off, slips out of her shorts. She stands astride me. "Pants," she says, and somehow I manage to work the button and the zipper and pull my jeans down to my ankles, and before I can even kick them the rest of the way off she has grabbed me and pulled me inside of her.

She moves and the moonlight's on her like silver sand spilling down polished mahogany. I grab her hips and her skin is somehow smooth and rough at the same time, like a snake's. She doesn't look at me, rides me hard, silent. Faster. I try to move with her but the wood is hard beneath me and she's fierce, arrhythmic, her fucking something entirely her creation and me just trying to keep up. Then she's grinding, arching her back, fingernails digging into my chest, and things are building up in me but too slow and she gasps, stops, writhes against me a moment more, and gets up. She walks to the edge of the ship and stands naked in the night, her shoulders rising and falling as her breath comes back to her.

I'm sitting there with my cock in my hand. "Hey," I say.

She dives. I hear the splash as she enters the pool below, and I go to the edge and she's swimming beneath the surface, a dark shape on the bottom of the moonlit pool. She climbs out the other side and I see that she's got Putin with her, and she walks to the river and waits.

I pick up Santana and jump into the pool, and the water wraps around me like a cold fist. I follow her path and climb out and stand beside Davia at the edge of the lazy river.

There are a dozen zombies on the other side. They reach for us, groan.

Davia taps Putin against the concrete bank of the river. She turns to me. Grins. Slips into the water.

I go with her, and we come out the other side, and the zombies are waiting for us. She takes the first one, a guy thick as a tree trunk, probably deadlifts eight hundred pounds. Davia's airborne with Putin above her and she brings the saw blade down and nearly splits his head in two. She's pulling the blade out when another one comes for her, and I take its head three-quarters of the way off with a sharp swing of Santana. The alcohol evaporates and leaves in its wake the high of the kill, the dizzy clarity of adrenaline rush. And then we're moving together, Davia and me, this dance this perfect synchronicity, and she's got the zombies behind me and I've got the ones sneaking up on her, and we don't have to talk or signal or anything—we just move. Putin's teeth an inch from my ear and Santana's black blade practically trimming Davia's Mohawk but neither of us afraid, neither slowing down, because we know the other is there, I am there and she is there and together we are a force of nature.

I don't know where she's been my whole life, but she's here now, and it's like she's been a part of me forever.

She kills the last one and turns to me, naked and blood soaked and smiling, and I shove her into the grass at the edge of the river and climb on top of her and I'm still hard, been hard this whole time, and now we move together, move as one with the moon above us and the bodies bleeding into the river while it whispers its chlorine secrets to the night. That zombie I almost decapitated is still moving, watching us with its blind eyes, and Davia sees it and I know she sees it and neither of us cares, we think *let the motherfucker watch*, and then Davia has her hands around my neck and her eyes locked on mine and she squeezes and everything explodes, and if the zombies tore the world apart right now it wouldn't matter. There'd be no better way to die.

* * *

Most people don't know when they're in the prime of their life, when they hit their peak, whether it's when they're the strongest or smartest or best-looking or if it's a moment—a big promotion or a world-class fuck. The moment comes and goes and it's all less from there, a seismograph full of bumps with all of them a bit smaller than that one earthshaker, the one that tears the scale in half.

Some people know it. Astronauts. Olympians. How do they go on? When you've stood on the moon or on top of the podium and there's nowhere to look but down, how do you find satisfaction in a lifetime of lesser things?

I'm no athlete, and I'll never do a moon shot, but I know where I'm at. I know I'm at the top. Spring spins to summer, and this summer—it's the peak. And I keep hoping it's a plateau that stretches out forever across a bronze desert beneath the sheltering sky.

It feels like time is an ever-moving thing, a river of lava scorching memories in the crevices of your brain, but it's not, when you really think about it. It's more like a movie. A movie looks like one continuous thing as it's playing, but if you slow down, concentrate, you see that you're really watching a series of pictures. Twenty-four images per second, too fast for your eye, your brain, so you just turn it into a movie. Naturally your brain would do that. It does it all day. Moments stack up on top of one another too fast to contemplate until you look back on them, try to piece them together in your head but find they never come back exactly the way they were before. It's like someone's cut up the film and scattered it across the booth above the theater and you're scrambling around on your knees, grabbing pieces and trying to line them up, but you're missing big chunks, minutes or hours at a time, and the audience is getting restless below you and they want the full story, but you can't tell them because all you've got is a big pile of moments.

So how can I tell you the story of that summer? How can I make you see it the way it was for me? I can't. All I can give you are the moments.

Heat wobbling up from the asphalt at midday and Rodney's shadow a black ball beneath him, blood on his white shirt, not his blood. Takes a cigarette from Mo even though he doesn't smoke and Rodney says Gracias and Mo says You're welcome.

Lupita and Rain in the kiddie pool in Disney bathing suits they took from the Alvin's Island down the beach, the tourist shop in a building shaped like a giant shark. They leap and pirouette in the shin-deep water and sing songs from the cartoons, belting them out like they're on Broadway.

A zombie on the beach with its legs torn apart by buckshot—whose gun, I don't know. Maybe Queen Walmart. The zombie still moving and swatting at the sea gulls that peck and poke its knees.

Canned baked beans warmed over coals and mixed with a shot of whiskey. Sweet and tangy with fire in your throat. Camping on the shore of the apocalypse.

And Davia. A blade with a blade in her hand. Her body against mine and her vodka-soaked tongue in my mouth. Her breath in time with mine as we clear the lazy river, night after night a new crowd waiting to be cut down. Santana and Putin and Rip and Davia and the darkness that stretches on forever in the eyes of the zombies and the edges of the world.

* * *

Someone's phone connects in June. President Grassley has organized the scattered military and they're taking back a dozen cities a day. Old-ass Chuck Grassley. I didn't even know he was still alive before the outbreak started, and now he's turning the tide. They clear a city, bolster their numbers with new recruits, mostly nineteen-year-old kids itching to play the real-life version of *Resident Evil.*

They clear New York. DC. Atlanta. Getting closer each day.

End of June, a pair of A-10s flies down the beach. A strafing run, the gunfire knocking against the hotels like giants shaking oil drums full of rocks. We go out there afterward. The zombies' bodies are obliterated by those massive bullets, arms and legs ripped clear off at the sockets, heads popped like balloons, holes blown in their torsos big enough to toss a football through. I feel sorry for them. It's not like when I kill them with Santana. More like those assholes who hunt wolves from helicopters. There's no sport in this.

They never had a chance.

Phone gets a signal pretty regularly now. Pensacola all-clear on July 1. A-10 runs a few times a day. Dothan clear on the second. Ground vibrates when their missiles hit a building somewhere nearby, bring it down in a whirl of fire and dust. Tallahassee on the third.

We are surrounded.

*　*　*

The kids are out of sparklers and the bottle rockets have all been lit. Mo lets Lupita light the last big boomer. It thuds from its launcher and whistles into the sky and explodes like a flare hanging over a rice paddy in Vietnam, a red sun trickling sparks into the river, and everyone cheers.

Then the light vanishes. Darkness hangs heavy and people move quietly back to their places in the park. A jet engine roars in the distance; then silence again.

Davia is breathing deep, something close to a snore but not quite. She's drunk, but so am I, and I hold her close and feel something inside of me that might be love, but it's got so much sadness in it that I tell myself that can't be what it is.

The troops are coming from every direction. Coming to take it all away.

"Davia," I say.

She moves her face against me, something you'd almost want to call a nuzzle except that a battle axe can't nuzzle you without cutting. "Hmm?" she says.

And I almost tell her. It's on my lips.

She looks up at me. Those eyes like galaxies imploding.

"I don't want it to end," I say.

She touches my face, and her fingers are the probing antennae of some underwater creature. Something dark and unknowable.

Something beautiful. "It has to end," she says. "Everything ends. When it doesn't end, all that's left is the zombie."

And then she sleeps, and I listen to them, the people who ended but didn't end, the zombies, all of them out there in the dark in their ceaseless revolutions, forever following that river, not knowing that the end is just the beginning viewed from another direction.

* * *

We hear them at sunrise.

First it's the gunfire. A smattering of small arms and some sort of big beast coughing loud over the rest of them. Every now and then a boom and a rumble as something collapses.

Then engines. The ground vibrates and Davia and I stand up in the pirate ship. Below us, the rest of the kingdom wakes; the people crawl from sleep around Lazy River and wait.

Last is the music. They're blaring something metal, heavy drumbeat and screeching guitars, and it's a minute before I can make it out.

Rodney looks up at me, mouths *What the fuck?*

It's Rob Zombie. "Dragula." Maybe that was cute when they started out, but you know they've been playing it on repeat since they started rolling into cities weeks ago. Today it feels cheesy. A mockery of the war we've been winning for months.

They come into view on the street. A whole parade of equipment—twenty Humvees and twice as many trucks and jeeps and two huge tanks—plus a couple hundred men walking between them. Men, no. They look like kids. A bunch of twentysomethings practically skipping along with their

M16s, cheering and whooping when they spot a zombie and fill it with ten pounds of bullets from a dozen different guns. A guy in aviator shades and a cowboy hat stands in the back of one of the Humvees. He swings an M2 machine gun toward one of the hotels and peppers the side of the building. Explosions of plaster, dust drifting in the morning air, holes the size of baseballs.

Then he swivels the gun our way. Sees me up on the pirate ship. He's probably two hundred yards away, but we make eye contact. I know he sees me. He knows I see him.

I give him the finger.

He looks behind him and waves, and half the caravan veers off the road. They idle for a moment, waiting for one of the tanks, and it screes across the parking lot and bounces over the big concrete elephant turds that mark the parking spaces and comes plowing right through what's left of the fence, bringing it down and dragging it along behind it, rending a fifty-foot hole.

We didn't clear the zombies last night since we were too busy drinking and fireworking. There are probably thirty or forty spread out around the perimeter of the park. Every one of them turns at the sound of the fence coming down. Heads for the tank.

The rest of the army pours in behind the tank and the song restarts and gunfire is everywhere. They're spraying the zombies mostly, but the bullets are flying out of control and one of them hits the ship and splinters the wood a few feet from Davia's head.

"Hey!" I say. I jump off the ship into the water and climb out and sprint across the park. "Cool it! Fucking cool it!"

All those kids are riled up, half of them going one way half the other and blowing the zombies apart, holding their guns at their hips and spewing lead like they're Rambo or something. Mr. M2 unloads on a couple of zombies, the big gun barking *tuk tuk tuk tuk* like a fist in the base of my skull every shot. I'm almost to the river and I've got Santana in my hand and I don't know what I'm planning to do with her, but the dude swings that gun at me and raises an eyebrow and waits.

I stop.

The gunfire ceases and M2 gets out of the Humvee. He's got no shirt, and now I see it's not a cowboy hat but some piece of a cavalry uniform like he thinks he's Robert Duvall in *Apocalypse Now* and I know he's just dying to say the line, and I swear if he does I'll cut him in half, the phony motherfucker.

He looks into the lazy river. It's full of zombie blood and bits. Nasty. "Where's the bridge?" he says.

"Fuck off," I say.

He scoffs. "That's no way to talk to your rescuers."

"No one asked to be rescued."

M2 takes his shades off and he's older than I thought he was, his eyes palest blue, heavy bags beneath them. He's grinning, though. Teeth stained with tobacco. He starts to say something.

And then a scream. Behind us. A woman. And then a man. "No. No!"

I turn and I can see everyone, all the citizens of Lazy River, every eye in the kingdom on the kiddie pool where Gabriela and Mo crouch over their daughter as she bleeds out into the chlorine-tinted water.

Gabriela picks Lupita up. The girl's body is limp. Blood pours from a hole in the middle of her. "Ayudame!" Gabriela looks to each of us, and we don't know what to do. "Mi hija! Ayuda a mi hija!" We don't know what to do because we all know it's too late.

"Ah shit," M2 says. "She should have got down. Why didn't you guys get down?"

And then Mo is running, el decapitador in both hands, some sort of inhuman noise coming from him, part roar and part wail, and the soldiers turn their guns on him as he nears the lazy river. He screams as he reaches the edge, leaps, flying upward forward skyward, the blade over his head now, his back arched, his eyes full of wrath.

The river is wide. Mo splashes into the middle of it. He comes up coughing, no decapitator. He takes a breath, goes back under, looking for it.

M2 sighs and climbs back into the Humvee.

By the time Mo finds the blade and begins wading the rest of the width of the river, the barrel of that huge gun is leveled at him. He reaches the far edge. Puts the decapitator down in front of him and rests his arms on the concrete and his head on his hands. He cries.

And that's the end. Our last morning in Lazy River. They pack us into the trucks like we're cargo and haul us away.

* * *

They've set the refugee camp up at the fairgrounds. Six blocks of tents, a hundred in each block. They're all named after characters in *The Walking Dead* because someone at HQ is just a fucking laugh riot. I'm in Rick Block, which isn't quite as good as Daryl Block but good enough. Least I'm not in Carl Block.

They put us four to a tent, but for some reason I'm not with anyone I know. Xan and Rain are in my block but way on the other side. I think Rodney's in Daryl. Lucky.

I don't know where Davia is. Last I saw her, she was standing at the far side of the park, over where we dumped the garbage and the zombie bodies. Putin in her hands. Breeze in her hair. She watched as they loaded me into the truck at the point of a rifle. As they shut the door behind me. When I looked out the window, she was gone.

We sit and look at each other, me and my three tentmates. Two of them look like they're just out of high school. One's probably fifty, bald with glasses, a hundred pounds overweight. I wonder what he weighed before.

"Where you stay at?" one of the kids says to me after a while.

"Lazy River."

"The water park?"

"Yeah."

"Fun. We were just at the Denny's."

"Where's the rest of your crew?"

"Dead." He's sitting on the edge of his cot, and he twists the sheet back and forth with one hand. "Fifteen of us there at one time. Now they're all dead."

"We lost a bunch too," fat guy says. "We went to the mall. But they got in. The zombies. Only a couple of us made it, up on the roof. They couldn't get to the roof." He turns to me. "How many'd you lose?"

"One." I look at my hands. My bare hands. They took Santana from me, put her in a bin when we entered the camp. Stuck a label on her, said they'd give her back. "We lost one today. Fuckers shot her when they came in."

"Yeah, but how many'd you lose to the zombies?"

I rest my hands on my knees, look at him a long time. "None," I say. "They didn't get a goddamn one of us."

* * *

A woman in uniform comes around with a clipboard after a while. Stands above my cot without looking at me.

"Name?" she says.

I tell her.

"Occupation?"

"Zombie hunter."

She rolls her eyes. "You and everyone else, tough guy. Your real job."

I look at the ground. "Customer service representative."

"That's more like it."

* * *

They serve us dinner in the big hangar where they used to hold the farmer's market. I'm waiting with a tray in my hand like I'm in second grade when Queen Walmart gets in line behind me.

"They got you too," she says.

"They did." Some cadet slops macaroni and cheese onto my tray. "They got us all."

"Took your machete."

"And your shotgun."

She nods. She had a freshness about her last time I saw her, a wild energy. Fierce. A lion. Now she looks beaten. "We were doing fine," she says.

We're moving down the line. Roast beef. Green beans.

"We were happy," she says.

End of the line and they hand me a glass of pink lemonade. "They're making out like they saved us," I say.

She takes her lemonade and swirls it in its plastic cup. "You didn't need to be saved."

"Neither did you."

"They ruined us."

I feel tears in my eyes, but damned if I'm going to let her see me cry. "They ruined everything," I say, and I take my tray and walk off through the survivors, hunched over their plates and eating quietly. Alone in a new world, the world they knew once but can never know again.

SUNDAY, OCTOBER 27

The sun's up high when the phone wakes me. It's Mo.

"Turn your TV on," he says. There's a ton of noise in the background.

I go out in the living room, and Rodney's on the couch watching some football pregame stuff. "It's on," I say. "What am I looking for?"

"Channel four."

Rodney turns the channel, and it's a helicopter view of the clay pits. Big woodsy area north of town with all kinds of dirt roads and clearings where the kids take their jacked-up pickup trucks and do donuts and dredge the tires whirling through three-foot-deep puddles of clay red as rust. There's a mix of military vehicles and police cars all around the edges of a clearing, probably thirty men with guns drawn. They all aim at the truck in the center. Bogged down in mud, the Guillermo's Gardens trailer still attached. "Shit, Mo," I say.

"I think it just took me too long to find a place," Mo says. "I was going to dump the trailer in the bay, but I couldn't get it to go over the edge of the bridge. Then I tried the scrapyards, but they were all closed up. By the time I thought to take it out here, sun was coming up. People out on their way to church. I guess they'd seen something on the news, called it in."

I can hear the helicopters through the phone. Voices of the men with guns. Yelling for him to come out.

"He'll rat us out," Rodney says.

I shake my head. He wouldn't. Not Mo.

Mo breathes into the receiver for a long time. Heavy. "You still got the zombies?"

"We got them."

"Good. It's a good plan, Rip. A good plan." On the TV, the door opens. Mo steps out. Up to his thighs in mud. He's got the phone to his ear, looks up at the helicopter, waves. "You see me?"

"Yeah."

"Cool." He waves again, and then he starts rooting around in the bed of the truck. The men are yelling at him, closing in with their guns. "Recuerdas ese cabrón que mató a Lupita?"

"I remember," I say.

"Ha. I thought you didn't speak Mexican."

"Guess I picked it up."

Mo smiles up at the camera. "You're a good guy, Rip. Listen. Tell Gabriela something. I couldn't get that guy who killed our niñita. So I've got a replacement. You watch, Rip. It's going to be great."

I know what he's going to do and so does Rodney, even though he can't hear anything that's not on TV, and Rodney and I look at each other and part of me wants to tell Mo to stop, to turn himself in, but where does that get him? Where does that get us? There's no other way now, and Mo knows it and so do we. "Por Lupita," I say.

Mo nods onscreen. He tosses the phone into the clay and the signal cuts out at my ear. Mo's got one hand in the bed of the truck, and the men are so close now their boots are in the mud. The helicopter banks and Mo is in the center of the screen and the camera zooms, cinematic, beautiful. He closes his eyes, opens them, and pulls el decapitador from the bed. It flashes in the sun and the camera's lens flares and then Mo's already halfway to the nearest soldier, and they start to fire and Mo slows but not enough. The soldier tries to run but his boot's lodged in that clay, that sucking red earth that grips like the dead, and Mo catches him where the neck meets the shoulder and the decapitator doesn't stop until it's almost to the soldier's hip.

And then the bullets do their job. Mo goes facedown in the clay and red bleeds into red, and the soldier's body topples on top of Mo's, and el decapitator pulls the body down until they all vanish in the bog.

The camera shows everything. No *viewer discretion advised* anymore. We've seen it all. We've lived it.

I get three beers from the fridge. Hand one to Rodney and open my own and pour the third out in the sink.

"For your dead homies?" Rodney says.

I smile. "He'd like that."

"We're so fucked." He starts laughing. "Totally fucked."

We drink.

"They're quiet in there," Rodney says.

I listen. I haven't thought of them at all this morning. Too focused on Mo. But there's no sound in the junk room.

Rodney puts his ear to the door. "You think they're sleeping or something?"

"They don't sleep." I listen too. Nothing.

"But like, a resting cycle or something. We never let them hang around long enough to see."

I grab the catch poles, hand one to Rodney. Untie the rope on the doorknob. "You ready?" Rodney nods and I swing the door open.

The room is destroyed. Furniture knocked over and everything from every shelf spread across the floor. Wallpaper torn in strips. Busted lightbulb in the lamp, blades of the ceiling fan broken in half, dangling like bugs' legs.

The bookshelf leans at a forty-five-degree angle, the top sticking through the shattered window into the morning air. The hurricane shutters yawn open.

No zombies.

"Shiiiit," Rodney says. He runs to the window, sticks his head out.

"How'd they figure out the shutters?"

"Don't know. But they gone, man."

We run outside. It's a perfect fall morning, crisp and cool with a low blue sky empty of clouds. A breeze sways the elephant ears and carries up a fresh salty smell from the bay. Rodney and I stand in the road and look both ways. An SUV comes by, family inside in church clothes. Kid in the back seat waves to us as they pass.

"Which way?" I say.

"Fuck if I know." He looks at his phone. "It's the middle of the day. Maybe they'll find someone to bite. Maybe we just start the plan early."

I shake my head. "Someone will spot them. Call the cops, shoot them, whatever. We've got to get them loose someplace tight, where they can bite a bunch of people before anyone has time to fight back."

"So we got to find them, then."

"Looks like it."

We walk toward town, Rodney checking the houses on the water side, me checking the side my house is on. I look in bushes, peer over fences into backyards. Where would I be if I was a zombie? Who knows. I'd never be a zombie.

A couple comes out of the house five down from me while I'm trying to see into their garden. Ten years younger than me, maybe. Dressed for church. She's pregnant. She's big enough he must have knocked her up during the outbreak. Why? What was the plan there? She rests her hands on her belly and narrows her eyes at me. "What are you doing?" she says.

"Dog," I say. I hold up the catch pole. "Lost my dog."

She looks across the street at Rodney. He's down on all fours, looking under somebody's deck. "And he's helping you?"

"Yep."

"Uh-huh."

We look at each other until the guy touches her, lightly, small of her back. She sighs, rolls her eyes. "Look somewhere else," she says, and they get in their car. They drive off.

"Rip!" Rodney's whisper-yelling from the other side of the road. Big house next to a vacant lot. They've got kids, have a big playground thing with a slide and swings and next to it a little plastic playhouse. "Tiffany!"

I run over there and look through the window of the playhouse. Tiffany Tetas is sitting in the corner, her knees pulled into her chest. Her head is rocking around like it's not attached right and there's blood coming out of her ear. Her eye has that empty anger. But she's just sitting there like a child. "What's she doing?"

"I'm telling you, man," Rodney says. "There's something going on in there. She remembers something."

I reach in with the catch pole and put the loop around her neck, give it a tug.

"Careful with her," Rodney says.

I coax her into standing and guide her out of the playhouse. We walk back up the road, keeping our eyes open for Thu.

We put Tiffany back in the junk room, and I retie my lock while Rodney nails some old plywood across the broken window. Then we go back out to the road.

"That him?" Rodney points.

There's someone standing in the road up past the vacant lot. Small, hunched. Yeah, it's him. Got to be. And beyond him, someone else. A woman.

She walks with purpose, right in the middle of the street. She's small but seems to take up all the space in both lanes, like she's bending the world around her, pushing through things with some power that would smash a car to a tiny cube if it tried to pass her. Thu turns, looks at her, says *riiiiiiig riiig* loud on that sharp fall breeze. He takes a herky-jerk step toward her, and I want to tell him to stop, that he doesn't know what he's getting himself into, that he's walking straight at death herself in all her gorgeous fury, but he's moving and she's moving and the collision is coming and there's nothing Rodney and I can do but watch the show.

Davia kneels at the edge of the street and comes up with something in her hand. Round and sparking in the sun. A hubcap, left there for who knows how long, maybe since that pickup truck crashed way back on the first day. She spins it, tosses it from one hand to the other as Thu takes his last few steps. Then she jumps into the air, twirling like a figure skater, the hubcap a chakram now, and she catches Thu above the ear and he stumbles, rights himself, but Davia swings the chakram up into his chin and he goes down. Davia stands astride him, brings the weapon down three more times. Then she stands up and shudders in ecstasy, that look on her face the one I know so well, and she leaves the body in the middle of the road and walks right up to me. "Rip," she says.

"Davia."

She's wearing full-length jeans but she's got her black wife-beater on again, and with the blood sprinkled across her face her arms she's the woman I knew before. "Let's talk," she says.

*   *   *

She goes in alone and leaves me and Rodney standing in the road.

"Least we still got Tiffany," Rodney says.

"One's all we need." I walk with him up to Thu's body. Davia destroyed him with that hubcap. Looks like his head got attacked with a meat slicer. We look around and there's nobody out, so I get Thu's legs and Rodney gets his arms and we carry him back to the house, toss him in the backyard where we tossed the family all those months ago.

Blood's still in the road. Probably our footprints. Doesn't matter. None of it will matter once we let Tiffany go.

Rodney gets an Uber and goes home to get his car. Inside, Davia is sitting at the kitchen table, her hands folded in front of her. I find a bottle of cheap vodka in the back of a cabinet and set it in the middle of the table and sit across from her. She looks at the vodka a moment, then at me.

"Is too early to drink," she says.

"Never stopped you before."

She sighs. "World is different."

I pour some vodka into a coffee cup and throw it back and it tastes like summer. "Wasn't that different a minute ago. You killed that one out there. Didn't it feel like old times?"

"But it is not old times. You know it is true. I know it is true." She laces and unlaces her fingers, drums them on the table. "Where you find zombie?"

"What makes you think he's mine?"

Her lip turns up, that smirk I love. "You think I am a fool? I see no zombie for months. And then first zombie I see is in front of your house." She cocks her head. "Is it present for me?"

"Would you like that?"

"I might." Now she pours some vodka into a cup. Drinks. When she puts the cup down, her smile is gone.

"Where did you go, D?"

She looks out the window. There are a few high white clouds scudding across the blue now. The house is quiet. I can hear the ice machine turning out cubes in the freezer. If Tiffany Tetas still breathed, I'd hear her breathing. "You think I just go with soldiers? I go live in refugee camp?" Davia finally says.

"The camp sucked, yeah. But we were only there a little while. And then we got to go home."

"You want me to go home? To the dorm? Back to work at the hotel?"

"You could have stayed with me."

"Oh, and we would be happy family. I be your pretty wife. We have cute little fat baby and go to Chunky Cheese on weekend."

"It's Chuck E. Cheese."

"Is stupid mouse. Who gives a fuck?" She looks at the blood on her arms. Traces her finger along the specks like she's shaping constellations. Santana is sitting on the kitchen counter, and Davia stands and picks her up. Takes her from her sheath and spins her with a flick of her wrist. Then she looks at me.

"I know. Don't you think I feel it too?" I stand with her and put my hand on hers, both of us holding Santana together. "Why do you think I had the zombie?"

Her face is close to mine. She blinks. "What do you mean?"

"We were going to start it again."

She takes her hand off mine, steps back. "Start what?"

"The zombie apocalypse."

"You are crazy man." She picks up the vodka and takes a swig from the bottle.

"You didn't have fun this summer?" It sounds stupider every time I say it. Like I just finished my last summer at camp, and now I'm too old to go back. I'm one of those aging hippies dying to recreate Woodstock, an athlete past his prime insisting on taking the field one last time. But it's all I've got. "You didn't like killing them?"

"Of course I like killing them." She takes the bottle into the bedroom and stands at the window. From there we can see the backyard, thick green with overgrowth. She drinks again. "I like killing them because after I kill them, they are dead. They do not hurt anyone else. That is our job. We kill them. We do not make more."

"But when there's no more to kill—"

"We have done our job."

I stand between her and the bed. She has her back to me. Santana's still in my hand, so I set her on the bedside table, put a finger on Davia's hip. "I didn't know what else to do."

"Do your job. Live your life."

"That was my life."

"Then get a new life."

"You were my life."

She turns around now. Our bodies are a few inches from each other and the sun split by the leaves casts shuddering shadows on the walls. Her hair is in her eyes and she pushes it away.

"You were gone," I say. "It was the only way I could get you back."

She looks up at me. "You destroy world for me?"

I touch her face. "I'd kill a thousand men. I'd burn every city to the ground. I'd be three of the horsemen if you'd be the fourth." And then I kiss her, and she kisses back hard and there are tears on her face but they're on mine too, and we fall into the bed. Our sex is like waves at night while the tide slips toward the moon. Slow where it once was fevered, quiet where it once was a scream. Different. Better. Worse.

Not the same. It will never be the same.

*   *   *

She sleeps when we're done, her head on my chest. I watch the shadows on the wall as the sun crosses the sky. The blades of the ceiling fan slice the air and spill it to the corners of the room. Davia's breath on my face. The afternoon slides by.

The light's turning orange by the time she wakes up. She looks at me, the gloaming painting her skin like glowing honey. She doesn't say anything. Just stares, her eyes deep in mine. Finally, she looks away. "I'm going back to Russia."

Like she's caved in my chest with Putin. "Why?"

"For a better life."

I want to argue with her, but she's right. Things are better in the NewSSR than they are here. She doesn't have to wait tables. She doesn't have to live in a dorm. The NewSSR: land of opportunity. "How would you even? Flights cost a fortune."

"I have connections." She sits up. Slides into her pants, pulls her wifebeater over her head. "We take care of each other. We are still comrades."

"What about the other day? You were in that business suit. What were you doing?"

She laughs. "I had interview. Office manager. It did not go well."

I picture her walking into the office with Putin strapped to her back. I can't imagine her any other way. Makes me smile. "You'd hate that job."

We hear Rodney's car pull up outside. The square echo of his door slamming shut.

"Let me go with you," I say. "To Russia."

"There is nothing for you there."

"You'll be there."

"Rip," she says. Now she touches my face, a gesture of pity. "I am not for you. We are not made for each other now. Maybe in the summer, yes, but not now. Be happy for what we had."

"We can have it again."

The front door opens.

Davia narrows her eyes. "I kill your zombie."

I smile.

Rodney shouts from the front door. "Oh shit. Rip!" And then comes a voice like an anchor dragged through a corrugated steel pipe screaming *raaaag raaaag raaag!* and scuffling and slamming, and Davia and I run into the living room and Rodney and Tiffany are in the kitchen, their hands around each other's necks. The door handle is ripped from the wood and lying on the floor, still tied to the toilet. Don't know how we didn't hear it. Maybe I slept after all.

"Help, dude!" Rodney says.

Davia darts into the bedroom and grabs Santana, but I hold up my hand. "Wait."

"What?" she says. Her eyes are already burning with the fire of the kill.

"Just. Wait."

Rodney's got Tiffany pinned against the counter, and he's talking to her like she's a scared dog. "It's all right," he says. "Calm down, girl. I got you. I got you. You don't need to be scared. I got you."

I get the catch pole and start to creep up on her.

"That's good," Rodney says. "That's good, Tiffany. Just be cool."

And here's the crazy thing: she listens. She calms down. Takes her hands off Rodney's neck and lets them hang at her sides.

Rodney lets go of her. Looks at her. "That's right. That's good. We good." He smiles at me. "See? She's still in there. Makes you wonder about killing all of them. If we—"

And then Tiffany bites his nose off.

Rodney falls on his knees screaming and blood is spilling all over the linoleum, and Tiffany swats the kitchen table away like it's a toy and the bottle of vodka shatters on the floor. She roars, something bestial and terrifying, and Davia comes at her with Santana, but the floor is slippery with vodka and blood and she loses her footing, misses with her swing, chops Tiffany in the arm instead of the head.

They fall to the floor together. Santana clatters under the cabinets. Tiffany climbs on top of Davia and snaps at her face like a rabid dog. Rodney stands up, tries to kick her off, but Tiffany grabs his leg and bites deep into the calf and he falls over again.

"Rip!" Davia yells.

I get the catch pole and try to loop it around Tiffany's neck, but she's squirming like a wild animal and I'm slipping on the floor now too, and Davia's yelling at me and Rodney's screaming in pain and the zombie won't stop with the fucking monster roar and why didn't they just make the loop on the catch pole a little bigger?

"Kill it!" Davia says.

"I can't kill her," I say. "She's the last one."

"Rip!" And she looks at me now and there's something I've never seen before. She's afraid. Tiffany is a weight on top of her and Davia's holding her off as best she can but she can't hold forever, and on her back in the slick of alcohol and blood with Putin miles away and Santana out of reach she is just a human, just a person about to die.

I drop the catch pole. Reach under the cabinet, and Santana's hilt meets my hand like she's been pulled to me by the Force. I step over Rodney, who's on his back now, breathing heavy. I walk carefully, the soles of my bare feet leaving red footprints. Stand astride Tiffany and Davia, both of them rocking fighting squirming between my legs. I raise Santana one last time, and I can hear her singing, and I think, *Go ahead, girl, make a devil out of me*, and I swing.

The blade sinks in. Tiffany goes down. The kitchen is quiet except for Rodney's rasps.

Davia crawls out from beneath the body. Covered in blood. She goes to the kitchen sink and washes it off her hands, her face. Then she turns to me, full of rage. "You were going to let me die."

"I didn't."

"You almost did. You wanted to keep your zombie. Keep your stupid little dream."

"But I didn't. I killed her."

"Too long, Rip." She shakes her head. "You waited too long." Then she's gone. I watch her through the window as she storms up the street, blood dripping from her hair.

"Rip," Rodney says. He's breathing slowly now.

"Hey, man." I kneel beside him. The hole where his nose used to be is oozing blood all over his face, into his mouth. I grab a towel and try to wipe some of it away, but it just comes back. I don't even bother with the leg.

"I got the bug. I can feel it." He rubs his hands on his thighs. "It's in your veins. Goes so quick. But it feels kind of good. Numb. Light."

He doesn't have much time left. We both know it. We've seen it before, so many times.

"I fucked that up, didn't I?" Rodney says.

"Yeah. You kind of did."

"Thought I could talk her down."

"You just had a crush on her, that's all."

He laughs and his teeth are stained with blood. "Told you the black guy dies."

"But you made it to the end."

"Like *Dawn of the Dead*." He holds up his hand and I take it in mine. His grip is weak, but he squeezes me anyway.

"Ving Fucking Rhames," I say.

We sit like that while his breathing slows. He closes his eyes.

"Rodney," I say. I touch Santana. "Do you want me to finish it?"

He shakes his head. "It was a good plan, Rip. Stick with the plan."

"Tiffany's dead. So's Thu. Plan's over."

"Nah. You got one left." He smiles.

"You don't want to be one of them, Rodney." I yank Santana out of Tiffany's skull. "I won't do that to you."

"Yes you will. It's the only way. We got to do the plan. Otherwise it's just—"

And now he coughs a bunch of blood and I'm not sure if he's going to be able to talk again.

"Unsustainable," I say.

He nods. His breaths are shallow, far apart. His eyes unfocused. His lips move. I can't hear him, so I put my ear down close to his mouth. "I want to see what it's like," he says.

Then his hand is limp in mine. His chest is still.

The sun is nearly down and the room is full of blue evening light. I want to sit with him like this, hold his hand while the dark comes on and his blood spreads to the far corners of the earth. But there's not time.

I get the catch pole and put it around his neck. Sit in the kitchen chair, brace myself.

It's almost dark when his hand twitches. His head jerks, left twice, then right. He opens his eyes. Black as holes cut in the far side of outer space. He looks at me.

"Hey," I say.

And Rodney says *aaaaaarrrrrlllg*.

* * *

I try to rig the catch pole so that Rodney and I can watch TV together. He's at the end of it reaching for me and I knew he was strong, always known it, but this strong, damn. It wears me out just trying to move him.

"Come on, Rodney. Work with me, man."

I guide him around and yank back on the pole and he falls into the couch, and I get the other end of it kind of wedged in a bookcase. The rope's still tied to the toilet, so I wrap it around the bookcase and the catch pole and I jerry-rig it pretty tight and he's stuck. I get two beers and sit down beside him, a few feet of space between us.

Rodney reaches for me with both hands. I hold out the beer and he grabs it, but he just squeezes it in his fist and swings it back and forth, sloshing beer all over the place. *Rolg. Ralg*, he says.

I sit back and turn the TV on. It's some big-budget talent show. The people onstage are doing the "Thriller" dance in full zombie makeup, and the judges are eating it up.

"It's not going to be the same without you," I say.

He stops reaching and his bottle clatters on the ground, rolls under the couch. A puddle of beer leaks into the rug. His eyes have that emptiness that all zombies' have, but when I really look at him, it's like he says. There's something in there. A luminescent jellyfish bobbing through an empty ocean at midnight.

Maybe something of Rodney is left. I don't know. Maybe I just want him to be there.

"When we made this plan, I always figured we'd do it together. Me and you and Mo, all of us, and Davia'd come back and maybe Gabriela would get back together with Mo and we'd be a family again. It wasn't supposed to happen like this."

The talent show ends and it switches to the nightly news. Mo's standoff is the lead story. They play the footage from the clay pits, but this time they cut it off right before the bloody stuff starts. Then they show pictures of us at the Air Force base. Mo so obvious, stalking around there without his mask, and me and Rodney easy enough to recognize if you know it's us but anonymous to everyone else. They freeze-frame each of us at the moment where the view is clearest, zoom in. My eyes look right into the camera. It was yesterday, but somehow I look so much younger, like the guy in the video is another man in another life.

There's a reward. Ten thousand bucks for information leading to our capture.

"We got a bounty on our heads!" I lift my beer. "Jesse James and Billy the Kid!"

Rodney doesn't say anything.

I turn the TV off. It's dark in the house. Moonlight comes through the window and casts silver shadows on the floor.

"I'm sorry, Rodney," I say.

Grolg?

"I'm sorry."

MONDAY, OCTOBER 28

It's a long night. I don't sleep, just sit on the couch with Rodney. When the sun comes up I eat some Pop-Tarts and watch the clock. At eight, I strap Santana to my waist and load Rodney into his car. Maneuver him into the back seat and wedge the pole against the dashboard so that he's pinned back there.

We drive downtown. Everyone is on their way to work. Cars waiting at lights, people on their phones texting talking checking Instagram or whatever. People in and out of McDonald's and the coffee shop. The streets bustling like they did before. Like the outbreak was a dream, like it never happened.

We pull up in front of the call center. I look at Rodney in the rearview mirror. "What you think, man? Show the boss who's boss?"

Rodney looks out the window and back at me. He snaps his teeth and lunges at me and the wire digs into his neck.

"Okay! Okay. Just hold up. Wait a minute and you can Hulk out."

I lead him inside. The receptionist smiles up at us, but as soon as she sees Rodney, her face falls. "You can't just walk in here with him like that."

"I'm not asking permission."

"Doesn't matter. You can't come in."

"He works here. So do I."

She rolls her eyes. This girl's new. Can't be more than twenty years old. Never got her name, but I guess she got mine. "You got fired," she says.

"I'm picking up my paycheck."

"Bullshit. You're obviously up to no good. You probably turned Rodney into a zombie somehow, and now you're going to let him loose upstairs in some crazy revenge fantasy." She stands, picks up the phone on the desk. "Not happening. I'm calling security."

I pull out Santana and smash the phone to pieces.

She puts her hands on her hips. "I've got my cell in my pocket."

"Take it out." I hold Santana's tip an inch from her nose. "Go ahead."

She doesn't blink. She pulls her phone from her pocket, shows it to me. Unlocks the screen.

I don't feel my hand shaking but I can see the blade quivering in front of her. Rodney's yanking around at the end of his pole and I'm trying to hold him with one hand and the machete with the other and finally I just say, "Fuck off," which is pretty lame but I can't come up with anything else.

The receptionist smirks. Laughs under her breath as she dials.

I lead Rodney up the stairs and wait at the top. Gather myself. "You ready?"

He looks through the glass door into the fluorescent white of the call center. *Riiiiip*, he says.

The word slips into my ears and slides right down my spine into the middle of me. "Did you say my name?" I try to turn him so that he's looking at me. "Rodney. Rodney! Are you in there?"

He turns and stares at me for a moment. Blinks, opens his mouth and closes it. Then he says *riiiilg* and tries to tear my throat out again, so yeah, that's that.

I push him through the door. The lights are bright overhead and the computer screens are on and a few of the phones are ringing, but the room is empty. I look at the clock. Eight thirty Monday morning. Weekly productivity meeting. Rodney and I scoot between the desks toward the meeting room at the back of the office. It runs the length of the back wall and is separated from the main room by a bunch of tall windows. A couple of conference tables are in there and a big screen where the boss puts up her PowerPoints. It's perfect, actually. Small, confined, only one way in and out. They'll all be zombies before they know what's hit them.

Everyone's in there, framed by the windows. Twenty of my former coworkers, not like they were friends or anything but colleagues at least. Whatever. Rodney gets them now, or I let him go somewhere else and another zombie gets them later. They were dead when they woke up this morning.

The boss is at the front of the room. The screen says *Diversity: Be a HERO* and has a bunch of people of different races smiling in their business suits.

The door's open, and she's right next to it. She'll be the first.

Then I get this image of her kids. Zombie mom coming home. Tearing them apart, turning them into miniature zombies. Someone, maybe me, having to kill them. Dead zombie kid like that one in my backyard.

Faint, far away, the sound of a siren.

No. This is the way it has to be.

I free Rodney from the catch pole and shove him toward the door. He lets the momentum carry him forward, limps on his busted leg, a low growl rumbling in his chest filling the call center. He stops at the door, puts his hands on the frame. *ROOOOOOAAAAAARRRRG!*

I get chills. You fucking tell them, man.

The boss looks at Rodney and sighs. She turns back to the employees. "I'm sorry, y'all. You try to lead a workshop. First I can't get the clicker to work, and now this. If it's not one thing, it's another, isn't it?'

I watch them through the big windows. They laugh. A guy spreads cream cheese on his bagel.

"Just hold up one sec, okay?" The boss bends over and comes back up standing lopsided, her high-heeled shoe in her hand. Rodney shuffles into the room and the boss stands square with him, holds the shoe like a shot put, waits.

Rodney lunges. The boss punches.

Rodney's body goes stiff, and then he falls flat on his back. The stiletto is buried to the heel in his eye. He twitches a bit, and then he's still.

The boss pulls the shoe out and it drips blood on the carpet. "Oh, now it's all grody!" she says, and she gets some napkins from the catering tray and wipes off the gore and puts the shoe back on. "Okay," she says. "What does it take to be a diversity HERO?"

No one pays any more attention to the zombie on the floor. They eat their pastries and drink their coffee.

"Tree squirrels," I say. I don't know who I'm talking to.

The sirens are louder outside now. I run back down the stairs, out the front door. I hear the receptionist yelling behind me, "You better run!"

I get in Rodney's car and haul ass down the street all the way to the end of the marina. Stop beneath the statue of Mayor The Rock. The waters of the bay ripple and swell, the way they always have, the way they always will.

No more zombies. No more anonymity. That's it. So what else is there to do?

One more beer.

I follow the bay around to Bungalow. Park the car in the gravel lot and walk across the docks and look down into the algae-tinted shallows. Blue crabs skitter across the bottom, waving their claws at minnows. Seaweed sways in the current. Beautiful things.

Bar won't open for hours, but I've got my fingers crossed, and for once today, I'm lucky. The door to the big walk-in fridge behind the bar is open, and Bob's in there loading a keg onto a dolly. He looks up when he sees me. "Didn't think I'd see you again, Rip."

"And here I am."

"And here you are." He wheels the dolly into the bar, and I help him load the keg into the cooler and tap it. He fills a couple of glasses with foam before he gets a decent pour. Hands it to me. "Catawba White Zombie," he says. "Seems like everyone wants to make a zombie beer these days."

I taste it. Crisp and wheaty and dry.

"So you saw about Mo," Bob says.

I nod.

"They're still looking for the other two guys." He pours himself a beer, clinks his glass against mine. Looks at me a long time before he drinks. "I don't know who those other two guys are. I don't want to know."

"Only one of them left, anyway."

His lips quiver. He hides them in the glass as he drinks.

We sit out on the porch and listen to the sirens as they move around town.

"Did you really get four in one shot?" I say.

Bob laughs. "I really did. But it was luck. Luck, maybe a little help from Jah."

"That was something." A cop car crawls down the road on the other side of the bayou, its lights flashing. "We really had something. I thought we could get it back."

"You can't get it back, Rip. None of us can." Bob sets his beer down and leans his elbows on the table. "Look at me." I do. "We're all going in the same direction. We all wish we could go back. But when it's gone, it's gone. You don't fight to get it back. You find joy in the new. There's always something waiting for you up ahead, but if you spend all your time looking back, you're going to miss it."

Footsteps on the planks, rattling their way up the dock.

Bob smiles at me. I put my hand on his shoulder. "Every little thing is gonna be all right?" I say.

"Ha."

I down the last of the beer. The sun reflects like a firework on the water and Santana hums at my waist.

And then she's there, Putin over her shoulder, hair freshly shorn on the sides, the Mohawk hanging loose and wild and free. Davia's eyes are full of everything, all the hate and love that ever swam in her brain manifest in that glare, and she takes the blade from her shoulder and taps it on the planks and for a moment I'm sure that this is it, that she's come to end me. The way I cut her last night was too deep, and the wound is infected, so now she's got to sever the limb completely to heal; she's got to rend me from her life with the teeth of her blade. She blinks, the future playing out behind her eyes, all those different possibilities unspooling sure and silent as orbits.

I smile. Wait for the blow.

It doesn't come. "Get up," she says. "You come with me."

TWO YEARS LATER

So this email says:

You call this beer? It tastes like it was wrung out of the bears'
fur and mixed with the soccer player's sweat. I don't know what
you commies are putting in it, but it doesn't hold a candle to
American ingredients. I'm switching to Bud Light. I don't care
how much it costs.

Don't know what I'm supposed to say to this one really. It's
a complaint, but he doesn't want anything, isn't upset by something in particular. Guy just doesn't like Three Bears Light.
Whatever. I copy and paste a canned response and send it off
and sit back in my chair.

The call center looks a lot like the one back in Spanish
Shanty, except it's got propaganda posters all over the walls—
muscular comrades and women with noses and cheekbones that
could cut steel stomping over the bodies of zombies that are
obviously meant to be American, fat and clothed in sweat pants
and tank tops from the Gap—and the people answering the

phones, my colleagues, speak sixth-grade-level English in their snow-capped accents. The Union's flag hangs on the wall, a lot like the old Soviet flag, red and yellow with the star and hammer, but they've replaced the sickle with a machete. A nice touch.

Yuri comes over to my desk. He's got a blond crew cut, wears jean shorts everywhere he goes. Tall but not that tall, fit but not that fit, like Ivan Drago's little brother. "You come to Plyazhnyy Domik after work?"

Plyazhnyy Domik's our bar. "Not today. Patrolling. Want to come with me?"

He rolls his eyes. "I am sick of patrol. You always want to patrol. We never find any."

"I'll bring the beer."

He drums his fingers on the desk. "You bring vodka?"

"I'll bring some vodka."

Now he's smiling. "Okay. We patrol."

* * *

Davia led me from Bungalow's porch out to the parking lot. A beat-up blue Volvo sat in the gravel, its trunk open. An old man leaned against the car. He had eyes that knew the dark side of the world and a nose that looked like it'd been broken a hundred times. He smoked a cigarette. "He is still alive," he said.

"Fuck you," Davia said. Then she looked at me. Pointed to the trunk. "Get in."

"They won't let him on board," the man said.

Davia took Putin from her shoulder and buried the blade in the side of the car. She screamed at the man in Russian while he smoked the cigarette down to the filter.

He flicked the butt into the dirt. "Fine," he said. "Is your money."

She was breathing hard now. She turned to me. "Get. In. The. Trunk."

So I did.

I was there for hours, banging around against a tire iron and one of those things you spread across the windshield to keep the sun out. A crack of sunlight came through for a while, but eventually night came and that too was gone. I took Santana from her sheath on my waist now and then, held her across my chest, her warmth flowing into my body my heart.

We finally stopped after it had been dark for a few hours. I heard the doors open and shut, heard them speaking to each other. Davia and several men, arguing in Russian, Davia's voice getting louder, more agitated by the minute, until they were all yelling at each other, a cacophony echoing through the night.

And then Davia said something and they all stopped. Were quiet for a moment. And she said something else.

The trunk opened. Davia was there with four men. The air was salty and warm and a misty rain drifted across the orange streetlamps behind them. Beyond that, a freighter laden with shipping containers sat quietly against the black ocean.

"Where are we?" I said.

No one answered. Two of the men grabbed my arms and dragged me from the trunk, led me to a shipping container on the pier. They opened the doors and threw me inside. Only a little bit of space in there among the boxes. Thousands of boxes of Pringles.

Davia stood behind the men. She turned, walked away from me as the doors swung shut.

Weeks went by with me in that shipping container as the freighter pitched and rolled and yawed its way across the ocean. Sometimes the door opened and one big Russian or another slipped me some food, fresh water. I ate a lot of Pringles. Pissed in the empty cans and shit in the empty boxes. It was not fun.

One day the door opened and Davia stood against a blinding blue sky. She wore a thick ski parka and one of those furry Russian hats. The cold rushed around her and filled the container, and she tossed me a yellow foul-weather jacket. I threw the jacket on and followed her to the stern. The air so cold it stung my nostrils, the quiet broken only by the steady rumble of the ship's great engines, the massive props churning the water from blue to white. She leaned against the railing and watched the wake spread out behind us. I stood with her. The shore to starboard was rocky and covered in a thin layer of snow. To port, the sea stretched to the horizon, dotted here and there with silver-blue patches of ice.

"They say that fifty years ago, you needed an icebreaker ship to sail this route," Davia said. She watched a chunk of ice spin in the wake and disappear below the surface. "Not anymore."

"Where are we?" I said.

"The Barents Sea. You get off tonight. We follow the Pechora River and stop in Naryan-Mar. Then you leave."

"Are you coming with me?"

"No."

"Then why did you do this? Why help me get away if you're just going to ditch me?"

"You chose your woman," she said, glancing at Santana. "You chose wrong. You can't take it back. You don't deserve me." Her face was cut from stone pulled from the bottom of a frozen lake. "But I don't want you to die in jail. You can die somewhere else."

The sea unspooled behind us. Seabirds dipped and dove in our wake.

"I thought we could have it again, Davia," I said. "I thought I could have you again."

She took off her hat, let the wind blow her hair like a wild halo above her head. "We had each other in one place, in one time. That is all it was. It's all anything is. A thing and a place and a time."

We watched the water as the sun climbed into the sky. "Will I see you again?" I said after a while.

"You sound like bad movie," she said.

"I know. Still."

Davia looked me up and down. Her eyes were full of the cold and the snow and the sea. I tried to see something in there: a clue, a promise, a hint of hope. It was like trying to see the dark side of the moon.

She shrugged. "Life is long." And she disappeared among the shipping crates.

The ship snaked its way up the river and docked in the middle of the night. A single Russian sailor guided me down the gangplank. I had Santana and the yellow jacket and a half-eaten can of Pringles. Nothing else. "What am I supposed to do now?"

"I don't know. Get job?"

"I don't speak Russian. Don't have ID. I've got nothing."

"No one cares," he said. He pointed to the sleeping town, the freshly-plowed streets lined with snow, the faceless apartment buildings lit yellow by the streetlamps. "Big business everywhere. You find job. Work, don't get in fights. You will be fine."

I wandered into Naryan-Mar, the snow crunching beneath my boots. In the town square, I found a bulletin board. Dozens of posts in Russian, one in English:

NEED! ENGLISH SPEAKERS FOR WORK! MONEY!

Good enough.

ACKNOWLEDGMENTS

There came a point while writing this book that I typed *THIS IS BULLSHIT AND YOU KNOW IT* and shut my laptop. I didn't look at the story again for nearly two years, and then I dug it out and sent it to Paul Lucas, my agent, who assured me it wasn't bullshit—it was pretty good, in fact, and needed to be finished. So, first and foremost, a heartfelt thank-you to Paul, who has fought for me and encouraged me through seven years and two books. *Apocalypse Yesterday* would not exist without him.

Thank you to Terri Bischoff at Crooked Lane for snatching the story up, and to everyone else at the publisher—Madeline Rathle and Melissa Rechter in particular—for their passion and hard work. I'm also grateful to Rachel Keith for her insightful editing.

Here's a weird one: Thanks to everyone at the Thomas E. Hannah YMCA, particularly the amazing Childwatch staff. I did most of my writing and revision in the break room at the Y while Childwatch took care of my daughter. I'd never have had the time to get this done if it hadn't been for that invaluable two hours a day.

Last but most important, I am grateful to my wife, Jill. She is a writer too, and a better one than me. She is my first and most trusted reader because she calls me on my bullshit. She pushes me. I rarely want to write, but I do it for her, for us, and it makes me better. She makes me better. I am there and she is there and together we are a force of nature.